I, Dan Remington, promise to take care of you, Kelly Russell, throughout your pregnancy. I promise to help you finish your schooling and become the person you dream of becoming. I promise to love our child and bring him or her up in a safe, loving home.

But I don't think I can promise to love you....

*Dan Remington*

Dan Remington

*Kelly Russell*

Kelly Russell

# ∧∧∧∧∧∧∧∧∧∧∧
## ⸎FAMILY⸎

1. HOUSEBOUND—
   Anne Stuart
2. MOONLIGHT AND LACE—
   Linda Turner
3. MOTHER KNOWS BEST—
   Barbara Bretton
4. THE BABY BARGAIN—
   Dallas Schulze
5. A FINE ARRANGEMENT—
   Helen R. Myers
6. WHERE THERE'S A WILL—
   Day Leclaire
7. BEYOND SUMMER—
   Karen Young
8. MOTHER FOR HIRE—
   Marie Ferrarella
9. OBSESSION—
   Lisa Jackson
10. TRUST A HERO—
    Muriel Jensen
11. GAUNTLET RUN—
    Joan Elliott Pickart
12. WEDNESDAY'S CHILD—
    Leigh Michaels
13. FREE SPIRITS—
    Linda Randall Wisdom
14. CUPID CONNECTION—
    Leandra Logan
15. SLOW LARKIN'S REVENGE—
    Christine Rimmer
16. UNHEAVENLY ANGEL—
    Annette Broadrick
17. THE LIGHTS OF HOME—
    Marilyn Pappano
18. JOEY'S FATHER—
    Elizabeth August
19. CHANGE OF LIFE—
    Judith Arnold
20. BOUND FOR BLISS—
    Kristine Rolofson
21. IN FROM THE RAIN—
    Gina Wilkins
22. LOVE ME AGAIN—
    Ann Major
23. ON THE WHISPERING WIND—
    Nikki Benjamin
24. A PERFECT PAIR—
    Karen Toller Whittenburg
25. THE MARINER'S BRIDE—
    Bronwyn Williams
26. NO WALLS BETWEEN US—
    Naomi Horton
27. STRINGS—
    Muriel Jensen
28. BLINDMAN'S BLUFF—
    Lass Small
29. ANOTHER CHANCE AT HEAVEN—
    Elda Minger
30. JOURNEY'S END—
    Bobby Hutchinson
31. TANGLED WEB—
    Cathy Gillen Thacker
32. DOUBLE TROUBLE—
    Barbara Boswell
33. GOOD TIME MAN—
    Emilie Richards
34. DONE TO PERFECTION—
    Stella Bagwell
35. POWDER RIVER REUNION—
    Myrna Temte
36. A CORNER OF HEAVEN—
    Theresa Michaels
37. TOGETHER AGAIN—
    Ruth Jean Dale
38. PRINCE OF DELIGHTS—
    Renee Roszel
39. 'TIL THERE WAS YOU—
    Kathleen Eagle
40. OUT ON A LIMB—
    Victoria Pade
41. SHILOH'S PROMISE—
    BJ James
42. A SEASON FOR HOMECOMING—
    Laurie Paige
43. THE FLAMING—
    Pat Tracy
44. DREAM CHASERS—
    Anne McAllister
45. ALL THAT GLITTERS—
    Kristine Rolofson
46. SUGAR HILL—
    Beverly Barton
47. FANTASY MAN—
    Paula Detmer Riggs
48. KEEPING CHRISTMAS—
    Marisa Carroll
49. JUST LIKE OLD TIMES—
    Jennifer Greene
50. A WARRIOR'S HEART—
    Margaret Moore

# ∧∧∧∧∧∧∧∧

## ⤳FAMILY⤳

# *Dallas* SCHULZE

## The Baby Bargain

DESPERATELY SEEKING DADDY

### *Silhouette Books*

Published by Silhouette Books
**America's Publisher of Contemporary Romance**

**SILHOUETTE BOOKS**
300 East 42nd St.,
New York, N.Y. 10017

RECYCLED PAPER

ISBN 0-373-82152-2

THE BABY BARGAIN

This edition published by arrangement with Harlequin Books S.A.

® and TM are trademarks of Harlequin Books S.A., used under license.
Trademarks indicated with ® are registered in the United States Patent
and Trademark Office, the Canadian Trade Marks Office and in other
countries.

Look us up on-line at: http://www.romance.net

**Printed in U.S.A.**

Dear Reader,

I was delighted when I found out that *The Baby Bargain* was being reprinted. This was a book that touched my heart and, judging from the mail I've received over the years, readers apparently felt the same way.

This is a story about two people who meet under less than ideal circumstances. They have nothing in common except loneliness and a shared need to belong somewhere—to have roots, a place in the world. Family.

I know some people believe that a family is born of shared blood and ancestral ties, but I've always thought that family is a matter of the heart. That's the way it is for Dan and Kelly, anyway. Two lonely people with few dreams, who find love and build a life together against all expectations.

I hope you enjoy reading this story as much as I enjoyed writing it.

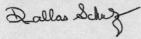

Please address questions and book requests to:
Silhouette Reader Service
U.S.: 3010 Walden Ave., P.O. Box 1325, Buffalo, NY 14269
Canadian: P.O. Box 609, Fort Erie, Ont. L2A 5X3

*Chapter 1*

Kelly Russell pulled her coat a little tighter, hunching her shoulders together as the worn fabric balked at closing. The coat was nearly four years old and it hadn't aged well. The gray polyester had looked cheap and shiny when new. It still looked cheap, but the shine had worn off years ago, leaving the edges frayed and the pockets threadbare.

Kelly had been a thin, angular fourteen-year-old when the coat was purchased. She was still thin but no longer angular, and it was an unfortunate fact that the coat hadn't grown as her body filled out. Now the mismatched buttons refused to close across her bust, allowing the cold, late-December wind to cut through her.

She shivered, sheltered even as she was by the library's wide porch. The winter weather seemed more bitter than it had in years past. Or maybe she just felt it more. Lately it seemed as if she was always cold, deep inside where no coat could warm.

Funny how she'd thought that this year might be different. Every year, as Christmas approached, her spirits lifted. She began to remember Christmases when she was a little girl, before her brother, Devlin, left home, before her mother died.

They had celebrated the holiday then with a tree and lights and deliciously exciting packages.

There hadn't been anything expensive in the packages—they'd never had the money for expensive gifts. Often as not, the boxes contained some necessity. But just the fact that they were gaily wrapped was enough to elevate the most ordinary pair of socks to new heights.

And once in a while there would be something truly wondrous waiting under the tree. The last Christmas before he left, Devlin had used some of the money he'd earned working on a farm over the summer to buy her the most beautiful doll she'd ever seen. All dark ringlets and bright blue eyes, it seemed the most incredible gift, almost magical. She'd treasured that doll as only an eight-year-old could. She'd thought that she would never own anything half as nice again in her whole life.

The wind skidded around the side of the building, slicing through her, reminding her that this was neither the time nor the place for dawdling along, lost in daydreams. Kelly shivered, clutching her precious stack of books to her chest as she hurried down the library steps.

It was stupid to think about the past. If she'd learned nothing else, she should have figured that out by now. Those Christmases were all a long time ago. Devlin had left the summer after giving her that doll. Her mother had died three years later. And the doll had gone the way of so many things from that time—into the trash where her father had thrown it while she watched. He'd said the doll was made in the image of a painted hussy and was unfit for his household.

Now another Christmas had come and gone. The new year lay just on the other side of sunset. Remembrance, Indiana, bustled with a final burst of holiday spirit. The Christmas lights lent a sparkle to the town, one that was reflected in people's eyes as they rushed home to get ready to go out and celebrate the coming of a new year.

Despite the cold that seemed to bite into her bones, Kelly was in no hurry to get home. No parties, no laughing friends, awaited her. Her father had declared that the only proper way to greet the new year was on your knees praying for the world's salvation, just as it was the only way to celebrate the Lord's birth.

Kelly had knelt until her knees ached. She didn't know if the world was any closer to salvation because of it, but she knew her youth was slipping away without her having even tasted it. As she watched the old year fade, she felt as if she was watching her life fade along with it.

She dodged a group of boys who were running down the sidewalk, laughing and shouting. It seemed as if even the children had someplace to go, something to look forward to.

Glancing in the direction the boys had come from, she felt her face flush and then pale. Diane Randall and Chad Levitt. Up until she had quit school a year and a half ago, Kelly had gone to school with the couple now walking toward her. The captain of the football team and the head cheerleader. A fairy-tale couple, right out of one of the many novels Kelly devoured in secret.

She'd read in the paper that Chad had been recruited by one of the "big ten" universities. She didn't know what Diane's plans were, but Kelly didn't doubt that she'd go on to do something wonderful and exciting. Some people were just born to live wonderful and exciting lives.

Kelly ducked her head over the books she carried as they drew near. She didn't want them to see her. Didn't want to see their pity or contempt. She knew what she looked like. She saw her reflection every morning in the tiny mirror in her bedroom. With her hair scraped back, no makeup and her plain, worn clothes, she looked old and unattractive.

With her head lowered, Kelly misjudged her path. Her forward progress was abruptly halted when she bumped into someone.

"Careful." The hands that steadied her were large and strong, the voice one she had once dreamed of. She raised her head, meeting Chad Levitt's dark brown eyes, remembering how she'd fantasized about him the year she turned fifteen.

"You okay?" he asked with impersonal courtesy.

Mute, she glanced from him to Diane, who was looking at her with a faint frown—but no recognition. The realization knocked the breath from Kelly. That Chad didn't recognize her was no surprise. After all, their paths had never really crossed. But she and Diane had stood next to each other in lines, had lockers that sat side by side. By virtue of their last names starting with the same letter, they'd been thrown together frequently, developing, if not a friendship, a friendly acquaintance.

When Kelly had quit school soon after her sixteenth birthday, Diane had helped her clean out her locker, her pretty features concerned. Kelly hadn't told anyone why she was quitting. She'd just gotten so tired. Tired of fighting her father, of dealing with his anger every morning. As far as he was concerned, an education was a waste of time, especially for a woman.

And she'd grown tired of never fitting in at school. She was always on the outside looking in. That wasn't going to change.

But she couldn't explain that to Diane—pretty, popular Diane. Diane had been kind. She'd even told Kelly to keep in touch. Not that Kelly had done any such thing. She'd taken the invitation exactly as it was meant, a kind gesture, certainly nothing to be acted upon. But she'd treasured the knowledge that she'd had an almost-friend.

Now Diane was looking at her without the slightest trace of recognition.

"Hey, are you okay?" Chad was starting to frown.

"Maybe she's deaf, Chad," Diane suggested, looking sympathetic. "Speak slowly so that she can read your lips."

"Are…you…"

"I'm fine," Kelly got out, her voice husky. "I wasn't watching where I was going. Sorry."

She dodged around them without waiting for a reply and hurried down the sidewalk, wanting to put as much distance between herself and the humiliating scene as possible. Tears burned in her eyes, cooling as they fell onto her icy cheeks.

She was nearly a block away before she slowed, angrily wiping her fingers over her face. It was stupid to be so upset. Why should they remember her? She'd been a nothing, a nonentity, a shadow. That's all she'd ever managed to be in school.

She had always known she wasn't pretty or sophisticated like other girls. She'd never had the clothes or makeup the girls in school had chattered about, and she'd never known how to giggle and flirt like they had seemed born knowing how to do. If her mother hadn't died maybe things would have been different.

But her mother *had* died and her father thought cosmetics were the devil's work. Kelly shuddered, remembering the one time she'd tried wearing makeup. She'd found a box of her mother's things and had been playing with some eye shadow and lipstick when her father walked into her room. It was the first time he'd taken his belt to her. There had been other times since then, more than she could remember, but the memory of that beating lingered in her mind, all the more terrible because she hadn't understood why he was so angry.

Not that she understood it any better now, but she'd come to accept her father's rages, the way other people accepted the flu—unpredictable and something to be endured.

Her footsteps slowed as she neared the edge of town. Bud's Tavern was just across the street. Neon signs advertising beer flashed in the gathering dusk. The parking lot was almost full but she knew more cars would somehow be wedged into it as the night wore on. Inside, people would be laughing and talking, dancing maybe, having fun.

Her father said places like Bud's Tavern were dens of iniquity. Kelly didn't dare disagree, but to her Bud's had always looked warm and cheerful. What would it be like to be part of the crowd inside? she wondered. Would it be fun and exciting or would she feel lost and out of place as she always had in a group?

Shaking her head, she turned away, her footsteps quicker now. If she didn't hurry, she was going to be late and her father would be angry. He already verged on disapproval regarding her trips to the library. It wouldn't do to give him a reason to forbid her to go again.

The trailer house where Kelly and her father lived was on the edge of town, set in the middle of an overgrown lot that was the only thing of value her father owned. Kelly made spo-

radic efforts to keep the yard tidy but it was a losing battle.
Three old cars sat in rusting heaps where the front lawn might
have been. A shed leaned drunkenly against a sagging fence.

The trailer house was as old and worn as its surroundings.
It had once been pale blue and white, and Kelly sometimes
thought it might have been bright and cheerful when it was
new. But now it was old. The paint had faded to a vague gray
and dents marred the sides.

The interior was painfully neat and just as painfully shabby.
Holes in the sofa had been covered with a blanket that had, in
its turn, developed holes of its own. The curtains were a heavy,
dark cotton that blocked out what little sunlight could penetrate
the overgrown trees. The tiny kitchen held a stove and refrigerator and enough counter space to make a sandwich.

Kelly barely noticed the shabbiness. Sometimes she remembered the little house they'd lived in when her mother was
alive. It had been dilapidated, too, but there had been a different
feeling about its disrepair. It was as if the house hadn't given
up hope of being restored to its former charms. The trailer had
given up hope a long time ago.

Her father sat in one corner of the sofa, hunched over his
Bible, his lips moving as he read. He didn't bother to look up
and acknowledge Kelly's arrival. She hurried through the
kitchen to the tiny alcove that served as her bedroom, putting
the library books on her bed and shrugging out of her coat.
Her shoes were damp but there was nothing to be done about
that. The sturdy black saddle shoes were the only ones she
owned. They would just have to dry while she wore them.

Dinner was a plain meal of beans and corn bread. The beans
were bland but filling. She was going to have to go to the store
in a day or two—a chore that she hated. She hated seeing
everyone else with their full carts while she counted every
penny she spent.

Her father ate without speaking, muttering some passage
from the Bible now and then, his eyes fierce under furrowed
brows. Looking at him, Kelly tried to remember what he'd
been like when she was a little girl. Had he ever smiled at her,
ever laughed? She couldn't remember.

She picked at her food, feeling something hot and painful in her chest. Was this how the rest of her life was to be? Sitting across the table from her father, unspoken to, unspeaking? Never tasting even the edge of life? Was she going to grow old and die without ever being young and alive, without ever dancing or laughing with a man or wearing a pretty dress?

"Get your coat, girl. They'll be expecting us at the meeting."

Kelly turned away from the shallow sink, wiping her shaky hands on her dress. Her father waited near the door, his dour face almost animated as he considered the evening of prayer that was to follow.

"I...I don't feel very well. Maybe I should stay home." The words were hardly more than a whisper as terror threatened to close her throat.

"What's wrong with you?" he demanded, a harsh scowl hooking his brows together over steel-gray eyes.

"I feel...sick." It wasn't exactly a lie. When she thought of the dark little meeting room with its cold cement floor and bare walls, she *did* feel sick.

He stepped forward, his fingers hard on her arm as he pulled her forward into the light. Fear had driven the color from her face, lending credence to her plea of illness.

"I wouldn't want my illness to interrupt the meeting, make us come home early or anything," she stammered.

"It is an important meeting." He released her abruptly, wiping his hand on his sleeve in an unconscious gesture as if he disliked touching her. "If the world's to be saved, it will be through the power of prayer. You know that, don't you?"

"Yes, Father," she whispered, keeping her eyes lowered.

"You'll stay here, then, and pray," he announced.

"Yes."

She hid her crossed fingers against the side of her dress, wondering if she was condemning her immortal soul to eternal damnation by lying about something as important as prayer.

But at the moment her immortal soul seemed a dim concept. If she didn't do something—anything—her whole life was going to be gone without her ever having lived it.

She waited until she heard the last hiccup of her father's battered old pickup truck before darting into her tiny room and pulling the door shut behind her. Her hands were shaking as she dragged the narrow box from under her bed, brushing away the dust that had gathered on it.

It had been almost three years since she had dared to pull it out. If her father knew she'd kept the things it contained... She shivered, forcing the thought away. He was going to be gone until after midnight tonight. Sometimes these prayer meetings lasted all night.

And it wasn't as if she was going to do anything really wrong, she reasoned with herself as she lifted the lid of the box. It wasn't a sin to want to have just a taste of fun, was it?

The box held very little, really. A shiny green satin doll dress that was all that was left of Devlin's Christmas gift and a faded picture of her brother and herself, taken when she was seven and Devlin had been a tall, lanky teenager. Ordinarily she would have lingered over the photograph, trying to flesh it out with increasingly fuzzy memories. But tonight her mind was on the future, not the past.

She drew another dress out, holding it up to herself as she knelt on the floor. Her mother had worn this dress to a dance in high school. Kelly had seen the pictures once.

The same pictures she'd watched her father burn after her mother was killed in a car wreck. Running away with her lover, he'd said. But she hadn't believed it. Devlin had gone away but her mother would never have left her—not without a word. If she'd been leaving, she would have taken Kelly with her.

She shook the thoughts away as she set the dress aside. She lifted out a pair of high-heeled pumps that matched the dress and the flat case that held all that was left of her mother's makeup.

Stepping out of her own plain dress, Kelly slipped the brightly printed dress over her worn underwear. The print was a wild mixture of pink and orange and green, all swirled together. What was it called? She frowned, trying to remember. Psychedelic. That was it. The bodice had a scooped neck and the skirt dropped straight from the high waistline.

She frowned, tugging at the short skirt, which exposed an extraordinary length of leg. Her dresses usually came to the bottom of her knee. Now she felt exposed. But she'd seen other girls wearing short skirts. She set her teeth. Just for tonight she was going to find out what it was like to be like the other girls.

Just for one night.

Dan Remington stared at the TV dinner he'd just pulled from the oven, his expression morose. New Year's Eve and he was sitting in his apartment with nothing for company but an ailing plant and a very healthy alley cat. He watched without interest as the cat leaped to the top of the table and boldly walked over to sniff at the TV dinner.

"You have the manners of a warthog, Grunge."

Grunge looked at Dan, gauging the seriousness of the accusation. Deciding, correctly, that Dan wasn't going to protest his presence, he returned his attention to the food. He sniffed at the vegetables, dismissing them as unworthy of his attention. The apple cobbler received dubious approval—the crust might be edible. The sliced turkey and gravy were tasted, considered and then approved.

Dan scratched behind one battered gray ear, knowing that the cat would just as soon be left alone. From Grunge's attitude, it was sometimes hard to tell who paid the rent on the apartment. Grunge had moved in soon after Dan, not precisely asking permission, but more as if he were granting a favor by allowing Dan to stay. Dan had never considered himself much of a cat lover but he'd found the big tom helped alleviate some of the loneliness.

Loneliness. Dan shook his head. He'd never expected to find himself turning to a cat for company. But then he had never expected to find himself so cut off from the people he'd known all his life.

Who was it who had said that you couldn't go home again? He was finding that more true than he cared to admit. He stood, leaving the cat to eat in peace. Moving over to the television, he flipped it on. Only a few more hours till midnight. The people in Times Square were looking smug. After all, they had a jump on the rest of the country. They got to shoo the old year out earlier than everyone else.

Dan snapped off the television and wandered over to the window. The park that lay across the street was dark and full of mysterious shadows. The snow that had fallen just before Christmas lingered only in sheltered places, catching the light here and there, giving the look of a patchwork quilt.

What was he doing here? Not just here in this apartment but here in Remembrance? There was nothing for him here. After nearly two years in a Central American prison, he'd come home, wanting nothing more than to pick up the threads of his life. It had been foolish of him to think that everyone else's life would have stood still just because his own had been dragged to a halt. People had moved on, changed.

He'd left, traveled for a couple of months and then somehow found himself back here. This was home. Or it had been all his life. Now it was just the closest thing to a home that he had.

Restless, he let the curtain fall, turning to look at the sterile apartment. If he moved out tomorrow, there would be nothing here to show that he'd once spent several months of his life here. If he disappeared tomorrow, his absence would leave a gap in no one's life.

His mother lived in Europe with her new husband, a man half her age who treated her as if she were made of gold. She would miss him but her life would go on.

And Brittany? Brittany would miss him. The love they'd once felt had changed, not without pain, into something approaching a friendship. Yes, Brittany would be sorry to see him go, but her life was wrapped up in Michael and little Danielle. She had a family, people whose lives were intimately entwined with hers. A husband, a child.

"That's what I want."

Grunge looked up from the tray, licking gravy off his whiskers. Well fed, he was willing to provide an audience.

"A family. Is that so much to ask?" Grunge licked one paw and began to wash his face.

"I suppose you think that's ridiculous." Dan scowled, turning away to glare at the blank television screen. "Maybe you're right. Maybe it's just the holiday season that's making me crazy."

Whatever it was, he knew he had to get out of the apartment. If he sat here watching plastic-faced celebrities chortle about the new year, he was going to put his foot through the television.

His sudden, decisive move to the coat closet startled Grunge who jumped, putting one foot down in the apple cobbler. He hissed his displeasure but Dan wasn't listening. Bud's Tavern might not be the best place in the world to spend New Year's Eve, but it was certainly better than sitting here with nothing but his own company.

Just for tonight he was going to get out and have fun. Even if it killed him, he was going to have a good time. At least for tonight.

# Chapter 2

Kelly swallowed and backed farther into the corner she'd found. It seemed as if it was the only space in the entire room that wasn't occupied by people laughing and talking.

Bud's Tavern wasn't quite what she'd expected. Of course, her idea of what she'd find in a "den of iniquity" had been vague. This certainly met some of them. There were lots of people and all of them seemed to be having a roaring good time.

But her dreams hadn't included the amount of sheer noise that filled the bar. Across the room, a small band blasted music so loud it seemed to preclude conversation, but that didn't stop anyone from talking. They simply raised their voices to be heard above it. Kelly didn't see how anyone could hear anything.

And she'd never anticipated breathing air she could actually see. She'd read the phrase "smoky barroom" in books but her imagination had never come even close to the reality. Smoke drifting from cigarettes swirled in a cloud near the ceiling, giving the multicolored lights a hazy look. It hovered everywhere, drawing a tattered veil around the edges of the big room.

Once her eyes had stopped watering and her lungs no longer burned, she was able to ignore the smoke, just as everyone else seemed to. But it was the only thing she had in common with the room's occupants.

She'd seen right away that her clothes were all wrong. It wasn't that her skirt was too short, as she'd feared. A lot of the other women were wearing short skirts, some even shorter than her own. But they were all narrow, snug little affairs of denim or leather. And they were generally paired with cowboy boots or spike heels and stretchy little T-shirts.

Kelly eased one foot out of its shoe, flexing her toes to relieve the cramp that was running up her instep. It had taken her nearly fifteen minutes of practice to be able to take more than two or three steps in the thick-soled shoes without falling over. They added nearly two inches to her own height of five foot two, if she could just keep from tipping over.

"Hey." Kelly looked up, startled, as a tall, willowy blond woman with perfectly chiseled features stopped in front of her. "Where did you get that dress?"

"It was my mother's," Kelly stammered out and then immediately wished she'd said something else.

"It's really hot. My mom threw out all her sixties stuff. Can you believe it?" The blonde looked disgusted. Kelly shook her head, trying to look as if she couldn't believe it. "You've done a great job with the makeup and everything."

"Thank you." Kelly groped for something more to say. After all, this was the first person to speak to her. This was what she'd come here for, wasn't it?

"Hey, Tiffany." The blonde turned in response to the shout, lifting one perfectly manicured hand. Kelly tucked her own ragged nails behind her back. Tiffany turned back for a last comment. "Great retro look, really."

Kelly watched her plunge into the mass of people, weaving her way expertly through the crowd. Even from a distance, she exuded the confidence Kelly was so sorely lacking. It was clear that Tiffany was perfectly at home in Bud's Tavern. Whereas Kelly was anything but.

Still, she'd been nice. For a minute there, she'd almost felt as if she wasn't out of place. Retro look? Tiffany had made it sound like a compliment. Was it possible that she looked like she was making some sort of a fashion statement? The thought almost made her smile.

She fished for her shoe, edging back as one of the waitresses headed toward her corner. One of the first things she'd realized was that one didn't come to a bar without planning on drinking.

Even if she had known what to order, she didn't have any money. So far no one seemed to be paying any attention to the fact that she wasn't drinking. In fact, no one seemed to be paying any attention to her at all.

Aside from the brief moment when Tiffany had spoken to her, she might as well have been invisible. Her fantasies had never been quite like this. She'd been a little sketchy on details but she'd certainly never imagined herself feeling so out of place, so invisible. If it wasn't for the fact that she'd been jostled and bumped more times than she could count, she might have begun to wonder if she was even here at all.

*If a girl goes into a bar but nobody sees her, is she really there at all?*

Kelly almost giggled at the absurdity of the question. Her forehead felt clammy and there was a vague buzzing in her ears. She should have eaten more at supper. Her stomach felt hollow. She watched a waitress go by with a tray of drinks and licked her lips, suddenly realizing how thirsty she was. A glass of water sounded like heaven but she didn't dare ask for it, didn't dare risk drawing attention to herself.

Maybe if she went to the ladies' room, splashed a little water on her face, she'd feel better. But the sign for the rest rooms was all the way across the room. Just the thought of trying to make her way through all those people made her feel dizzy.

Everywhere she looked, people leaned against walls or stood next to the bar or sat in booths, or rocked back and forth on the tiny dance floor. Everyone was laughing and talking, smiling and drinking, apparently having the time of their lives. Everyone was with someone else.

She had been lonely most of her life but she'd never been quite so aware of being alone. Here, in this crowd of people, her aloneness was so obvious, so real. She felt as if she were the only person in the world who didn't have someone to talk with.

Dan tried to remember what impulse had led him here, to this noisy bar. He'd had some vague thought about getting out among other people being good for him. After all, it was New Year's Eve, a time to celebrate and have fun. So was he having fun yet? he asked himself cynically.

He picked up the shot glass of whiskey and downed the last swallow. If he remembered correctly, the cat had eaten most of his dinner. Too much alcohol on an empty stomach was not a good idea. He picked up a handful of pretzels from the bowl on the bar and signaled the bartender for a refill.

Lifting the fresh drink, Dan caught a glimpse of himself in the mirror that lined the back of the bar. He lowered the drink slowly, frowning at his reflection in the smoky glass. Was it just his imagination or did he look totally out of place, like an ill-tempered wolf in a group of happy puppies?

His scowl deepened. He wasn't any older than most of these people. Not in years, at least. But in terms of experience, he felt decades older. Two years in a Central America prison, accused of being a spy, was enough to drum the youth out of almost anyone, he supposed.

He'd thought that coming back to Remembrance, coming home, he would be able to put those years behind him. He'd been a fool. You couldn't go home, you couldn't go back. All you could do was keep going and hope you found some reason for continuing.

He turned away from the mirror, downing the shot of whiskey as he leaned back against the bar. What were they all celebrating, anyway? A new year, new problems, new bills. What was to celebrate? A year just past, spent alone. A year coming up, spent the same way. No home, no roots, no one to care all that much what happened to him, no one whose life was intimately tied to his.

Looking around the crowded bar, it seemed to Dan that

everyone was with someone else. Everyone had someone to talk to, someone to laugh with. Everyone but him.

And her.

He narrowed his eyes, studying the girl on the other side of the room. He'd seen her when she first came in; the wild colors in her dress were enough to catch his eye even in this overcrowded room. He'd noticed her a time or two since then. At first he'd assumed she was waiting for someone, but no one showed up.

She'd backed herself into a corner, looking as out of place as he felt. Acting on an impulse, Dan slid off the bar stool. Carrying his drink, he made his way across the room, side-stepping a couple who stumbled off the dance floor into his path.

The closer he got to the girl, the stronger was the impression that she didn't belong here. She didn't look like the other women in the place. And it wasn't just that. Even to his uneducated eye, her clothes and makeup were odd. Beneath the thick mascara and heavy black eyeliner, her eyes were large and a soft, warm brown. The wildly patterned dress had a scooped neckline that exposed as much breast as it covered. From the high waistline, the skirt dropped in a bell shape to a point considerably above her knee. Dan had a vague idea that he'd seen similar dresses on old *Laugh-In* reruns.

But despite the makeup and dress, there was something about her. Something almost…lost.

The band was taking a break, making conversation possible.

"Hi." As openings went, it was simple, if not original.

She blinked and then her eyes widened as she realized he was speaking to her.

"Hello."

"Are you waiting for someone?"

"No."

"I'm Dan Remington." He held out his hand.

"Kelly. Kelly Russell." Her fingers felt small in his. Small and cold.

"Can I buy you a drink?"

"That would be nice."

"Anything in particular?"

"No. I don't have a preference."

Dan signaled a waitress and ordered an Irish coffee before turning back to Kelly.

"Do you come here often?"

"No." Something in the question seemed to amuse her and he found her fleeting smile as appealing as the rest of her. She didn't seem to feel any need to fill the silence with polite conversation while they waited for their drinks, and he found that pleasant, too.

In truth, Kelly couldn't think of anything to say. Certainly conversation with an attractive man had been part of her tangled fantasies. But in those fantasies she'd always known just what to say, dazzling him with her wit and charm.

When the waitress brought the coffee, Kelly clutched it to her, almost scalding her tongue on the hot liquid. The smooth bite of the whiskey flooded her mouth, hitting her empty stomach with a bounce and then racing through her veins without pause. She felt her face flush. Where she'd felt cold and clammy before, she was suddenly warm and cozy. She gave Dan a shy smile.

"It's very good. Thank you."

When was the last time he'd had a woman thank him for buying her a drink? Dan smiled back at her, feeling suddenly that the evening might not be a total waste, after all. The speakers popped as the amplifier was turned back on. The band was preparing to start another set.

"Do you want to dance?"

Kelly nodded, finishing the last of the Irish coffee with a gulp. She didn't know how to dance, but she'd watched the couples on the floor earlier and it didn't look all that difficult. Besides, she was suddenly feeling much more confident.

As the evening wore on, Kelly's confidence increased in direct proportion to the level of alcohol in her bloodstream. She was finally getting a taste of what life was really like and it was everything she'd thought.

Dan Remington had given the man in her daydreams a face. He was tall, with streaky blond hair and eyes as blue as a summer sky. His smile was easy but she thought she read something behind it, a loneliness maybe, that she understood.

They didn't talk much. Words didn't seem necessary. It was as if they were communicating without them. When the band moved into a slow tune and Dan slipped his arms around her, Kelly felt as if she had come home at last. Through the haze of three Irish coffees, she knew that her whole life had been directed toward this one moment.

A small voice in the back of her mind cautioned her. This was one night only, one night out of a lifetime. Tomorrow everything would be as it was, as it had always been, as it probably would always be. She might never see this man again. But she shoved the voice away, refusing to let common sense intrude on the magical spell that seemed to be weaving itself around the two of them.

For Dan, the magic was a little more prosaic, a little more easily understood. He wanted to forget. For tonight, he wanted to forget everything that might have been, everything he'd once dreamed of having. He wanted to forget the loneliness.

Kelly didn't insist on meaningless conversation. She was soft and warm in his arms, a shield from the chill of being alone. And the wistfulness he thought he glimpsed in her eyes told him that she knew what it was to be alone—to be lonely.

As the lights dimmed for another slow tune, Dan drew her into his arms, feeling her settle against him. It felt right to hold her in his arms, to feel her slender body against his. He didn't allow himself to question how much of that rightness was whiskey induced. For this one night, he needed to forget.

On the darkened dance floor, his mouth found hers. She jumped as if startled, her mouth stiff beneath his. He would have drawn back but her lips suddenly softened. She seemed to melt against him, warm and pliant.

For Kelly, the kiss was a revelation. In all her vague dreams of what a kiss would be like, she'd never imagined anything approaching reality. Dan's mouth was firm, just like his body against hers. He tasted of whiskey, a sharp, smoky taste that threatened to melt her bones.

His tongue came out to trace the soft swell of her lower lip and Kelly shuddered at the intensity of feelings that sprang to life. Her head was spinning with sensations she'd never experienced.

When the music ended, Dan led her off the floor. The table they'd been using was now occupied by a group intent on bringing in the new year with a noisy bang. Dan wedged a space for them at the bar, signaling the bartender and ordering two more drinks.

The small voice of reason suggested to Kelly that she'd had more than enough to drink already but it was easily ignored. She was having fun—for the first time in years. There was a not unpleasant buzzing sensation in her head, and Dan's arm around her waist was all that kept her feet from floating right off the floor. She couldn't remember the last time she'd felt so good.

They danced again, kissed again and drank some more. It occurred to Dan that he'd had more than enough to drink, though it would have been difficult to tell by looking at him. His walk was steady, his speech was clear and his eyes had no trouble focusing. But he could feel the effects of the alcohol.

The loneliness that had become his constant companion these past months had faded to a shadowy presence in the back of his mind. He felt younger and freer than he had in years. He felt like acting his age. He grinned at the thought, feeling suddenly reckless.

"What is it?" Kelly's question made him realize that he was grinning foolishly to himself.

"Just a thought. Let's dance." He guzzled the last of his whiskey before leading her onto the floor. He didn't want to dance, didn't have the slightest idea what the music was. It was just an excuse to put his arms around Kelly's slender waist, to feel her nestle up against him.

It was sweet torture to hold her like this, to feel the soft brush of her against his body, to feel the slender length of her back under his hands. It came to him suddenly that he couldn't remember ever wanting anyone the way he wanted her. His body ached with the need to have her close without the irritating barriers of their clothes interfering.

Kelly trembled as his mouth found the sensitive shell of her ear. His teeth nibbled at the lobe, sending shivers down her spine, making her knees weak. There was a heaviness in the pit of her stomach that she had never felt before, a kind of burning ache.

When the song ended, Kelly stumbled off the dance floor. Her legs didn't seem to belong to her. In fact her whole body seemed to belong to someone else. Someone young and pretty, someone who belonged with all these beautiful, happy people.

Midnight was approaching and, with it, the level of noise grew until the building nearly shook with the volume of it. The band had moved into a loud, raucous medley of sixties hits, the speakers rattling the rafters.

The room was packed with people. Their places at the long maple bar had been taken. Dan stopped a few feet away, drawing Kelly close, leaning down to talk directly into her ear as it was the only way to be heard.

"Let's get out of here. We can go to my place. It's not far."

"Your place?" A faint warning bell rang in Kelly's mind.

"I want to be alone with you."

The warning bell drowned in a rush of pleasure. He wanted to be alone with her. Hadn't she always known this was the way it would be? With the knowledge that came of several Irish coffees, Kelly was sure that destiny had finally taken a hand in her life. Why else would she have come here and met Dan?

"Yes, all right." He couldn't hear her breathless consent but he could see it in her eyes. They paused long enough at the door to find their coats, pulling them out from beneath the dozen others that had been stacked on each iron hook. Seeing Kelly's inadequate cloth coat, Dan draped his own sheepskin-lined denim jacket over her shoulders.

Dan had walked the few blocks from his apartment to the bar. Considering the amount he'd had to drink, it was just as well he had chosen not to drive. The air was cold, with a frosty bite that smelled of snow, though the sky was clear. Wrapped in Dan's coat, his arm around her, Kelly felt warmed to the bone. She leaned her head on Dan's shoulder and pushed all thoughts of reality out of her head. She'd promised herself this one night and she was going to grasp everything it had to give with both hands. Let tomorrow take care of itself.

The walk to Dan's apartment building was short. The streets were empty. With midnight just around the corner, most people had already settled in to greet the new year.

If Dan had been in any condition to think about it, he might have expected the cold air and brisk walk to cool the need that burned in his veins. But a delicate scent that could only be Kelly's seemed to fill his head, drawing him deeper, making the ache in his gut more acute. The heavy denim of his coat made her appear even more fragile, even more feminine.

And he wanted her like he'd never wanted anyone in his life.

As they approached his apartment house, Kelly stumbled when one of her thick heels caught on a crack in the sidewalk. Dan caught her, the coat falling open as she fell against him. For an instant, her breasts were pressed against his chest. He could feel the taut buds of her nipples through his shirt.

It was like setting match to flame.

Kelly gasped, startled, as his arms swept around her, crushing her to his body. Her head fell back with the suddenness of the move and she had only a glimpse of Dan's face before his mouth closed over hers.

This was not like the kisses they'd shared on the dance floor. There was nothing tentative here, nothing questioning. She quivered, her whole body going limp as his tongue slid into her mouth, sweeping across the sensitive flesh of her lower lip, testing the ridge of her teeth before plunging inside.

Lights seemed to flash beneath her eyelids and the low ache in her stomach became a burning pressure. Hardly knowing what she was doing, she brought her arms up to circle his neck, her movements made clumsy by the bulky weight of his coat.

Without breaking the kiss, Dan bent to scoop her up in his arms. He carried her up the walkway, finding his way more by instinct than sight. Her slight weight barely slowed him going up the stairs.

He had to put her down momentarily to find the keys to the

front door. Kelly leaned against the doorjamb, her breathing ragged. The warning bell rang frantically, the sound drowned out by the pounding of her own pulse in her ears.

The door was pushed open and Dan swept her into the hallway, kicking the door shut behind them. The denim jacket and Kelly's own coat landed on the floor with a soft thud. His hands framed her face, his mouth slanting across hers, his tongue plunging inside.

Kelly was helpless to do anything but respond. She was caught between the wall at her back and Dan's scarcely less taut frame. His hands swept up and down her sides as he kissed her, long drugging kisses that drained but at the same time filled her body with a strange burning sensation.

His fingers found the zipper on the back of her dress, sliding it down the length of her spine. The garment slipped down her arms. Kelly shivered, wrenching her mouth free as his hands slid between the two of them to cup her breasts. Her fingers dug into his shoulders, her whole body rigid.

For an instant, sanity almost made itself heard. She was rushing toward something for which she was woefully unprepared.

If Dan felt her sudden tension, he misunderstood its cause.

"Beautiful," he murmured. "So beautiful." His thumbs brushed across her nipples.

The sensation was so intense, it was almost painful. She felt his touch, not only at her breasts, but deep inside, like an echo in the pit of her stomach. She continued to shiver, her back arching in an unconscious gesture of surrender.

He'd called her beautiful—no one else had ever said she was beautiful.

"Unbutton my shirt," he muttered against her throat.

Her fingers shaking, Kelly did as he asked. When the shirt hung open to where it was tucked into his belt, she flattened her palms against his chest. She felt the shudder that went through Dan at her touch. It gave her a wonderful feeling of power to feel this man tremble because of her.

Her hands slid to his shoulders as he drew her forward until her breasts were gently crushed against his muscled chest. For a moment, neither of them moved, neither of them breathed.

"I want you." With those words, Dan scattered the last varning bell in Kelly's mind. She had never felt wanted, truly vanted, in her life.

"Yes." The word was a surrender. An offering. A plea.

She couldn't have said how they got from the hallway to the edroom. It didn't matter. Her dress had disappeared some- vhere along the way, along with her underwear, leaving her aked and vulnerable. She didn't care. She was beautiful and e wanted her.

Dan lifted her onto the bed before stepping back to strip off he rest of his clothes. And then he came to her, his muscled ody pressing her down against the sheets. She'd never felt nything so intense in her life. A million nerve endings sprang o life, each sensitized to his slightest touch.

She cried out when his mouth found her breast, drawing the ipple inside and suckling. Her fingers twined in his hair, her egs shifting restlessly. She felt hollow and aching inside. Empty and needful. She whimpered when Dan's hand slid cross her stomach to tangle in the soft curls at the top of her highs. She would have closed her legs in automatic reaction o this invasion but his fingers found the warm dampness of er and she could only tremble in helpless reaction to his touch.

Dan's head was spinning with need. He'd never wanted a oman like this, never felt such a powerful, burning need. It vas as if something beyond his control had brought him to this voman, this moment.

Her skin was soft and warm. She fluttered beneath his touch, er response holding an element of uncertainty that might have iven him pause at another time. But he couldn't seem to think f anything beyond his searing need.

He rose above her, his hips sliding between her thighs. In er arms, he'd find a cure for the emptiness that nagged at him. Ie'd be whole again. At least for tonight.

Kelly's hands settled hesitantly on his shoulders, her eyes vide in the moonlight that spilled in through the open curtains. he bit her lips as she felt him press against her. Suddenly the varning bell returned, clanging through her mind, but it was oo late.

Her hands shifted to his chest in an uncertain protest, but th gesture was lost on Dan who didn't recognize it for what i was. With desire pounding in his veins, believing she felt th same, he thrust deep.

Kelly gasped, her nails digging into his chest as pain stabbe through her, shattering the haze of passion that had led her thi far. She tried to twist away but there was no escaping the sud den possession of her body.

Her teeth drew blood from her lower lip as he moved above her. The pain had eased but her body felt invaded, stretched filled in ways she'd never imagined.

Above her, Dan was aware of the sudden rigidity of her body. He struggled to find a reason for it but his body wasn' interested in explanations. She fit him like a glove, all damp heat and soft friction. It had been so long.

Kelly bit back a whimper as she felt him swell within her, his body convulsing over her. There was a long moment when he lay above her, his breath coming in shallow pants. She closed her eyes, praying for this to end, praying that she'd wake up in her own narrow bed to find that this had all been nothing more than a vivid dream.

Dan rolled to the side, aware of her small gasp of discomfort as he withdrew. There was something wrong, something he should remember. His hand came out to catch her arm when she moved to leave the bed.

"Don't." He had to pause to put the words in order. "Don't go." The whiskey he had consumed earlier was suddenly hitting him like a sledgehammer. His speech was slurred, his vision fuzzy. But this was important.

"Need to talk," he managed, trying to fight the fog that seemed to be creeping over his mind.

"Not now," she mumbled, pulling back as far as his grip would allow.

"Later." Yes, they could talk later. In the morning. In the morning he'd be able to remember what it was that was so important. In the morning his brain would make sense of it all. They'd talk then.

Kelly held her breath, her eyes never leaving his face as his drifted shut. The hand on her arm loosened and she slid off the bed as if it were hot coals. Snatching her panties off the floor, she shoved her hair back from her face, trying to remember where her dress was. It was lying in the bedroom doorway and she scurried over to it, jerking it on with shaking hands.

What had she done?

The pleasant alcoholic fog that had made everything seem so right, so inevitable, had been shattered along with her virginity, leaving her nothing to hold between herself and reality.

She'd slept with a man she'd just met. No. Not *slept* with him. No pleasant little phrases. She'd had sex with him. Nothing more, nothing less. She'd let him pick her up in a bar and bring her back to his apartment like some kind of cheap tramp.

She swallowed back a sob, struggling with the zipper that ran up the back of the dress. The same zipper she'd rejoiced in feeling him slide down.

The straps on the thick, chunky shoes defeated her shaky fingers and she finally just snatched them up, stuffing one in each side pocket of her coat where they bulged awkwardly.

With a last wild look toward the bedroom door, Kelly fled the apartment. The cement steps were icy on her bare feet but she didn't notice the discomfort. She had to get home.

By the time she reached the overgrown driveway that led up to the trailer, she was chilled to the bone. Her feet were numb and she wondered vaguely if her toes were frostbitten. It didn't seem terribly important. All she wanted was to reach the shelter of her bed and pull the blankets over her head. She wanted to go to sleep and wake up in the morning to find that none of this had happened.

Her father's truck was parked in front of the trailer and Kelly almost collapsed. If her father caught her...if he ever guessed what she'd done...

She crept around to the back, thankful that she'd thought to leave the window over her bed unlocked, though she'd planned to be home long before her father got back from his meeting. But then nothing had gone quite the way she'd planned.

It took her frozen fingers several seconds to find the edge of the window and get a solid grip on it. It slid open with a soft scraping sound that made her catch her breath. But no light was turned on and there was no sound to suggest that she'd been discovered.

Kelly lifted herself over the windowsill, sliding onto the bed. The air felt hot on her skin though she knew the little heater at the other end of the trailer barely kept the temperature above that outside. Kneeling on the bed, she eased the window shut, feeling her shoulders sag as it clicked into place.

She'd made it. Now all she had to do was forget this night had ever happened.

A soft click behind her flooded the little cubicle with light. Still on her knees, Kelly spun toward the light, her eyes wide and frightened. Her father sat on a chair just inside the doorway. He'd obviously been waiting for her to come home.

And just as obviously, he could read at least some of what had happened from her appearance. She lifted a hand to her face, aware of the forbidden makeup that must be smudged under her eyes. Her hair was a wild tangle about her face.

She shrank back against the wall as he reached for his belt but she didn't protest. She knew there was nothing she could say or do to stop what was about to happen.

# Chapter 3

March swept in like the proverbial lion, bringing with it snow flurries and below-freezing weather. Winter might have to surrender its hold but it wasn't going to do so without a fight. The land hunkered down to wait out winter's temper tantrum, knowing that spring lay just around the corner, no matter what the thermometer was saying.

Dan scowled out at the chill, gray sky, asking himself for the thousandth time why he didn't just pack up and leave. He could move to a warmer climate. Arizona was nice this time of year. There was nothing to keep him in Remembrance— nothing and no one.

"Hey, Dan. You wanna give me a hand with this engine?"

Casting a last frown at the sky, Dan turned in answer to Lee's call. He'd gone to school with Lee, who was struggling to get his own auto-repair business going. Dan's desultory help had somehow become a full-time job and he'd been working in Lee's repair shop since just before Christmas.

It wasn't the job that was keeping him, he thought as he helped Lee steady the engine they were lowering into a '67 Mustang. When he'd returned from the dead, his mother had given him everything she'd inherited from his father's estate. Her new husband was rolling in money, she'd told him bluntly, and she wanted him to have the money his father had left her. He was comfortable, if not wealthy.

He'd thought of taking some of that money and starting his own business. His father had been a pretty successful contractor with his own company. That had been sold at his death, of course, but there was no reason Dan couldn't start up his own company.

But what good would it do? he asked himself cynically. He could just as easily take the money and travel around the world, have a high old time for a few years and then die poor but well traveled.

He wiped his hands on a greasy rag, trying to shake the depression that was an all too frequent companion these days. He had to make some decisions about his life. He couldn't keep drifting like this. It was all very well and good to spend a few months helping Lee get his business going, but it was just another way to avoid making any decisions, any commitments.

"Why don't you go to lunch, man? I can handle it alone for a while."

Dan nodded in answer to Lee's suggestion. He wasn't particularly hungry but he welcomed an interruption to his thoughts. He stripped out of the overalls that protected his own jeans and flannel shirt. Pulling on his denim jacket, he hurried across the street to Rosie's.

A classic American greasy spoon, Rosie's was complete with cracked red vinyl booths and peeling black-and-white checked linoleum. The waitresses were all well into middle age with teased hair dyed improbable shades of red and lavender. Rosie's was also the best place in town—some said in the county—to get a good hamburger with all the trimmings.

Which meant that, at twenty after twelve, it was also one of the busiest places in town. Every seat at the counter was occupied, as were all the booths. Well, he could order his lunch to go.

"Dan!"

He turned toward the sound of his name, recognizing Brittany's voice and half wishing he could pretend to be deaf. She was seated at a booth in the back. As Dan made his way toward her, he wondered how it was possible that she seemed to grow more beautiful every time he saw her.

"Brittany. How are you?"

"Fine. Why don't you join me?"

"Sure." His hesitation was brief. He slid into the seat across from her, reaching for a menu, although he already knew what he was going to order.

"How have you been?" Brittany asked. "We haven't seen you since before Christmas. I thought you might have left town without telling anybody."

"I've been busy, I guess." Dan shut the menu and looked across the table at her. The sheer beauty of her was almost a blow. Wide-set gray eyes, a beautifully molded mouth and a thick mass of black hair that seemed made for a man to lose himself in. "How have you been? And Michael?"

He made himself add the last. He and Michael Sinclair had once been best friends, closer than most brothers. But that had been a long time ago, before he'd spent two years in that hellhole of a prison. Before he'd come home to find Michael married to the woman he'd loved, father to the child Dan hadn't known she was carrying.

"I'm fine. I've sold two articles since January."

"That's great. Next thing I know, I'll be seeing your name on the bestseller lists."

"Well, it's a long way from articles to bestsellers but you never know."

She broke off as the waitress came to take their orders, picking up the conversation as the woman left.

"Michael's fine, too. He and Donovan are working on a design for a new housing development outside Indianapolis."

"That's great." Dan tried to infuse the proper enthusiasm into his voice. It wasn't that he begrudged Michael his success. He knew as well as anyone how hard Michael had worked. He'd joined his father's architectural firm but he'd had to earn his place there. Still, it hurt to know that Michael had all the things that could have been his. That *would* have been his if it hadn't been for that damned plane crash.

"How is Danielle?" Really, the question was a masterpiece. A casual listener would never have guessed what it cost him to ask it. But Brittany wasn't a casual listener and she knew exactly how difficult it was for him to be a casual visitor in Danielle's life. She was Dan's child by blood and Michael's by every other standard that mattered.

"Danielle's fine. She's growing so fast. Sometimes it seems as if I just turn around and she's grown another inch."

"I know. I saw her a couple of weeks ago." Dan shrugged in answer to her questioning look. "I just happened to be going by her nursery school while the kids were out playing. She's turning into a real little beauty."

"Danielle didn't mention seeing you."

"I didn't talk to her. I figured the teachers would probably call the police if a strange man started talking to one of the kids. I was just driving by."

"You're not a strange man," Brittany denied firmly. "You're…a friend of the family. Danielle knows you."

"Well, I didn't really have time to stop, anyway." Dan dismissed the incident. Not for anything in the world would he admit that he often drove by the nursery school when the children were outside. Brittany would probably think he was losing his mind. And maybe he was. But it was a sort of bittersweet pleasure to see Danielle. For a moment, he could almost imagine what his life would have been like if things had gone the way they should have.

"Michael misses you." Brittany interrupted his thoughts. "The two of you were best friends once."

"That was a long time ago. It's nobody's fault that things went the way they did, Brittany. I don't blame Michael for what happened. In fact, I'm glad he was there for you and Danielle," he said, surprised to realize how much he meant it. "But things have changed. We're not the same people we were."

"I still think—"

"Don't," he cut in, a smile taking the sting out of his words. "Don't think about it. I don't."

It was a patent lie but he really didn't want to talk about the friendship he'd once had with Michael or think about the way his life might have gone. He was grateful for the waitress's arrival with their meals. Even more grateful that Brittany didn't insist on picking up the conversation when the waitress left.

They ate in silence for a few minutes. A comfortable silence, Dan realized, a little surprised. He could sit across the table from Brittany and no longer be overwhelmed by a sense of what might have been. At some point they'd managed to make the shift from lovers to friends.

"Are you dating anybody in particular?" Brittany asked, her elaborately casual tone completely failing to mask her curiosity.

He wished he could have told her he was. But he couldn't remember the last time he'd been on a date, the last time he'd even met a woman he wanted to date.

He had a sudden memory of big brown eyes and silky soft skin. The girl from New Year's Eve. Funny how she popped into his thoughts at odd times. But he couldn't even remember her name. And he wouldn't really say they'd had a date. An encounter maybe, an incident, one of the more confusing experiences of his life, but definitely not a date.

"No, I'm not seeing anyone," he said at last, a slight frown creasing his forehead.

"I could introduce you to a couple of women I know," Brittany offered casually.

"I don't need a matchmaker," he snapped, stung that Brittany, of all people, should be offering to fix him up with a date.

"Sorry." Her eyes reflected her startlement at this reaction. To his horror, he saw the shimmer of tears.

"No, no. I'm the one who's sorry," he said hastily. "I shouldn't have snapped like that. For God's sake, don't cry." He shoved a handful of napkins at her, his expression so panicked that Brittany laughed, a slightly watery sound but reassuring.

"I'm not going to burst into tears." She dabbed at her eyes

with the edge of a napkin. "Don't mind me. I'm just a little overemotional these days."

"Is something wrong? You said everything was going all right. There's nothing wrong with Danielle, is there, or Michael? You're not sick."

She laughed again at the rapid-fire questions, shaking her head. "Nothing's wrong. Nobody's sick." She hesitated, her cheeks flushing softly. "I'm just a little pregnant and it's got my emotions all topsy-turvy."

In his concern, Dan had leaned across the table toward her and now he sat back with a thump. He felt her words as if they were a physical blow, knocking the wind from his lungs. Pregnant. He groped for something to say.

"A little pregnant? Isn't that like being a little dead? I mean, there's no halfway with that sort of thing, is there?"

"I guess not." She laughed a little, still flushed. "I'm just not quite used to the idea yet, I guess."

Glowing. He'd heard the term used when people talked about pregnant women but he'd never actually noticed it himself. But Brittany was definitely glowing. When he'd first seen her and thought she was even more beautiful, he'd been seeing the glow pregnancy gave her. Had she looked like this while she was carrying *his* child?

Looking at him, Brittany must have been able to read something of his thoughts. Her smile faded, replaced by a look of concern. She reached across the table to touch the hand he'd unconsciously clenched.

"Dan..."

"Congratulations, Brittany." He deliberately cut her off, knowing it was rude and not caring. He didn't want to listen to her tell him that he'd find a wonderful woman soon. In fact, if he didn't get out of here soon, he was going to do something he'd regret, like break the table in two with his bare hands.

"Look at the time." He glanced at his watch without seeing it. "I told Lee I wouldn't take too long. Lunch is on me."

He threw a few bills on the table and started to slide out of the booth, pausing when he caught the look of distress in Brittany's eyes. He was behaving like a first-class bastard. His face softened as he reached out to catch one of her hands.

"I'm really happy for you, Brittany. Truly happy. No one deserves this more than you and Michael." He stood, still holding her hand and bent to kiss her on the forehead.

She clung to his hand for a moment, her eyes serious. "Don't be such a stranger. Come and see us."

"Sure," he promised, knowing he had no intention of doing any such thing.

Dan left the diner and started across the street to the garage, changing his mind at the last minute and angling away from it. He wasn't ready to talk to anyone. He shoved his hands into his pockets, hunching his shoulders against the cold as he strode down the sidewalk.

Brittany was pregnant.

The knowledge settled like a lead weight in the pit of his stomach. It wasn't that he begrudged her and Michael this happiness. It wasn't even the thought that, had things turned out differently, this child might have been his. He'd come to terms with the fact that he couldn't change what had happened.

In his more rational moments, he even faced that maybe what he and Brittany had had wouldn't have survived the stresses of marriage. She'd been so young. And he'd had so much growing up to do. That was one thing you could say in favor of Central American prisons: people tended to mature very quickly in them.

No, he was genuinely glad for her. But seeing her so happy, so settled, made him wonder when he was going to find even a portion of that happiness. Maybe it was being the only one to survive the plane crash that had killed his father and everyone else on board; maybe it was the time in prison that had made him realize how short life could be.

He wanted a home, a family, the things that really counted in life. He wanted something to anchor him, a reason to get up in the morning, something to look forward to as the years went on.

When was he going to find any of those things?

* * *

Kelly shook convulsively. The gas station bathroom was unheated and the bare tiles seemed to intensify the chill outside, driving it bone deep.

But it wasn't the cold that made her shake. Crouched against the wall, Kelly was hardly aware of the temperature. The cold she felt was lodged deep inside her, spreading outward to drive the color from her skin, leaving her as pale as the white porcelain fixtures.

It was early in the morning, so early the sun itself still held a sleepy look about it. Kelly had crept out of the house just after dawn, leaving her father sleeping. She hadn't slept at all last night. Knowing what she was planning, terrified that if she fell asleep she might not wake up in time to slip out of the trailer before he awoke, she'd lain awake all night, listening to his mutterings, counting every tick of the clock.

And now she'd gotten her answers from the little pink-and-white box. The test tube sitting on the edge of the cracked sink confirmed what she'd already guessed. The gap in her schedule, the nausea in the mornings, the feeling that something had changed...

It had taken her nearly three weeks to scrape up the money to buy the box that was now spelling her doom. She'd concealed it in the toolshed, awaiting an opportunity to sneak out first thing in the morning. She hadn't dared to bring it into the trailer, sure that her father would somehow sense its presence.

Kelly shivered again, her knuckles turning white where they gripped the edges of her coat. If her father found out... Just the thought made her dizzy with fear. She pressed her forehead against her updrawn knees.

She was pregnant.

Even thinking the words made them seem too real. She wanted to push them away, deny them, make their reality a lie.

Pregnant.

She drew a harsh, sobbing breath. It had to be a mistake. God couldn't be so cruel. He couldn't punish her like this. Not just for that one night. Hadn't her father already punished her enough? She ground her forehead against her knees, clenching her teeth to keep the sobs back.

If he found out she was pregnant, he'd kill her. There was no doubt in her mind about that. She had to get away before he found out, before it became impossible for her to conceal it from him any longer.

A baby. She was expecting a stranger's baby. She knew almost nothing about him. He'd told her his name and where he worked. Not very much to know about the father of her child. She'd tried so hard to forget that night, blocking it from her mind as if just to think about it would make it real.

But it had been real. No amount of pretending could change that. She carried the reality inside her. Along with a despairing fear.

Rocking back and forth on the cold tile, she felt hot tears slide down her icy cheeks. There had to be a way out. If only she could think of it. There had to be some way out.

"Hey, Dan." Dan turned as Lee called his name. "There's somebody here to see you."

Dan lifted his hand in acknowledgment, feeling a stir of curiosity. He couldn't imagine who would be here to see him. He hadn't kept up many friendships. Unless it was Brittany. He'd half expected her to seek him out since their conversation two days ago. One thing about Brittany, she could never bear to leave anything unfinished. Especially when it came to someone she cared about.

He wiped his greasy hands on an equally greasy rag that did more to redistribute the grease than remove it. If it was Brittany, he was going to lie to her and tell her that he was dating someone.

But it wasn't Brittany. In fact, it wasn't anyone he knew. He studied his visitor as he walked across the garage. She was standing outside the office, her shoulders hunched inside her thin coat, though the sun had come out with springlike warmth this morning.

She was small, not much more than five feet. The thin coat was worn and much too small even for her thin frame. Her feet were stuck into a pair of old men's work boots that were several sizes too large. Her dark hair was dragged back from her face with a rubber band that was pulled so tight it actually made his scalp hurt to see it.

She was too thin, the bones of her face too sharp, too stark. Her eyes were large and dark and might have been pretty if the rest of her hadn't looked so worn and beaten. She was young, not more than eighteen or nineteen, and obviously very poor.

She was also a complete stranger.

She watched him approach, some expression flickering across her pale face that he couldn't quite catch. Fear?

"I'm Dan Remington," he said as he stopped in front of her.

"I know." Her voice was low, husky and vaguely familiar. Was she related to someone he knew? He waited for her to say something more but she only stood there, staring at him with those big eyes.

"What can I do for you?" he asked at last when the silence threatened to stretch to unmanageable lengths. He tried a smile on her. It had no effect.

"I'm pregnant."

The words were flat, without inflection. She might just as easily have said that the sun was out. Dan stared at her, waiting for her to add something, to explain her flat announcement. When nothing was forthcoming, he groped for an appropriate response.

"Congratulations."

# Chapter 4

He knew immediately that he'd said the wrong thing. A slow flush crept into her cheeks. Her body seemed to tighten as if from the impact of a blow.

"Look, I'm sorry. I—"

"You don't remember me, do you?" she cut into his stammered apology.

Dan stared at her, feeling a creeping sense of disaster. There was something *almost* familiar about her. But he couldn't place the familiarity, couldn't quite bring it into focus.

She must have been able to see the answer to her question in his eyes. She didn't wait for him to speak. She turned and started to walk away, her back rigid with humiliation. There was something painfully dignified in that thin little figure despite the tattered clothes and clumsy boots.

"Wait!" Dan caught up with her in a few strides, catching her arm before he remembered his greasy hands. He dropped her elbow with a muttered apology though he didn't really think she cared if he put a mark on her coat. She stood in front of him, her features stiff.

It wasn't hard to read her expression now. Pride, anger, hu-

miliation and a kind of underlying desperation that tugged a
Dan's heart. But she had to have the wrong man. He didn'
know this girl. Certainly not in the way she apparently though
he did.

She said nothing, waiting for him to speak. The ball wa
clearly in his court and he groped around for a moment befor
finally lifting his shoulders in a weak shrug.

"Look, I'm sorry."

"New Year's Eve."

Three simple words but they exploded with the force of
grenade. Dan felt their impact as an actual physical blow.

"You were the girl in the bar." The words weren't a ques
tion but she nodded, her eyes focused on the view just past hi
shoulder. Dan stared at her, trying to sort through his tangle
memories of that night. She wasn't wearing any makeup an
the clothes were different. Her whole carriage was differen
That was why he hadn't recognized her. But with her ha
down...

He sucked in a deep breath. In an instant, his world had bee
picked up, given a good shake and set down in an entirely ne
pattern.

"We have to talk. Wait here," he told her, his face grim. I
the few minutes it took him to strip off his stained coverall an
sluice the grease off his hands, Dan kept his mind carefull
blank. It wasn't as difficult as it might have seemed. In fac
he wasn't sure he could have summoned up much by way o
intelligent thought if he'd tried.

He told Lee he was going out and that he probably wouldn
be back for the rest of the day. From Lee's expression, it wa
clear that he'd guessed something was wrong but he didn't as
any questions. One of the benefits of old friends, Dan though
They knew when to ask a question and when to mind their ow
business.

The girl was waiting where he'd left her, her shoulde
hunched inside the coat. As he approached, Dan realized th
it was the only way she could get the cheap garment to clo
across the front.

Her coat was too small, her boots were too big. She was to

in, too pale *and* she was too young. His mouth tightened into
grim line. He must have been out of his mind.

"Come on." He reached to take her arm but she shied away,
if his touch might burn. Dan's fingers clenched as his hand
opped away. "We can talk at Rosie's across the street," he
id without expression.

She nodded without looking at him. He shortened his stride
match hers. The too-large boots forced her to take short,
uffling steps. If it hadn't been for the smooth line of her
eek, she might have been mistaken for an elderly bag lady
uffling along some inner-city street. For some reason the
ought made him feel both angry and guilty.

Midafternoon was not one of Rosie's peak hours and they
d their choice of booths. Dan led the girl to the booth all the
ay in the back. It was only as he was sliding into the seat
ross from her that he remembered this was exactly where he
d Brittany had sat two days ago. When she'd told him *she*
as expecting a baby. Maybe there was something about this
oth that lent itself to discussing pregnancies. He made a men-
note to avoid it in the future.

The waitress arrived before Dan had removed his coat. She
ew Dan and gave him a friendly smile, sliding a curious
ance at the girl across from him.

"What can I get for you, hon? Coupla coffees to take the
ill off?"

"Coffee for me," Dan said. When the girl said nothing, he
sitated for a moment before continuing. "And a cup of tea."

"Comin' right up."

"I'm old enough to drink coffee," the girl snapped as soon
the waitress was gone.

"I didn't say you weren't," he said, his tone sharp. "If you
nt coffee, I'll call her back."

"Oh." She subsided back against the booth, a tinge of color
ming up in her cheeks. "No. I don't really like coffee, any-
y. Tea will be nice. Thank you." She added the last as
nctiliously as a child at a tea party.

Dan almost groaned. How the hell old was she, anyway?
e'd removed her coat and the curves that were just visible

beneath the shapeless gray dress were somewhat reassurin
Still...

"How old are you?" he asked abruptly.

"I'm eighteen." She seemed surprised by the question b
she answered promptly.

Eighteen. Geez, he should be shot. It could have been wors
of course. She could have been sixteen, or a well-develope
fifteen.

The waitress returned, setting steaming cups in front of ther
"The apple pie is real good today, hon." She was looking
the girl as she spoke, a faint frown in her eyes, and Dan kne
she was thinking that a good slice of pie might help fill o
the hollows under her cheeks. Maybe the girl realized the san
thing. She flushed and shook her head. With a shrug, the wai
ress left them alone.

Neither of them spoke for a moment. It was left to Dan
break the silence.

"Look...ah..." He stumbled to a halt, realizing too late th
he didn't know her name. She lowered her head and he sa
her knuckles whiten around the sturdy mug in front of her. I
flushed, cursing his clumsy tongue and his lousy memory.

"Kelly," she said with painful dignity. "Kelly Russell."

"Kelly." He certainly wouldn't forget it again. He stared
his coffee, wondering just how one went about conducting
conversation like this. Maybe honesty was the best policy.

"I was pretty drunk that night," he said quickly. "I'm n
making excuses. I just want you to understand why there a
some gaps in my memory. Some pretty substantial ones ob
ously."

"There isn't that much to remember," she said in a flat lit
tone that sounded as if she was trying to pretend none of th
mattered. "We met at the bar. We talked a little. We dance
It was noisy and you suggested going back to your apartme
We...we..."

"I remember," he broke in when she couldn't get the wor
out. And he did remember. He remembered how right she
felt in his arms. He remembered her trembling response. Th
odd hesitancy at the end. And afterward, the feeling that son

hing had gone wrong somewhere. He'd tried to talk to her but he night's drinking had finally caught up with him.

When he'd awakened the next morning, she'd been gone. ince he hadn't been able to recall her name and he'd known othing else about her, there had been no question of trying to nd her. If he was honest with himself, there'd been a certain mount of relief in the realization. He didn't normally pick omen up in bars and take them home with him.

He had done his best to forget that night. And he'd suc-eeded reasonably well, only remembering her at odd moments. had begun to seem almost as if it had happened to someone lse. Only it hadn't been someone else—and that wasn't all he membered.

"You were a virgin," he said bluntly. He glanced up from is coffee to see the color sweep into her cheeks in a fiery ood.

"Yes." Embarrassment reduced her voice to a strangled hisper.

"Oh, God." Dan thrust his fingers through his hair, sitting ack against the booth. He'd really hoped to hear her deny it.

Kelly cradled the cup of tea, trying to absorb some of its armth into herself. She couldn't remember the last time she'd lt truly warm. Winter seemed to be dragging on forever.

She stole a glance across the table at her companion. He was aring at the scuffed tabletop, one hand cupped around his ffee mug, the other clenching and unclenching on the table.

None of this was going the way she'd thought it would. It d taken her two days to screw her courage up to come find m. And, in reality, it wasn't courage that had brought her re. It was desperation. She had nowhere else to go, no one se to turn to.

It hadn't occurred to her that he might not remember her. It as stupid of her to think that the night that had shattered her e had meant anything to him. And it wasn't until she'd seen e lack of recognition in his eyes that she had realized how fferent she looked.

She reached up to smooth back a strand of dark hair that d slipped loose from it's pins, conscious of her pallor and the dark circles lack of sleep had put under her eyes. She looked completely different from the girl he'd met that night. She felt completely different—as if she'd aged years in the past two months.

Had he *really* thought she looked beautiful that night? Or had she been nothing more than a warm body to greet the new year with?

"Are you sure you're pregnant?" She jumped as Dan's question broke the tense silence.

"I'm sure. I took one of those tests."

"They're not a hundred percent accurate, are they? It could still be a false alarm, couldn't it?"

"I'm sure." She made the statement as definite as possible, hoping he wasn't going to ask her to explain. The intimacies they had shared made him no less a stranger and she didn't want to discuss the changes in her body with him, the odd awareness that couldn't be explained.

Her tone must have convinced him. He thrust his fingers through his hair again, looking so shaken that, at another time, she might have felt sorry for him.

"I don't mean to sound rude or unkind but I have to ask. Are you sure I'm the father?"

"I'm sure. There was only that one time with you." She flushed but her eyes were steady. She'd been prepared for that question, prepared for him to have doubts. She'd even braced herself for the possibility that he might refuse to accept the responsibility, that he might not be willing to help her.

"I guess we were just lucky, huh?" He downed the last of his coffee, setting the mug on the table with a snap. "I'm not trying to deny my responsibility. It's just that this is all a bit much to take in." He gave her a crooked smile that held an unselfconscious charm.

Kelly felt an odd pain in her chest at that smile. She'd forgotten that smile, forgotten the loneliness that seemed to linger behind his eyes, forgotten the disarming way his hair tended to fall down over his forehead.

Over the past two months, there had been times when he'd become nearly an ogre in her mind. She'd wanted him to be an ogre. She'd needed someone to blame. If he were the bad guy, then it was his fault that her life had been turned upside down, his fault that she'd done something so foolish, so self-destructive.

Looking at him now, she realized she couldn't blame him for what had happened. He hadn't coerced her into going home with him, hadn't forced her into his bed. She'd been looking for an escape, a few hours when she could pretend to be someone else. Someone attractive and likeable. And he'd given her that.

It was just bad luck that the price had turned out to be so high.

"If you're pregnant, I'm as responsible as you are," Dan said firmly. "More really. I should have known better."

"All I want is some money," she told him, hoping he couldn't hear the way her voice threatened to shake. She broke off as the waitress appeared to refill Dan's cup. She set another cup of tea down in front of Kelly without asking, clearly believing that Kelly needed it. Dan spoke as soon as the waitress left.

"You're going to need more than money. I realize I'm probably not your favorite person at the moment but I do want to help you. You're going to need a lot of help for the next few months—and after. Babies are expensive. There's going to be medical expenses—hospitals and doctors." He waved one hand in a vague gesture that encompassed all the cost that went along with having babies.

"That's not going to be necessary," Kelly said before he could continue.

"Don't be stubborn about this. I want to help. I insist on it. This is my responsibility."

"All I want is money." Her fingers were locked so tight around her mug that her knuckles hurt. "I want an abortion. I just need the money from you to pay for it." Kelly didn't look at him as she said it. She had spent two days thinking about it and she knew it was the only possible solution. The *only* way. Still, she rushed the words out, feeling them catch in her throat.

There was a moment of silence when she could hear the low

murmur of conversation from the only other occupied booth. Two men sitting next to the front window, absorbed in an earnest discussion.

"No!" She jumped at the explosive denial, her eyes flying to Dan's face. His skin was flushed, his eyes a bright, angry blue. "Absolutely not."

Dan was as surprised as Kelly by the strength of his reaction. There had been no time to think, no time to consider. The refusal simply exploded out—a gut-level reaction to her words.

"It's the best solution," she said, trying to sound firm.

"No." There was flat denial in his voice.

Kelly stared at him, frustrated and feeling a stir of anger. She'd spent so much time analyzing, looking for other ways, trying to decide what was the best thing to do. Now he was throwing all her painful decisions out the window in the time it took to draw a breath.

"This is my decision."

"You're carrying *my* baby."

"It's my choice."

"You came to me. That makes it my choice, too."

She glared at him, feeling the tears that came all too easily these days burning in the backs of her eyes. Why was he making this even more difficult?

"There's no other way."

"There's always a choice. I'll help you."

"You can help me by giving me the money I asked for. A couple hundred dollars. You'll never see me again."

"I won't give you the money for an abortion." His jaw was set in a rigid line and Kelly felt the tears well up. She blinked, forcing them back.

"You're not being reasonable. I didn't even finish high school. I have no skills, no job, nothing."

"What about your family?"

The angry color ebbed from her face, leaving her ashen. Her eyes dropped to the table. "No. They can't know about this."

"Okay. So I'll help you. I said I would help you."

"With the medical bills and things like that...we're talking about a lifetime commitment."

"I'll help you. I'll be there for you and the child. I'll do anything you want but I won't give you money to have an abortion."

"It's the only way," she said stubbornly. "It won't cost that much."

"It's not the money."

"You're not being fair. I'm the one who has to carry it. And then have it and then try to manage. It's my choice."

"You're right. It is your choice."

"You'll give me the money?" she asked.

"No."

"But you said it was my choice."

"It is. But I won't help you."

"Are you going to take the baby and raise it?" she snapped, forcing back the tears that threatened to spill over.

She thought her question would end the discussion, make him see how unreasonable he was being. He stared at her, stunned by the suggestion, his expression blank. He didn't say anything for the space of several slow heartbeats and then he nodded slowly.

"Yes. Yes, I will take it."

"What?" Kelly sat back, feeling breathless, as if the air had been knocked from her.

"I'll take the baby and raise it. It's my child."

"But you can't."

"Why not? Because I'm a man? Single fathers aren't as rare as they used to be."

"You just can't." She shoved the cup of tea away, splashing it over the rim of the mug, creating a dark transparent pool on the table. "You don't want this child."

"As a matter of fact, I do." Dan was surprised by the conviction he felt. He *did* want this child. This was what he'd been needing. A reason to put his life in order. A family, something to build a life around. This wasn't quite what he'd had in mind but there was no reason it couldn't work.

When she'd told him she was pregnant, he'd thought in abstract terms. She would need help. It was his responsibility. It wasn't until she'd suggested the possibility that there might not *be* a baby that it had suddenly become real.

This was his child she was talking about, his flesh and blood. He felt a wave of excitement. It didn't matter that he hadn't planned on this, that the circumstances could hardly have been worse. He wanted this child, wanted it with more passion than he'd felt about anything in a very long time. He'd lost one child when Michael had married Brittany. Danielle was his daughter only by blood. He'd learned to accept that. But he wasn't going to lose another child. Not if he could help it.

"Don't you see? This is perfect." He leaned forward, determined to make her agree. "I'll take care of you during the pregnancy. I'll provide you with a place to stay if you can't stay where you are. I'll pay the medical expenses, give you money to live on, anything you want. Then once the baby is born, you give me custody. I'll give you enough money to get yourself established, get training, whatever you need."

"That's like I was selling my baby to you," she protested.

"It's *my* baby, too," he reminded her firmly. "And nobody would be doing any buying or selling. If we were married or living together, I would do the same thing, wouldn't I? And if we got a divorce after the baby was born, I'd be expected to make a settlement. And there'd be no reason why I wouldn't get custody of the child. Our child. In fact, if it will make you feel better, we can get married."

"No. No, I don't want that." Kelly hid her shaking hands in her lap, staring at the spilled tea. She'd thought that she'd grown numb over the past few weeks, that there wasn't much that could shock her anymore. But she'd just been proven wrong.

Never in her wildest dreams had she thought of Dan offering to take the baby. She'd thought he'd probably be relieved that she wasn't going to have the child, that she wanted so little from him. No paternity suits, no demands, no awkward intrusions into his life. But he'd just suggested turning his life upside down, changing it irrevocably. He'd even suggested marriage.

*That* was one thing she knew she didn't want. She'd made

one mistake and it had been a big one. But that didn't mean she had to compound it by getting married for all the wrong reasons.

"Think about it," Dan urged. "It's the perfect solution. You don't really want to have an abortion, do you?" he added gently.

She shook her head. No, she didn't want that, had never wanted it. It had seemed the only choice, the best thing to do. How could she bring a child into the world when she had nothing to offer, no future for herself or the baby?

But what he was asking... She twisted her hands together in her lap. To give up her child... *Don't be such an idiot,* she scolded herself. *He's offering the baby a chance, at least.* Could she carry a child under her heart for nine months and then give it up? Could she do anything else?

Kelly could feel Dan's tension across the table. He was practically willing her to agree. She pressed a hand to her stomach. She hadn't let herself think of the life she carried. She'd forced herself to think only in hard, practical terms.

It was only now that he was offering her this oh-so-practical alternative that she realized that there had been a tiny, half-formed dream in the back of her mind. The dream of finding someway that she could keep the baby, someway that she could escape her father and have her child and raise it.

She'd give it everything she'd never had, all the love and affection, all the caring, that hadn't been hers. It had been a hopeless fantasy, which was why she'd never let herself admit to it. It had hovered in the darkest corners of her thoughts, too foolish to entertain, too precious to give up entirely.

And suddenly Dan was offering her that dream. Only it had been taken and twisted around. He was offering her baby a chance at the life she'd wanted for it. And he was offering her a way to escape her father. But to get those things, for herself and her child, she would have to give up that child. It didn't even occur to her that Dan might allow her to see the child once he had custody.

Dan watched her down-bent head, trying to read her thoughts. He wanted her to agree, couldn't remember the last time he'd wanted something so much. It suddenly came to him that he'd thought something similar on New Year's Eve—that he hadn't been able to remember ever wanting someone the way he'd wanted her.

He wasn't a man who put much faith in fate, but if he had been so inclined, he might have wondered if maybe fate hadn't taken a hand in his life that night. This was a chance at the home and family he so desperately wanted.

And who was to say that this couldn't even work out well for Kelly? From the looks of her and the way she'd reacted when he mentioned her family, her life could use a little help, too. He could provide her with a new start.

She had to agree to this. She just had to.

As if the urgency of his thought reached her, Kelly lifted her head. Her eyes were wide and dark, showing the turmoil she felt.

"You truly want this baby? You'd be good to her?"

"I truly want this baby and I'll be a good father to him *or* her. I inherited some money from my father, not a fortune but enough. The child would never want for anything."

"Money isn't everything," she said slowly, unaware of the impact the clichéd statement had coming from someone who so obviously had very little of it. "Love and affection are a lot more important. That's what a child really needs," she added, her expression wistful.

"There would never be a moment when this child didn't know it was wanted," he said quietly.

She looked at him searchingly, as if trying to read his sincerity. Dan met the look without flinching. He wasn't sure what she might read in his eyes. Could she see how desperately he wanted this child?

"All right." The word was so low he had to strain to hear it. She lowered her eyes from his, but not before he'd seen the glitter of tears.

He felt a wave of fierce exultation when he realized what she'd just said. He was going to be a father, in the fullest sense of the word this time. This child would never call another man "Daddy."

He wanted to jump up and shout the news to the world. He felt like passing out cigars and pastel balloons. But he couldn't do any of those things. He knew Kelly's decision had been difficult, though not, he suspected, as difficult as her original choice had been.

He reached across the table to catch her hand in his. It was freezing cold and trembling. She didn't look up and he knew she was fighting back tears.

"Thank you," he said simply.

"Just see that you treat her right," she told him, her tone suddenly fierce. She pulled her hand away, sliding to the end of the booth.

"Wait a minute." Dan stood, catching her arm when she would have walked away. Kelly turned back, pulling away from him as if his touch was painful.

"I have to go," she muttered without looking at him.

"We have to work some things out."

"Not right now. I have to get home before my father gets back and finds me gone."

"Okay, but we need to talk. Where do you live? How can I get in touch with you?"

"You can't!" The look she threw him held something approaching terror. "Please, I'll call you in a day or two and we can work out the details. Now I really have to go."

"Let me give you my number." He found a pen and grabbed a napkin off the table, hastily scribbling his home number and the number at the garage. Kelly took it from him, stuffing it into her pocket without looking at it.

"You'll call? You won't change your mind?" Dan didn't try to conceal the urgency he felt. What if she just disappeared, taking his unborn child with her? He would never know what happened.

"I won't change my mind. I don't have any other choice," she said firmly. She turned and hurried away as quickly as the heavy boots would allow.

Dan watched her leave, clenching his hands against the urge to go after her. It took every ounce of willpower he had to watch her walk out the door of Rosie's and disappear. She literally carried all his hopes for the future.

# Chapter 5

Dan straightened from under the hood of his Corvette and stared at the phone on the wall, willing it to ring. It remained stubbornly silent, a fact that Lee regretted as much as he did, though for different reasons. Business at Lee's garage had been slow for the past two days. Lee was working on a truck, the only job they currently had. Dan was giving his own car a totally unnecessary tune-up.

A Corvette was probably not the best car for a family man, he thought, frowning down into the engine compartment. He wanted his child surrounded by something a little more substantial than fiberglass. He would need something solid, a wagon maybe. Of course when the child got older they might get something a little snappier.

Maybe he could keep the car, give it to his son or daughter for their sixteenth birthday. His scowl deepened. No, he didn't want to be the kind of parent who gave their children everything they wanted. A kid needed to learn the value of hard work, of earning something for themselves.

His own father had given him a job working on one of the construction sites so that he could earn the money to buy his first car. He had resented it, knowing his father could have given him the money outright. But he'd busted his butt for nearly six months and nothing in his life had ever felt quite as satisfying as paying for that car with money he'd earned himself.

He wanted to give his own child that same sense of independence, of accomplishment. He grinned. His child. He liked the sound of that phrase. He'd told Kelly that he wanted the child without giving it any thought. Now he'd had forty-eight hours to think about his snap decision and he hadn't felt a twinge of regret for his snap decision.

So why hadn't she called? Why hadn't he insisted on knowing where she lived? It had been stupid of him to let her walk away like that, when he had no way of finding her. Of course, he could always call every family named Russell listed in the phone book. But that didn't guarantee he'd find her.

"Problem with the car?" Lee stood on the other side of the car, looking at the immaculate engine, seeking a reason for the heavy frown Dan had been wearing all day.

"No. It's fine." Dan answered distractedly. "I was thinking about something else."

"Wondering why the phone doesn't ring?" Lee's dark eyes studied his friend.

"Things are kind of slow around here, huh?" Dan reached to lower the hood, letting it shut with a thud.

"I didn't realize you were so passionate about my business," Lee commented, absently wiping his greasy hands on an equally greasy rag.

"What do you mean?"

"Well, you checked the phone half a dozen times yesterday to see if it was still working. And every time it rang, you sprinted for it like you were trying for an Olympic medal. And you've done the same thing today."

Dan shrugged, reaching for the jar of waterless hand cleaner and smearing it over his hands. The sharp scent filled the air, competing with the odor of grease and new rubber from the rack of tires that lined one wall.

"I'm expecting a call," he admitted.

"Something important?" Lee leaned back against the truck he'd been working on.

"Yeah, it's important." That was the understatement of the year. Why didn't she call? He glanced at the phone again. It was getting dark out. Why hadn't he heard from her?

"Something to do with that little girl who was here a couple of days ago?"

"She's not a little girl," Dan snapped, feeling the phrase bite at his conscience. He felt guilty enough about what had happened without Lee making Kelly sound like a child. He rinsed the cleaner off his hands.

"Sorry." Lee's gaze sharpened at Dan's tone. "She a friend of yours?"

"More or less." Dan reached for a towel, turning to look at Lee as he dried his hands. "It's funny, you don't look like my father but you're beginning to sound like him. Is there a reason for this catechism?"

Lee laughed, lifting one hand in apology. "Hey. I didn't mean to sound like a cop. It's just that you've seemed different the past couple of days. More alive than I've seen you in a long time."

Before Dan could find an answer to that, a car pulled into the parking lot and Lee turned to greet what he sincerely hoped was a new customer.

*More alive.* Dan rolled the phrase over in his mind. Yes, it pretty well described how he felt. Ever since coming back to the States, he'd been drifting. There had been nothing left of his old life and he hadn't been able to find a new direction so he had just drifted, mentally at least. Now he had something to focus on, something to strive for.

He frowned at the phone. If only Kelly would call.

As if on cue, the phone rang. Dan lunged for it, telling himself that there was no reason to think that it was Kelly, any more than any of the other calls had been her. But this time he was rewarded.

"Is Dan Remington there?" The voice was muffled and slightly shaky, as if she were nervous.

"Kelly? This is Dan." His fingers knotted around the receiver. He felt almost dizzy with relief. She'd called.

"I...I'm sorry to bother you at work." His relief was tempered by uneasiness. She sounded...odd.

"Are you all right?"

"Can you come get me?" Her voice wavered.

"Where are you? Are you all right?" Dan scribbled down the address she gave him, aware that she'd twice ignored the question of how she was. "Kelly?" His voice was sharp.

"Can you come get me?" There was a note of something he couldn't quite define in the question. Fear? Panic?

"I'll be right there." He set the receiver down hard enough to draw a ping of protest from the phone. Ripping the address off the notepad, he turned toward his car, digging the keys out of his pocket.

"I gather you're on your way out," said Lee, who'd come back into the building.

"Yeah. Sorry to give you such short notice but I won't be back today."

"No problem."

Dan backed the Corvette out of the garage and into the small parking lot, spinning the wheel so hard that the tires squealed a protest. He felt a sense of urgency he couldn't explain and didn't try to argue with.

Kelly cradled the receiver to her cheek, though the line had gone dead. Her knuckles were white with the force of her grip. He had said he'd be right here. How long would it take him to get here from the garage? How long could she wait? She leaned into the corner of the phone booth, hoping that she looked as if she were using it for its intended purpose and not as a refuge.

The mild weather had continued and the temperature hovered in the sixties, but Kelly hugged her coat closer around her body. Shivers coursed through her frame. How long would it take Dan to get here?

In fact, it took Dan less time to arrive at the address Kelly had given him than he had thought it would. Luckily traffic was light.

The address turned out to be that of a convenience store. Dan pulled the Corvette into a parking space and started to get out, but Kelly had already stepped out of a phone booth and was hurrying toward the car. He leaned across the seat, pushing open the passenger door for her.

She was wearing the same coat she'd had on two days ago and the same thick boots, but this time she had a scarf wrapped around her head as if she were cold. The scarf was a faded navy blue, ragged around the edges, and she'd pulled it forward until it obscured her features.

"I got here as soon as I could," he said as she slid into the car. He felt as if he should apologize, though he knew it hadn't been more than ten minutes since she'd called.

"Thank you." Her voice still sounded muffled, almost as if she had a cold. She didn't look at him, didn't push the scarf back, didn't loosen her coat, though the interior of the car was comfortably warm.

Dan put the car in reverse and backed out of the parking lot. He glanced at Kelly. She was sitting as rigidly upright as the low-slung seats would allow. A convulsive tremor jerked her thin body.

"Are you all right?"

"Fine," she muttered in that oddly thick voice.

His frown deepened. "Where do you want to go?"

"I don't care," she whispered.

Dan glanced in the rearview mirror and then pulled over abruptly, stopping next to the curb. Reaching out, he twitched the scarf from her head. She gasped and shrank back against the seat, ducking her head, but he'd already seen enough to tell him that *fine* didn't begin to describe her condition.

His hand was gentle but implacable as he cupped her chin, lifting her face so that the light fell on it.

"God Almighty." The words were more prayer than curse.

No wonder her voice had been muffled. Her lips were swollen and bruised. One eye had swelled almost shut, the other

as puffy. There was a cut on one cheekbone and blue bruises
arked one side of her jaw.

"Who did this to you?" His voice was hoarse. Rage like
'd never known before threatened to choke him. He could
ar the sound of his own pulse pounding in his ears.

She shook her head, trying to pull away but he refused to
t her hide.

"Who did this?" he demanded, his eyes a fierce, angry blue.

"Don't. Please." She shrank back, lifting one hand, afraid
at he was going to strike her.

Dan released his light hold as if burned. "I would never hit
u. I've never hit a woman in my life." He sounded as shaken
he felt. "Tell me who did this to you," he asked again,
ore gently.

She shook her head, pressing her fingers to her battered
outh as tears welled up in her eyes. She began to cry, slow,
inful tears that ran silently down her pale cheeks.

Dan started the Corvette, aware that his hands were shaking.
'm taking you to the emergency room."

"No!" She reached out to clutch his arm, her fingers digging
ough the light flannel of his shirt. "No, I don't want to go
a hospital. I don't want to see anyone."

"Kelly, you need to see a doctor." He set his hand over
rs, intending comfort, but she jerked away from the light
uch, wrapping her arms around herself. She rocked back and
rth, those painfully silent tears trickling down her face.

"I don't want to go to a hospital. I won't, I won't, I won't."
ere was an edge to her voice that made it clear she was on
e verge of hysteria.

"Okay, okay. I won't take you to a hospital. I'll take you
my apartment. You'll be okay there."

Kelly huddled in a corner of the car, crying silently. Dan
ove with one eye on her, one eye on the road and his thoughts
n between rage and concern. He wanted to get his hands on
oever had beaten her. He wanted to tear them limb from
b. And he wanted to take Kelly to a hospital. She should
ve a doctor take a look at her, make sure she was all right.

And the baby. His hands tightened on the wheel. Was t
baby all right?

He couldn't think about that now. His first concern had
be taking care of Kelly. If he took her to the hospital, she w
likely to go into hysterics, which couldn't be good for her
the baby. He'd take her home, get her calmed down and th
could go from there.

Ben. Dan felt a wave of relief. Ben Masters was a friend
his, a doctor who had been there for him when he came hor
and had seen him through some rough times. He could call hi
if it looked as if Kelly needed medical attention.

Dan parked the Corvette in front of his apartment buildi
Kelly didn't move, didn't even seem aware that the car h
stopped. He hesitated, wondering if this was such a good id
after all. He shook his head, thrusting open his door.

She started when he opened the door, pulling back agai
the seat.

"This is just my apartment," he told her soothingly. "You
be able to clean up and we'll get some ice on that eye. You
be okay here."

She stared at him blankly for a moment, as if having troub
sorting his words into something she could understand. Da
hand clenched on the edge of the door frame. He wished
knew who had hit her.

Kelly swung her legs out, her movements stiff, as if she we
a very old woman. Dan held back the urge to help her, reme
bering how she reacted to his smallest touch. But when s
stumbled against the curb, he caught her automatically, one a
around her waist as she fell against his chest. He expected
to immediately jerk away, to see that look of fright in her ey
But it seemed she'd expended the last of her strength. She
against him, her eyes closed, her breathing quick and shallo

Muttering a curse directed toward whoever had done this
her, he bent to scoop her up in his arms. She didn't prote
He wasn't even sure she was aware of what was going on.
pushed the car door shut with his foot. As he carried her
the walkway, it came to him that he'd carried her to the d

New Year's Eve, too. It was too bad the circumstances were different.

The curtains in the window of the apartment below his witched violently. So Mrs. Barnett had been watching the reet more than her television. She'd certainly been rewarded r her inattention today. Within the hour, every old woman in e small building would know that he'd carried a woman to s apartment.

Most of the apartments were occupied by retirement-age omen, a fact that meant the building was generally very quiet. also meant that, as the only young, unattached male in the ilding, his movements had been carefully scrutinized since oving in nearly a year ago.

His life had been so dull he thought he'd pretty well dis- uraged them. Sheer boredom had made him a less than hot pic. But that would all change now. If it had been just a little er, it would have been too dark for her to see anything.

He set Kelly down in front of the door, keeping one arm ound her waist as he thrust the key into the lock. She leaned ainst him, seemingly incapable of supporting her own eight. Lifting her again, he carried her into the apartment, cking the door shut behind them. He brought her into the droom and set her on the bed.

She sat without moving, her hands limp at her sides, her ttered features without expression. Dan frowned down at her, ondering again if he'd made the right decision in bringing r here.

"Let's get these off." He knelt in front of her, unlacing the rk boots with quick jerks. She seemed hardly aware of him moving them, but when he reached for her coat, she pulled ck with a whimper of protest, clutching the ratty cloth.

"All right." Dan pitched his voice low and soothing. "You n keep the coat on. I'm going to call a friend of mine who's loctor and ask him to come over and take a look at you."

"No," she mumbled, his words snapping her out of her de- ondency. Her eyes flickered with awareness as she drew far- r back onto the bed. "I don't want to see anyone."

"Kelly, you have to see a doctor. You could have serio■
injuries."

"No." She made an effort to draw herself upright, winci■
as her bruised body protested the move. "I'm fine," she sai■
apparently unaware of how ridiculous the claim sounded, mu■
fled as it was by her swollen mouth.

"No, you're not." Without thinking, Dan reached up ■
brush back a lock of hair that had fallen over her forehead. S■
winced back, her eyes frightened, freezing the movement. H■
fingers curled into his palm before he let his hand drop aw■
from her.

"I would never hurt you, Kelly," he said quietly.

She said nothing, watching him warily. Clearly she did■
believe him.

"You should see a doctor."

"No." The word was little more than a whimper of prote■
She turned away, wrapping her arms around her knees a■
pressing her battered face against them.

Dan stood. Looking down at her, he felt a sense of hel■
lessness, a feeling he'd grown familiar with during the tw■
years he'd spent in prison. It was not a sensation he enjoye■
Kelly began to rock back and forth, seeking comfort in t■
gentle rhythm.

Dan's hands clenched into fists at his sides. He wanted ■
reach out and gather her up and tell her that no one was ev■
going to hurt her again. His mouth twisted. He was a fine o■
to promise her protection, considering the results of their br■
acquaintance on New Year's Eve.

Still, he was all she had at the moment.

"Kelly, you've got to let someone take a look at your i■
juries. If not a doctor, then it's going to have to be me."

For all her response, he might not have spoken at all. ■
waited but she didn't lift her head. It was as if by wrappi■
her arms around herself she had shut out the rest of the wor■
Considering what the world had done to her lately he could■
say he blamed her.

Someone still had to look at her injuries. He turned on ■
heel and left the room. When he came back a few minu■

ater, he was carrying a bowl of warm water, a wash cloth and
a bottle of alcohol. He set everything on the floor next to the
bed.

Ben's answering service had informed Dan that Ben was
unavailable but would return his call at the first possible moment. He'd left a message, saying it was urgent that Ben call
him. Meanwhile, he could take Kelly to a hospital, which
seemed likely to throw her into hysterics—or he could try to
tend her injuries himself.

He snapped on the lamp next to the bed. The sudden rush
of light in the darkened room seemed almost painfully brilliant.
Kelly hadn't moved. She was still crouched in the middle of
the bed, curled protectively into herself. He set his teeth and
reached for her. She started when his hand touched her shoulder, pulling back.

"Kelly, I'm not going to hurt you." He made the words firm
but gentle, trying to pierce the wall of her fear.

"No," she whimpered, trying to pull away as he drew her
forward.

"I'm not going to hurt you," he repeated.

For a moment, it seemed as if his words had gotten through.
She didn't protest as he pulled her coat open. Dan thought they
might be able to get through this with a minimum of stress.
But when he started to ease the coat off her shoulders, she
seemed to explode.

"No!"

She came off the bed, her arms swinging wildly. He had
been expecting passive resistance, protests and tears, but the
sudden violence caught him off guard. He ducked back, muttering a curse as her hand slammed into his nose hard enough
to send a jolt of pain all the way to the back of his head. His
heel bumped into the bowl of water and he staggered back, half
falling. The back of his head hit the wall with a resounding
thump.

Her breath coming in deep, sobbing gasps, Kelly scrambled
off the bed. Blinking to clear the momentary fuzziness from
his vision, Dan lunged after her. He caught her at the bedroom
door, one arm snaking around her waist.

"No! No more!" She turned in his hold. Dan caught a quick glimpse of her face, her features twisted with fear, all sanity gone from her eyes. Though he knew she wasn't really seeing him, that her fear was directed at terrors he could only imagine. having that look directed at him struck with all the force of a blow to the stomach.

"No more!" Her nails caught him across the side of his face. He jerked his head back but didn't loosen his grip.

She fought like one possessed, her terror giving her more strength than he would have thought possible. He was hampered by the fact that he was trying not to hurt her, trying to keep her from hurting herself. But it was still a vastly unequal struggle.

In a matter of moments he had her stilled. One arm wrapped around her holding her arms down to her sides, the other hand pressed her face into his shoulder. Gently crowded backward until she was trapped between his hard frame and the wall. Kelly gave one last convulsive jerk before stilling her body.

"I'm not going to hurt you. No one's ever going to hurt you again." He murmured the words over and over again, his hands gentle on her, offering more comfort than restraint.

Whether the words finally got through or she had simply exhausted her thin store of strength, Dan didn't know. Whichever it was, she suddenly went lax against him.

"It's okay. I'll never let anyone hurt you again." He stroked her hair, using both touch and voice to reassure her. She shuddered convulsively and Dan tensed, wondering if the struggle was about to begin all over again. But the only struggle going on was an internal one.

The sob that burst from her seemed to have worked its way up from the very depth of her soul. Dan's arms tightened around her as the storm of emotion finally broke loose. Holding her, feeling the force of her sobbing, he wondered how long she'd been holding this inside. Months? Years?

He was helpless to do anything more than hold her, offering her what comfort he could. He stroked her hair, cradling her in his arms and whispering wordless sounds of comfort.

The very force of the outburst dictated that it be brief. The wild weeping subsided into quieter sobs and then at last stilled, except for an occasional shaky breath.

Kelly lay against Dan, her eyes closed. She hadn't cried like that even when her mother died. She felt limp and drained, tired deep in her soul. Beneath her cheek she could hear the steady beat of Dan's heart. There was something reassuring in the sound, something solid in the feel of him.

He had said he would never hurt her, that he'd never let anyone else hurt her. The words, only half heard during her wild weeping, came back to her now. They lay over her soul like a soothing balm. He'd meant it. And she had known it without him having to say the words. It was just that when Dan had come toward her, she'd seen her father's face distorted with a terrible rage, his fist raised.

It was the first time he'd struck her with his bare hand. She'd thought nothing could be more terrible than the beatings, nothing could be more frightening than the sound of his belt striking her skin. But this had been worse. Always before, she'd almost believed that he thought he was doing what was best for her immortal soul, that there was an element of caring—however twisted—behind his actions.

This time she'd had none of that feeling. He'd been driven by rage, pure and simple. What a fool she'd been to think that she could keep her pregnancy from him, even for a few days. In the tiny trailer, there was no way to hide the fact that she was ill in the mornings.

He hadn't known about Dan before. He'd thought that her New Year's Eve excursion hadn't gone beyond a drink and a little dancing. He'd beaten her for that and then made her pray for forgiveness until her knees ached.

But she hadn't been able to hide the morning sickness, and it hadn't taken her father long to put two and two together. He'd confronted her this morning and read the answer to his question in her eyes.

Kelly shivered, remembering his rage, the way he'd come at her as if crazed. She'd thought he would surely kill her, so terrible had been his anger.

"It's all right. You're safe now. I'll take care of you," Dan murmured in her ear. The nightmare images receded a bit. She was safe now. Dan wouldn't let anyone hurt her. He'd promised. He'd promised to take care of her.

His arms were gentle but strong about her. If she just kept her eyes closed and imagined that this was another time and place, she could feel protected. Loved. But she had to remember that his concern wasn't for her. It was for the child she carried. If she let herself forget that, only disaster would follow.

*But would it be so terrible just to pretend for a little while?* She was so tired, so terribly tired. Would it really be wrong to just rest here and let him take care of her?

In the end, she didn't have to answer the question. Her exhausted body answered it for her. Dan felt the tension slowly draining out of her. Easing back until he could see her face, he realized that she'd fallen asleep, literally on her feet.

He lifted her and carried her to the bed she'd left so explosively a few minutes before. It was a struggle to get her out of the coat, which was too tight across the shoulders. It was a measure of Kelly's exhaustion that she showed no signs of waking during his maneuvering.

He had the urge to simply cut it from her, but for all he knew there might be some sentimental value in the garment. Though he couldn't really imagine being sentimental about a coat that must have been plug ugly when it was new and had only gotten worse with age.

Once he'd finally managed to peel it off, he tossed the coat in the direction of a chair. In contrast to the coat, the dull gray dress was too big. It hung on Kelly's thin frame like a sack. Kelly didn't stir as he lifted her to slip the dress over her head. It joined the coat.

The light fell with merciless clarity across the bed. Kelly lay there clad in only worn cotton panties and a bra that was so small her breasts threatened to spill out of the cups. She looked young and fragile and too thin.

Dan felt new anger spill through him. Her upper arms were bruised, obviously from someone grabbing her painfully hard—to shake her? There was an angry purple bruise on her ribs—had the bastard kicked her? Easing her onto her side, he wallowed hard against the bile that rose in his throat when he saw her back. The faded yellow of old bruises underlay the darker tint of more recent blows, making it clear that this wasn't the first time she'd been beaten.

He knelt by the bed, letting his hands fall against his thighs, his head lowered as he struggled to control the fury that swept over him. What kind of a man could do this to a woman?

She'd seemed nervous when he'd asked about her family and she had hurried away from their last meeting, saying she had to get home before her father found out she was gone. Had her father done this to her? And why?

He wasn't naive. He was well aware of the terrible things parents could do to their children. Even so, he found it impossible to imagine a father inflicting such a brutal beating on his daughter. His pregnant daughter. Had he known she was pregnant? Was that why he'd done this to her?

Dan rubbed one hand over his face, trying to wipe away the thought that he might be even partially responsible for this. There was nothing he could do about it now except try to make Kelly comfortable. He hoped he had done the right thing in bringing her here instead of taking her to a hospital.

She stirred when he put an ice pack against her swollen eye, her forehead pleating in discomfort, but she didn't wake. He kept the ice against the eye, hoping the chill would help take some of the swelling down. It was obvious from the state of her injuries that several hours had elapsed between the beating and her call to him. Had she been unconscious? Could she have a concussion?

Where the hell was Ben? Dan sat back on his heels, frowning down at Kelly's sleeping figure. Should he gather her up right now and take her to the hospital? She'd been so adamant about not wanting to go there. But she couldn't argue with him while she was unconscious.

His frown deepened. He had the feeling that very little attention had ever been paid to what Kelly wanted in her life. It would be almost like betraying a trust to sneak her to the hospital now. Where was Ben?

He did his best to clean up Kelly's injuries, but most of them

were just going to need time to heal. The bruises would fade
the small cuts wouldn't even leave scars. Physically she was
going to be all right. Heaven only knew what kind of emotional
scars she must carry.

Dan left her sleeping and went into the kitchen. He poured
water into a pot, set it on the stove to boil and then stood
staring at it like a zombie, trying to keep his mind blank.

Seeing Kelly, seeing the bruises that marked her skin
brought back too many images from his past. Two years in a
Central American prison had left him with more than a few
scars of his own. Scars he could generally ignore. Tonight
however, they had all come rushing back.

The smell of the prison—unwashed bodies, fear, despair
The prisoners who were there at dusk and gone by morning
and no one had dared to question what might have happened
to them, lest they disappear the next night. He'd been luckier
than some.

The sound of the water hissing against the sides of the pan
brought him out of the past. He shook his head, dumping a
healthy amount of instant coffee in a cup before pouring the
boiling water over it. He carried the steaming cup to the table
that sat in the alcove that was called, somewhat optimistically
the dining room.

He collapsed into a chair, putting his elbows on the table
and resting his head on his hands. He felt almost numb. The
past couple of days had spun his life into a new pattern and he
had the feeling that he was only seeing one edge of it.

First, he'd found out he was going to be a father. No—first
was that talk with Brittany. The realization that they'd some
how made the change from former lovers to friends, finding
out that she was pregnant—that had been the beginning.

Then Kelly had shown up with the news that she was car
rying his child. And suddenly he'd had something to build a
future for. For two days he'd built plans around the child she
carried, dreamed dreams for his son or daughter. He though
he'd forgotten how to dream but he hadn't. The skills might
be a little rusty but they were still there.

And now here was Kelly, lying in his bed, hurt and scared

He felt responsible. She had told him nothing. Not who had beaten her or why. But it wasn't hard to guess that it had been her father. And if she had been beaten because of her pregnancy, then the responsibility was his.

Dan rubbed his hand over his face before picking up his coffee. The steaming liquid couldn't burn away the feeling of guilt. Through his own carelessness, Kelly's life had been thrown into turmoil. He'd had no business bringing her back here that night, no business getting so drunk that he hadn't been able to recognize her inexperience, her youth.

He'd seen her fear two days ago when she mentioned her father. He should have insisted on taking her home, should have seen for himself that she was all right. The fact that he'd been stunned by the news she'd given him was no excuse. If he had taken her home, met her father, maybe he'd have seen the man for what he was and he could have insisted on Kelly leaving with him.

Then again, maybe the man would have seemed perfectly civilized. Only a fool thought that abusive parents looked like what they were. Still, there must have been *something* he could have done to prevent this from happening.

He rubbed at the pain beginning to throb in his temples. He almost welcomed the headache. It seemed the least he deserved. He lifted his coffee cup and took another swallow, almost choking when a low cry came from the bedroom. Steaming coffee splashed onto his hand as he set the cup down too hard, already half out of the chair.

When he reached the bedroom, Kelly was tossing restlessly, frowning and whimpering. Dan felt his pulse slow to something approaching normal. She was having a nightmare. When he'd heard her cry out, he had thought it was a cry of pain. She muttered something indistinguishable, throwing one hand out as if warding off a blow.

He eased down onto the edge of the bed as Kelly twisted more frantically. He could imagine the terrible images that haunted her sleep. He'd had more than his share of nightmares since he'd gotten out of prison.

"It's all right, Kelly. You're safe." He pitched his voice

low, hoping to penetrate her terror. He'd covered her when he left the room earlier but her tossing and turning had thrown most of the blankets off. Dragging the sheet loose from the foot of the bed, he lifted Kelly and wrapped her in it, lifting her so that she lay across his lap.

"No one's ever going to hurt you again. I swear it." He leaned back against the headboard, his arms holding her close against his chest, murmuring quiet reassurances to her. She whimpered once, stirring in his hold and then quieted. Her head rested on his shoulder, her body relaxing against his as the nightmare faded, chased away by the strength of his arms.

Dan continued to hold her long after she was sleeping peacefully again. It occurred to him that not only was he holding Kelly, he was holding his child—their child. It was a pleasant thought. His eyes drifted shut. He'd just lie here until he was sure Kelly's nightmare wasn't going to return.

Outside, a full moon shone down as frost gathered on the winter-deadened lawns, proving that winter still had a bite. Inside the dim bedroom, Kelly slept, held safe in Dan's arms. Her head rested on his shoulder. One hand lay outside the sheet, resting on her still-flat stomach. Dan's palm spread over it as if protecting both her and the tiny life she carried.

# Chapter 6

Dan woke suddenly, startled by some sound he couldn't quite remember. Kelly was still wrapped in his arms, sound asleep, her head nestled in the hollow of his shoulder. The sound that had pulled him awake was repeated. Someone was knocking rather violently on the door.

He sat up, groaning at the ache in his neck. Easing Kelly down onto the pillows, he swung his legs off the bed, rubbing his neck as he stood. Who on earth would be pounding on his door at four in the morning?

Pulling the bedroom door half-shut behind him, he hurried to the front door, yanking it open just as the man on the other side was lifting his hand to knock again.

"Ben." Dan sagged against the doorjamb.

"What's the emergency?" Ben's eyes went over Dan in a quick professional survey. He had a medical bag in one hand. "You look like hell but you don't look like a reason for me to have driven straight here from Indianapolis. The answering service told me it was urgent."

"It is. It was." Dan wiped a hand over his face, trying to erase the grogginess from his thoughts. "Come in."

"Thanks." Ben stepped into the hallway, shutting the door behind him. He followed Dan into the kitchen. Dan turned the heat on under the pan of water that was still sitting on the stove. Coffee. That was what he needed to get his mind going. Lots of caffeine.

"What's the problem?" Ben asked as Dan turned to lean against the counter. "Did you sleep in those clothes? What happened to your face? You look like you've been in a fight with that ugly cat of yours."

"Yes. That's part of the emergency. And, no, I haven't." Dan reached up to touch his cheek. He'd forgotten about the scratches Kelly had inflicted during that brief struggle. Come to think of it, his nose ached, too. "You want some coffee?"

"I want an explanation but coffee will do for a start. I've just spent three days at the world's most tedious convention. All I really want is to go to sleep without having to listen to some bore drone on about some obscure medical concept of which he knows nothing. Instead, I drove straight here from the airport, thinking that you would probably have bled to death from some wound you were too damn dumb to go to the hospital for."

"Sorry about that." Dan handed Ben a mug of steaming coffee.

"Oh, I'll survive," Ben admitted grudgingly as the scent of the coffee reached him. "What's going on?"

"Well, it's a long story." Dan gestured for Ben to have a seat and then took the chair across the table from him.

He told Ben the whole story, starting with meeting Kelly on New Year's Eve. He didn't spare himself in the telling, taking full blame for everything that had happened, admitting that he'd been drunk, that he hadn't even recognized her when she'd shown up two days ago. He told Ben about wanting the baby, about the bargain he'd struck with Kelly. And then the call late the previous afternoon.

"I know I should have taken her to the emergency room but she was nearly hysterical. She'd obviously hit the end of her rope. So I brought her back here."

"How did you end up with the scratches on your face?" Ben asked, his expression stern.

"She didn't want me to take a look at her injuries. God, don't look at me like you think *I've* been pounding on her," Dan protested, seeing doubt in Ben's eyes. "I've never hit a woman in my life and I sure as hell wouldn't start with one who was pregnant with my child."

"Okay, I believe you. Sorry if I looked doubtful. I get suspicious at four-thirty in the morning."

"I wouldn't blame you if you didn't believe me," Dan said morosely. "Lord knows, I've done enough to ruin her life."

"Well, you can't change what's already happened. Where is she now?"

"She's in the bedroom. She finally fell asleep a few hours ago. She's had a nightmare but she didn't really wake up. As far as I know, she's slept okay since then. Is it a bad sign that she's sleeping so heavy? I mean, she's not likely to fall into a coma or something, is she?"

"It doesn't sound likely," Ben said, shaking his head. "People don't normally lapse into comas at the drop of a hat. From the sounds of it, she's probably just exhausted. I'm no obstetrician but I seem to recall that pregnant women generally need more sleep, even when they haven't been through what she has."

"Do you think I should have taken her to a hospital?"

Ben shrugged. "That would have been the safest thing, certainly. Why don't I take a quick look at her?"

Kelly didn't stir when they entered the room. She slept like the dead, an analogy that didn't make Dan happy. Ben sucked in his breath when he got a good look at her face. His hands were gentle as he checked her pulse and listened to her heartbeat with the stethoscope he pulled out of his bag. He felt her ribs through the sheet. He lifted one eyelid and shone a small flashlight on the pupil. Kelly muttered, pulling her head away. For a moment, it looked as if she might wake but then she stilled, her breathing even.

Ben stood, staring down at her for a moment before turning

to gesture Dan out of the room. Dan barely waited until he'd shut the door before pouncing.

"Well, is she okay?"

"She's not in a coma. She's exhausted and her body is recharging. Her pupils look okay. Her lungs sound good. She may have a cracked rib but that's impossible to say without X rays and it may not be worth the risk to the baby." He shrugged. "Overall, she looks too thin and I'd say she needs a lot of rest and some good, solid food. Probably some prenatal vitamins."

He scribbled a number on a piece of paper. "Dr. Linden's got a practice in my building and I hear good things about her. Why don't you give her a call first thing in the morning?" He stopped and shook his head. "This is morning. Give her a call when the office opens and tell her I sent you. She'll squeeze Kelly in as soon as possible."

Dan took the paper, creasing it between his fingers. "But you think she's okay? And the baby?"

"I think so." Seeing the haggard look in his friend's eyes, Ben put his hand on Dan's shoulder. "Look, she's young and she seems pretty healthy, all things considered. Babies are tougher than movies and television would have you believe. There's no sign of any bleeding. My guess is that she and the baby are going to be fine. I still want you to get her to Dr. Linden as soon as possible."

"I will. Thanks. I really do appreciate this."

"That's what friends are for." Ben hesitated at the door, turning to look at Dan, his eyes searching. "You really want this baby, don't you?"

"Yes," Dan said simply.

"Why?"

From anyone else, Dan might have resented the question. But he'd known Ben Masters a long time. He'd stayed with Ben when he got back to Indiana. And Ben had been there for him when he'd found out that the child Brittany and Michael were raising was his.

"It's a second chance," he said slowly. "A piece of what I've always dreamed of."

"That girl in there isn't Brittany and this child isn't the one you might have had with her," Ben said bluntly.

Dan's fingers crumpled the phone number Ben had given him. "I know that."

"So long as you do," Ben said, unintimidated by the flare of anger that lit Dan's eyes.

Dan leaned against the door after Ben had gone. Ben obviously thought he was more than a few cards short of a full deck. Maybe he was right. Maybe he had no business asking Kelly to carry this child, to give it to him. After all, he might make a lousy father. The only thing he could be sure of was that he could never hurt his son or daughter the way Kelly's father—if it had been her father—had hurt her.

Dan pushed himself away from the door, rubbing one hand over his face. It was nearly dawn. He'd had only a few hours of sleep. He was in no condition to try and make any life-altering decisions. A hot shower, two or three gallons of coffee and then maybe his brain would be functioning again.

Kelly woke slowly, working her way up through layer after layer of cotton wool. She felt warm. That was the first thing she was aware of. For the first time in weeks she felt warm all the way through. She stirred, snuggling deeper under the layer of blankets, letting the warmth soak into her bones.

The bed felt good, not like the sagging mattress she had at home. The pillow was fluffy and didn't smell of incipient mildew, and the blankets were soft and smelled of sunshine, not like the scratchy woolen blankets she usually slept under.

She wasn't in her own bed. The thought seeped in slowly, bringing with it the first tinge of uneasiness. She pushed it away. She didn't want to think, didn't want to wake up. She just wanted to sleep until she felt rested all the way to her toes.

But Morpheus, once having retreated, proved impossible to coax back. There were too many questions starting to force their way into her mind. And hard on their heels were answers she didn't want to face.

Kelly opened her eyes slowly, studying the pale ceiling above. She knew where she was. She was in Dan Remington's bedroom. The same room where her life had been irrevocably changed. Sunlight poured in through the light curtains, a cold, crisp light that promised spring but held the bite of winter.

In her memory, the room had been bigger and darker. It had looked more ominous, less like the normal, rather plain bedroom it was. Dan must have brought her here after she'd called him yesterday.

Yesterday.

She closed her eyes, wanting to block out the memories that came flooding in. She'd been so sick yesterday morning. She hadn't been able to force the illness back until after her father was gone. He was between jobs again. Sometimes she thought he spent more time between jobs than he did working.

She had come out of the bathroom, pale and dizzy, and he'd been waiting for her, looming over her in the tiny hallway. He'd guessed the reason for her illness. She'd known it as soon as she saw his eyes, the terrible, terrible rage in them. She might have run then but there was nowhere to go.

He had seemed possessed. He'd called her sinful and evil, a true child of Satan, just like her whoring mother. And then he'd begun to hit her. She shuddered, her throat aching with remembered terror. She hadn't been able to get away from him, hadn't been able to do anything but crouch in a corner, making herself as small as possible, and pray for unconsciousness.

She wasn't sure if she'd actually passed out or if she'd simply retreated so far into herself that she didn't really notice when he actually left. When she finally became aware of herself, she'd dragged her aching body to the kitchen sink and bathed her bruised face in cold water until the chill made her shiver.

She had to get away. If she was still there when her father returned, he'd surely kill her. She'd dressed clumsily and stumbled out of the trailer. Her only thought had been to call Dan. She had no one else to turn to. There was no one else she could call.

Kelly drew herself farther up on the pillows, moving cautiously, waiting for the nausea, typical of the past few days, to strike. When her stomach only twinged in warning, she dared to draw a deeper breath. Though the bedroom was a comfortable temperature, the air felt cool on her blanket-warmed shoulders.

Her dress lay tossed across the arm of a chair, along with her coat. Dan must have undressed her. The thought made her flush, as much for the condition of her worn underwear as for the thought of him seeing her nearly naked. Then again, he'd seen her more than nearly naked on New Year's Eve.

Her frown turned into a wince as the movement pulled at her bruised face. She reached one hand up to explore the damage. Some of the swelling had gone down. Her left eye was partially open but she could guess at the bruise that must surround it. In fact, she suspected that she looked like hell, which pretty much described how she felt.

She was just trying to get up the courage to get out of bed to find a mirror and a bathroom when she heard a sound in the hallway. Clutching the covers over her shoulders, she shrank back against the pillows as the door was slowly pushed open. Dan eased into the room, his tense expression relaxing when he saw her.

"You're awake," he said, his relief obvious. "I was getting worried. How do you feel?"

"Fine," she choked out the lie past the nervous lump in her throat. She wasn't sure how she was supposed to react in this situation.

She and Dan had been intimate with one another, yet they didn't know each other at all. They weren't strangers and they certainly weren't friends. Nevertheless, she'd called on him when she needed help and he'd been there for her.

"You slept a long time."

"Did I?" She glanced around for a clock, startled when she saw that it was well past noon.

"Sleep was probably the best thing," Dan said, coming farther into the room.

He stopped at the foot of the bed. Kelly's fingers tightened over the blankets. Why was it that she never remembered how blue his eyes were? And why was it that blue eyes always seemed so much more penetrating than any other color? She felt as if he could see inside her with just a glance.

"You look better," he said softly.

She reached up to half cover her face, aware that she must look even worse than she felt.

"If I look better now, I must have looked like death warmed over before," she said, surprising them both with the dark humor of the comment.

Dan smiled but his eyes remained watchful. "How are you really feeling? Any pains or cramping?"

He was worried about the baby. Kelly felt a sharp little pain near her heart. How stupid of her not to have realized it before. He hadn't come to *her* rescue. He'd come to the baby's rescue.

"The baby's fine," she said dully, her eyes dropping to where the blankets were tented over her knees. She was aware of him moving around the bed until he stood next to her.

"I was worried about *you*," he said quietly.

She lifted her shoulders without looking up. It would be nice if she could believe him but, after all, he had no real reason to care about her personally.

She started as the bed dipped beneath his weight. She lifted her head, her heart beating too quickly. He was too close, too big. His shoulders seemed to loom before her, cutting off the light, cutting off the air.

Catching the flare of fear in her eyes, Dan reached out one hand in an automatic gesture of reassurance. But Kelly ducked back as if from a blow.

"It's all right, I'm not going to touch you," he said tightly. He pulled his hand back, white lines bracketing his mouth. It didn't matter that he knew it wasn't really him she was so terrified of. Every time she cringed from him, it stabbed right through to his gut.

"I'm sorry," she whispered, her knuckles white with the force of her grip on the blankets.

"Don't apologize."

Silence stretched between them. Dan stared at the night table, telling himself over and over again that she'd been through lot. Her reaction to him wasn't personal. He was aware of Kelly stealing glances at him.

"Did I do that?" she asked finally.

"What?" Seeing the direction of her gaze, Dan lifted a hand to touch the scratches on his cheek. "These? Don't worry about it."

"I'm sorry."

"Don't worry about it," he said again.

"It wasn't you," she said after a moment, her voice so low he had to strain to hear.

"I'd never hurt you. I know our—" he stopped, searching for the right word "—our relationship hasn't exactly been one to build trust. You hardly know me. But I'd never hit you. I can promise you that."

"I believe you."

She might believe him, but he knew it was going to take more than that to make her trust him—and he wanted her trust. It surprised him to realize just how much he wanted it.

"Who did this to you?" Kelly jumped at the question, her face paling beneath the bruises.

"It's not important," she muttered.

"It is important. No one has a right to do this to someone else." Dan saw her wince at the edge of anger clearly audible in his voice. He stopped, drawing in a slow breath before continuing in a neutral tone. "Was it your father?"

"I don't want to talk about it."

"I have to at least know who did this, Kelly."

"Why?"

"Why?" The question threw him off balance. How could he explain why? It seemed so obvious that he had to know something so important. "Because I need to know."

"I don't see why," she insisted, her jaw set in a stubborn line.

"Kelly, he's done this before. I saw the old bruises. You can't let him get away with this. No matter who he is."

"I don't want to think about it. I don't want to talk about it."

Dan stared at her, frustrated in the face of her stubborn re-

fusal. He'd spent most of the morning relishing the idea of
bringing the man to justice. Visions of putting him behind bars
had accompanied numerous cups of coffee. He'd thought Kelly
must surely feel the same. Now here she was refusing to even
tell him who it had been.

"Was it your father?" he asked finally. She said nothing
staring at the blankets, her jaw set. Dan reined in his exasper
ation, reminding himself that she'd probably had enough of
people bullying her. The important thing was that she was safe
and relatively unhurt. The fact that he wanted to get his hand
on the man who'd beaten her was not really all that important

"Okay." The bed shifted as he stood, shoving his hands in
the pockets of his jeans. "I won't ask any more questions. I
and when you feel like talking about it, we'll talk."

She cast him a wary look from under her lashes, as if won
dering if he was really going to drop the subject. He met her
gaze openly, doing his best to look reasonable and nonthrea
tening. It wasn't a look he'd ever really tried for before, bu
he must have managed at least a reasonable facsimile because
some of the wariness faded from her eyes.

"Thank you."

"You're welcome," he said, very solemnly.

It was worth controlling his desire for vengeance to se
something approaching a smile flicker across Kelly's face. I
occurred to him that he hadn't seen her smile much. Even o
the night they'd met, she hadn't smiled a whole lot. Or was
just that he'd been so wrapped in his own problems that h
hadn't noticed?

"I guess you'd like a chance to clean up," he suggested.

"That would be nice," she said, that shy near-smile flick
ering over her face again.

"The bathroom is next door." He hesitated, frowning. "Ca
you manage? I could help you."

"No. Thanks," she added, trying to soften the abrupt refusa
"I'm fine, really. Or close enough," she amended when h
gave her a doubtful look.

"Well, if you need me I'll be within yelling distance," h
said, as much to reassure himself as her, she thought. He wer

to the closet and pulled out a gray flannel shirt and a pair of jeans.

"These are going to be a lousy fit, but if you knot a belt around the jeans they should stay up." He spoke over his shoulder as he was digging through a drawer. "We'll have to do some shopping when you're feeling better. Get you some clothes."

"I don't need anything." Pride made her speak before she had a chance to think.

Dan turned from the dresser, a pair of thick white socks and a terry-cloth robe in his hand. He glanced at the chair where her clothes lay and then looked at her, raising one brow in silent comment.

Kelly followed his look. Her dress and coat lay tossed over a chair, somehow looking even more tattered and worn in the bright sunshine that spilled across them. Devlin's old boots lay on their sides beneath the chair, the only warm shoes she'd been able to find. Her flush was slow and painful.

"Don't make an issue out of it," Dan said quietly. "The deal was that I'd take care of you, support you, right? Well, clothes are part of that." He didn't seem to expect an answer, which was just as well. Kelly didn't think she could have said anything to save her soul.

Dan tossed the clothes on the foot of the bed. "You can use the belt out of the robe to tie up the jeans. Take your time and call if you need me. I'm going to heat up some soup."

Kelly watched him leave, waiting a moment to make sure he was really gone before she pushed back the covers and stood. She inhaled sharply as her bruised body protested the movement. Moving cautiously, she discovered that everything worked, if under protest.

With the robe wrapped around her and dragging on the floor behind her, she crept out of the bedroom and down the hall to the bathroom. Half an hour later, a warm shower and some ruthless work with the comb Dan had left out for her, she felt almost human.

After a few horrified moments staring at her reflection, she avoided the mirror. The bruises would fade, she told herself firmly. Besides, what difference did it make what she looked like? There was no one to care. Dan might be concerned but that was only because he wanted the child she carried.

*The deal was...* A deal. That's what they had. Her baby in exchange for escape for them both. She closed her eyes, setting her hand over her stomach. She'd tried so hard to divorce herself from the life she carried. But yesterday, when her father had come at her with such mad rage in his eyes, her first thought had been to protect the baby.

Kelly drew in a deep breath, squaring her shoulders as she opened her eyes. She'd struck a deal with Dan. A deal that was going to provide a future for her child and for herself. This was the best thing for both of them. It might not be easy, but most things in life that were truly worthwhile weren't easy.

This was the right thing to do. She had to believe that with all her heart. She didn't dare believe anything else.

Her nose led her to the kitchen, though it wouldn't have been difficult to find even without the warm scent of soup drifting out. Dan's apartment was not large. One bedroom, one bath, a fairly large living room and a kitchen with an alcove that functioned as a dining room.

Dan was standing at the stove, stirring the soup. It seemed odd to her to see a man doing such a domestic task. She couldn't ever remember seeing her father doing anything in the kitchen except possibly washing his hands. Cooking was a woman's rightful job, he always said, making it sound like a divine law.

Sensing her presence, Dan glanced over his shoulder. Kelly fought the urge to duck back around the corner.

"You're just in time for some of my world-famous soup," he said casually. "Have a seat. It'll be done in a minute."

He turned, leaning one hip against the counter as she shuffled farther into the room, her gait limited by the need to keep the thick white socks from drooping off her feet.

"How do you feel?"

"Better, thank you. I guess I look pretty awful."

"Well, the clothes are a little large," he said honestly.

"I meant this." She lifted one hand to her face, half covering the bruises that surrounded her eye.

"It'll heal." In a way, it was comforting to see the glint of anger in his eyes and know that it was on her behalf. She couldn't remember anyone ever being angry for *her*, unless maybe it was her brother, Devlin. But he'd been gone such a long time.

"Are you hungry?" Dan asked, turning to take a bowl from the cupboard.

"I don't know. I guess so." She eased onto one of the plain oak chairs.

"Well, I'm not much of a cook but I open a mean can." He set a bowl of soup in front of her and a plate containing a slice of buttered bread. "Eat up."

"Thank you." She picked up the spoon more out of politeness than hunger, but after a mouthful or two hunger stirred to life. She pushed back her sleeve as she reached for the bread, biting into it with relish.

Dan watched from the kitchen, feeling a smug satisfaction. He wondered how long it had been since she'd had a decent meal. Much too long, he'd be willing to bet. She was too thin, especially for someone carrying a baby. She needed some fattening up.

The fact that she was swallowed up by his clothes only emphasized her slightness. The shirt covered her almost to her knees and he could only imagine how she'd had to gather the waist of the jeans to keep them up. She shoved the sleeve back again when it threatened to droop over her hand. Tossing down the dish towel, he crossed to the table.

"Here. Let me roll those up for you." He waited until she'd looked up at him before holding out his hand for her arm. She hesitated a moment and then slowly lifted her arm so that he could reach the sleeve. She'd tried to roll it up but, one-handed, she hadn't been able to do a very thorough job.

Dan rolled the sleeve with a few deft motions, his mouth tightening when he caught sight of bruises he hadn't seen before on the inside of her lower arm. He said nothing, only lowered that arm and reached for the other.

"Thank you," she murmured when he'd finished.

"Shall I do the jeans, too? You're going to trip if you leave the legs dragging like that."

Wordlessly she turned sideways in the chair. Dan knelt at her feet, reaching for the clumsy roll of denim at her ankle.

"I guess I didn't do a very good job," she said. "It hurt a little to bend over."

Dan snapped the newly formed cuff tight with a quick gesture that made Kelly jump.

"Why won't you tell me who did this to you?" he asked, lifting his head, his blue eyes bright with anger.

"Why does it matter?"

"Because he shouldn't get away with this. No one should get away with something like this. Not even a father—especially not a father. It *was* your father, wasn't it?"

Kelly hesitated, lowering her eyes to where her hands twisted in her lap. "I don't want to think about it. I don't want to have to talk to the police and doctors. I don't want strangers reading about me in the newspaper and talking about me. I just want to forget."

Dan covered both her hands with one of his. She started and would have pulled away but he refused to let her.

"Kelly, what he did was wrong. Whoever he is, he had no right to hurt you. Do you think he *did* have a right? Do you think you did something to deserve this?"

She stared at his hand covering hers, her thoughts tangled. No, she didn't believe she'd done anything to deserve what had happened. And yet she kept hearing her father's voice saying that she had sinned, that she had to be punished.

"What I did was wrong," she whispered at last.

Dan's hand tightened over hers. "Is that why he beat you? Because of the baby?"

"Yes." The word was almost inaudible but it carried the impact of a sledgehammer blow. Dan felt it actually drive the breath from his lungs. He'd known it all along, but he'd had to hear her confirm it.

"Was it your father?"

There was a long moment where he thought she might refuse

to answer and then she nodded slowly. Dan swallowed hard. He could deal with his own rage and guilt later. Right now what mattered was making Kelly see that none of this was her fault, that she had no reason to blame herself.

"What *we* did was irresponsible and foolish. If there's any punishment to be meted out, it should have been mine. I shouldn't have brought you here in the first place, but once I did I had no business being careless. I, of all people, should know enough to take precautions."

He was silent for a moment, seemingly looking inward at things she couldn't see. He shook himself, his eyes focusing sharp and bright on hers.

"Don't you *ever* think that any of this was your fault. Or that you deserved what your father did. We made a mistake but what he did was flat wrong. The fact that he's your father doesn't give him the right to hurt you, no matter what you've done. Understand?"

His eyes held hers until she nodded. He squeezed her hands before releasing them and standing. "Your soup's getting cold."

Kelly turned back to the table, picking up her spoon automatically. "You won't try to—do anything about this, will you?" She stared at the table, counting her heartbeats while she waited for his answer.

"Not if you don't want me to," he said at last.

"Thank you."

"You don't have to thank me," he said roughly. "It's my fault you're in this situation to start with."

Kelly stirred her spoon through the soup, watching the patterns created in the broth. She would love to be able to lay the blame squarely on someone else's shoulders but that wasn't really fair.

"You didn't force me," she said quietly, not looking at him.

Dan shoved his hands into the pockets of his jeans, looking at her bent head. "How old did you say you were?"

The seemingly irrelevant question startled her into looking up at him. "Eighteen. Why?"

"You're sure as hell not like any eighteen-year-old I've ever

known. Sometimes you seem older than I am. Don't you want
to get mad at me? Throw things, call me names?''

"What good would that do?"

"It would make me feel better," he muttered.

The answer was so illogical but so understandable that Kelly
smiled, wincing when the movement pulled at the cut on her
mouth. She pressed her fingers to her lip.

Dan smiled with her, though his eyes held a darker look.
Looking up at him, Kelly was suddenly reminded of the first
time she'd seen him, the way the lights in the bar had caught
in the gold of his hair, the way his eyes had seemed as blue
as a summer sky.

She looked down, fingering her spoon. She didn't like to
remember the good things about the night. It seemed safer to
forget them. If she remembered too much, she might forget the
reason she was here, she might forget the reason he was being
so nice to her.

His only interest was the baby she carried. It could be disastrous if she ever let herself forget that.

*Chapter 7*

The waiting room looked more like a parlor than a doctor's office. The sofas would have fit neatly into any den and the end tables spilled over with luxuriant houseplants. There were four women seated in the room, all in various stages of pregnancy. Four women and Dan.

The nurse had called Kelly into Dr. Linden's office ages ago. Dan hadn't felt out of place while Kelly was with him, but after she left he felt as if he'd somehow grown too many arms and legs. He felt overgrown and gangly in a room scaled for women. The sofa was too low to the floor or his legs were too long. He seemed to take up too much room. He felt conspicuous, as if everyone was wondering what he was doing there.

He finally picked up a magazine that featured a laughing infant on the cover and opened it at random, focusing his eyes on the pages as if absorbed in the article there.

Was it taking too long? How long should an appointment like this take? Was Kelly all right? Maybe he should have insisted on talking to the doctor himself. Ben had said he'd call and give her Kelly's history, but maybe it would have been better if he'd talked to her. Not that he could have added anything to what Ben had told her.

Dan scowled at an ad for a car seat. Ben probably knew more about Kelly than he did. If it wasn't for Ben, he wasn't sure he could have gotten her to the doctor without tying her up. Ben had talked her into it, convincing her that it was the best thing to do.

She hadn't wanted to go to the doctor until the swelling around her eye had gone down, until the bruising was gone. Until, as she put it, she looked human. Ben had come by the apartment the night after his first visit, and Kelly had reluctantly allowed him to look at her pupils and to check the bruising over her ribs. He hadn't been happy about her decision but he'd admitted that it probably wouldn't do any harm if she waited a few more days.

Ben. Dan's frown deepened. After she'd gotten over an initial shyness, Kelly seemed far more comfortable with Ben than she was with him. Of course, she didn't share a history with Ben like she did with him.

Dan flipped a page, frowning down at a picture of a mother and father with their smiling infant. It was foolish of him to expect her to be anything but uneasy with him. Her brief acquaintance with him had hardly turned her life into a bed of roses.

His memories of New Year's Eve might be hazy from too much whiskey but he remembered enough to know that her first experience with sex hadn't been a totally wonderful one. He shifted uncomfortably, almost wishing he didn't remember that night as well as he did. If he'd known it was her first time, he could have taken more time.

Hell, what was he thinking? If he'd known she was a virgin, he wouldn't have taken her to bed in the first place. Even as drunk as he'd been, that would have gotten through.

If that evening wasn't enough to make her view him with less-than-rose-colored glasses, there was what had happened since. Her father had beaten her when he found out about her pregnancy. And she wouldn't have been pregnant if it hadn't been for his careless stupidity.

Actually, considering everything, it was a wonder she could even stand to be in the same room with him. He was grateful for the small strides they'd made. Given time, he could show her that he wasn't a monster. They'd created a child together. It would be nice if they could manage at least a friendship.

Besides, in the short time he'd known her, he'd developed a real admiration for her. She had a remarkable inner strength. Despite what she'd been through she hadn't been broken. She had survived. He'd been able to piece together only part of her past history, but what he knew had only made him admire Kelly even more.

She had a brother who'd left home when she was a child. The clunky boots were his. There was a certain wistful pain in Kelly's eyes when she mentioned him that led Dan to believe she hadn't heard from him in a long time.

Her mother had died in a car accident when Kelly was twelve. She'd admitted that much when he'd asked about her mother, but she'd said nothing more and something in her eyes had kept him from probing.

If there was a good age at which to lose your mother, twelve certainly wasn't it. It would have been especially hard for a young girl, just entering adolescence. That was a tough time for any kid without adding the death of a parent.

She'd been left with only her father. Dan's fingers crumpled the edge of the magazine, his expression so grim that the woman who'd been sitting on the other end of the sofa got up and moved to a seat across from him. Just the thought of Kelly's father was enough to bring rage boiling up inside.

Kelly didn't want him brought to justice and Dan had agreed to respect her wishes; that didn't mean he couldn't think of all the things he'd like to do to him. His smile held such a savage edge that the woman got up again and moved to a seat farther away.

Dan flipped a page, his smile fading. He'd give up all his fantasies about wringing her father's neck, if he could just be sure that Kelly and the baby were healthy. In the time she'd been staying with him, most of the bruises had faded.

He'd gone out yesterday and bought her a dress, since she

could hardly wear his jeans and shirt to the doctor's office. And the dress she'd been wearing when she had come to him was not only ugly, it was a vivid reminder of what she'd gone through.

His eyes softened, remembering her surprise that he'd thought of it. It hadn't mattered that the dress was a little too big so that she had to pull the belt to its tightest notch. She'd pulled it out of the bag, handling the soft green cotton as if it were handwoven silk.

She'd actually had tears in her eyes when she thanked him, Dan remembered, feeling a stir of anger. How long had it been since she'd received a gift? How long had it been since anyone had shown her simple affection? Since her mother died?

He shook his head, forcing his fingers to relax their crushing grip on the magazine. He couldn't do anything about what had gone before. All he could do was see to it that no one ever abused her again.

She was recovering. He could see a change just in the past few days. She no longer flinched every time he got close. She'd gained a pound or two, and there was even a hint of color in her cheeks.

As Ben had said, she was young and surprisingly healthy. She was healing quickly—at least on the outside. The scars that worried Dan were the ones on the inside. Given time, would those heal, too?

"Mr. Remington?" Dan's head jerked up at the sound of his name. The nurse was standing in the doorway to the inner office.

Dan stood, the magazine falling to the floor. He bent to pick it up, nearly banging his head on the center table as he did so. He fumbled the magazine onto the table, feeling like a fool, sure that everyone was watching him as he moved toward the door.

The nurse showed him into an office painted in warm peach shades, undoubtedly designed to soothe the nerves of anxious patients. It didn't seem to have any such beneficial effect on Dan. His imagination had been working overtime for days, creating any number of vague but horrific pictures. Being in the doctor's office only brought them to more vivid life. Thankfully he didn't have long to wait.

He stood as the door opened, braced as if for a blow. Kelly entered first but he could read nothing from her expression, as usual. He had a feeling she'd spent a lot of years hiding her feelings. Dr. Linden followed her, a slender woman in her early forties, with rather ordinary features and kind eyes.

"You must be Mr. Remington," she said, her eyes flicking over him in a glance that missed nothing. "Kelly tells me you're the father of her child."

"Yes," Dan admitted, feeling much as he had when his third-grade teacher had discovered that he was the one responsible for the toad that found its way into her desk. "Is everything all right? The baby, I mean. And Kelly?"

"They're both fine, Mr. Remington. Why don't you sit down and we'll discuss what I'd like Kelly to do. She's agreed that you should be here."

"Thank you," Dan said to Kelly.

"It's your baby," she said quietly as she sank into one of the chairs that sat across from Dr. Linden's desk.

She listened with half an ear as the doctor told Dan that she was prescribing vitamins. Kelly wondered if anyone but her had noticed that Dan asked about the baby first, adding her only as an afterthought. Not that she had any reason to expect anything else. It was just that he'd been so kind and thoughtful, it was easy to forget that his main concern was for the baby.

The baby she tried so hard not to think about. The baby she'd promised to give up. Kelly forced her thoughts back to the present.

"I spoke with Dr. Masters and he gave me Kelly's history, or as much of it as he knew," Dr. Linden was saying. She glanced down at her notes. "As I've already told Kelly, it would have been advisable for her to have seen me right away, rather than waiting as you have."

"Is there some problem?" Dan leaned forward in his chair, his body tense.

"As I told you, both mother and child seem to be in fine health, Mr. Remington. Remarkable health, really, considering what Dr. Masters told me. Kelly is a little too thin. I've drawn blood to test for anemia but, overall, I think they're both doing quite well.''

Kelly felt the breath Dan exhaled as he leaned back in his chair. Relief that the baby was okay, she reminded herself. She couldn't forget that.

''It says here that you should be eating plenty of fruits and vegetables and drinking lots of milk.'' Dan looked up from the booklet he was studying to frown at the hamburger that sat in front of Kelly.

''There's lettuce and tomato on the hamburger,'' she offered. ''And French fries are a vegetable.''

''I don't think that's what they've got in mind. But the milk shake is good. You'll need lots of calcium.''

Kelly dunked a French fry in catsup, biting into it without enthusiasm. She'd hesitated when he suggested going out to lunch after her doctor's visit. Every instinct told her that the less time she spent with Dan Remington, the better off she'd be. She had to keep some distance between them.

She'd only rarely eaten in a restaurant, and in her new dress she felt almost pretty. Dan had chosen a coffee shop not far from Remembrance's one and only mall. Kelly hadn't even been sure she was hungry, but the smell of food brought her appetite to life. It seemed as if all she did lately was eat and sleep.

''I suppose I should start looking for another place to stay,'' she said, thinking of the fact that he'd been sleeping on the sofa, which was about two inches too short for his long frame.

''What?'' Dan dropped the booklet and focused his full attention on her. ''Why?''

''Well, you're sleeping on the sofa.''

''The sofa and I are getting along just fine.'' Dan nodded his thanks as the waitress topped off his coffee. ''If that's why you're talking about moving out, forget it.''

Kelly stirred a French fry through the catsup, her eyes on the aimless movement. ''You never planned on me staying with you. That was just because—because of what happened.''

"I thought we'd been getting along pretty well together."

"We have. I mean, you've been very nice. But I don't want to intrude. I know you'd like to have your bed back. And you're probably sick of having me underfoot."

"You're not underfoot," Dan said, sounding vaguely irritable.

"Well, it wasn't part of the plan..."

"Would you stop making it sound like a war document?" Forgetting that the waitress had just filled his cup, he picked up his coffee, taking a gulp.,

"Dammit!" He set the cup down with a bang, cursing again as the scalding liquid splashed out onto his hand. Snatching up a paper napkin he dabbed at the burn.

His scowl brought a familiar tightness to Kelly's stomach. She lowered her hands to her lap.

"I'm sorry."

"What are you apologizing for?" Dan looked at her, one eyebrow raised. "Because I'm a clumsy idiot?"

"I didn't mean to upset you."

"You didn't upset me. I mean you *did* but I'm not *upset* upset. Oh, for crying out loud." He tossed the napkin down in disgust. "Just because I get upset doesn't mean I'm mad at you and it sure as hell doesn't mean I'm going to start pounding on you."

His words startled her into looking at him. "I know that."

"Do you? Then why is it that I end up feeling like Dracula?"

"I don't know," she answered honestly.

"Probably my own guilty conscience," Dan muttered. "Look, do you *want* to move out?"

"I...that was the idea."

"I know that was the idea. But I've given it some thought and I'm not sure it's such a great idea. I could find you a place but I don't like the idea of you living alone. What if you got sick or fell?"

"Lots of pregnant women live alone," she pointed out, not exactly arguing.

"Not while they're carrying my child," he said firmly. "I want you to stay with me."

"I'd be fine on my own."

"But you're not going to be on your own."

Kelly pushed away her half-eaten meal. "I don't want to intrude on your life like that."

"Intrude on my life? You're carrying my baby."

"Do you think I can forget that?" she snapped. Did he have to bring it up all the time? She could never pretend, even for an instant, that he was here because he wanted to be with *her*. Did he think she didn't remember that she was pregnant? There was never a moment when she could forget it, never a moment when her emotions didn't seesaw back and forth over it.

She stared out the window at the overcast sky, wishing she could get up and walk away. But there was nowhere to go, no one she could turn to. And the sad fact was that a part of her didn't even want to go.

"Kelly? Do you really *want* to move out?"

"Yes. No. I don't know." She shrugged, irritated that she couldn't answer more firmly.

"That's what I like, a really decisive answer." Dan's voice held a gentle amusement that only confused her more. Every shred of common sense said that she couldn't possibly like him. He'd torn her life apart, though she was willing to admit to sharing the responsibility for that. Still, she'd been the one to bear the punishment for their carelessness. She was the one whose body was going through changes that left her off balance and irritable.

She should dislike him. She *wanted* to dislike him. And then he'd look at her with that quiet amusement lurking in his eyes—such very blue eyes—and she'd remember the way he'd smiled at her New Year's Eve.

Even worse was the one occasion when she'd come out of the bedroom and found herself nearly nose to nose with Dan's bare chest. He'd just showered and the heady scent of soap and after-shave had enveloped her, sweeping her back, making her remember the feeling of his arms around her, the taste of his

1outh, the way his hands had seemed to know her body in
vays she'd never imagined.

No, she didn't want to live with him until the baby was born.
he wanted to put some distance between them. She *needed* to
ut some distance between them.

"No, I don't necessarily want to move out." The voice
eemed to come from someone else. That couldn't possibly be
er talking.

"Then what's the problem?" Dan asked, hearing the hesi-
ation in her voice.

"I just feel like I'm some sort of charity case," she said,
1e words almost bursting from her. "I mean, I'm living in
our house, I'm eating food you buy, wearing clothes you
ought me. I don't *do* anything."

"You're not a charity case." Dan reached across the table,
atching one of her hands in his. He felt her start, just as she
lways did at his touch, but he didn't release her this time.
Kelly, when I asked you not to have an abortion, I told you
d take care of you."

"I know. But I didn't expect it to be like this."

"How did you expect it to be?"

"I thought I'd get a job or something," she said, aware that
1e sounded vague to the point of foolishness. How could she
xplain that she hadn't been thinking with any clarity then? All
1e'd seen was that he was offering her the only out she had,
1e only escape for her and the baby she was carrying.

"What kind of a job?"

"Working in a bookstore or something. I don't know," she
1id, exasperated. "I don't know what I thought. But I feel like
parasite."

"You're not a parasite." Dan's hand tightened over hers.
The fact that you're pregnant is as much my fault as it is
1urs—more. It's only right that I take care of you."

He made it sound so reasonable. Kelly stared at their joined
1nds, noticing how his palm engulfed her fingers. It was a
cure feeling. Too secure. She pulled her hand away from his,
tting back in the booth.

"I can't just sit around for the next seven months," she said.

"Okay." Dan leaned back, a sudden sparkle in his eye: "Can you cook?"

"Yes. Nothing gourmet, but I can cook."

"Then you can be in charge of meals," he said, his smi suggesting that the problem was solved.

"It's not going to take me all day to cook meals for tw people. I'll do the housework, too."

Dan frowned and Kelly knew he was thinking that house work might be too much for her. She set her jaw. Maybe h saw the look or maybe he was tired of the argument. Whateve the reason, he nodded slowly.

"All right. You can cook and do the housework, as long a you don't do anything too strenuous. No heavy lifting or any thing like that."

Kelly nodded, feeling a small glow of triumph. She felt a if she'd won an important point. All her life, she'd let othe people dictate what she was going to do. It was time she starte taking charge, at least in a small way.

It didn't occur to her that it was rather remarkable that sh felt secure enough with Dan to argue with him. She had, witl out being conscious of it, come to believe that she was saf with him, that he wouldn't explode in a fit of fury if she dare to disagree.

The tangled memories of New Year's Eve were slowly bein overlaid with newer, gentler impressions. He'd been kind an considerate with her, treating her as if she were made of spu glass. Even if his main concern was for the baby, he'd don his best to put her at ease.

Whether she liked it or not, her life was inescapably er twined with his. No matter what happened in the next fev months, they'd created a life together. Nothing could eve change that. Nothing could ever fully dissolve that tie.

"I don't need clothes," Kelly protested, hanging back : Dan started toward the mall. They had finished their lunch be fore Dan sprang the news that they were going shopping. H stopped and turned to look at her.

"You can't spend all your time in my jeans or that dress.

"I could make some things, then."

"I don't own a sewing machine," Dan pointed out. "Are you going to make everything by hand?"

She lingered next to the Corvette as if it were home, regarding the mall with a combination of fascination and fear. She hadn't gone into a store to buy something brand-new for herself since her mother died. Since then, what few garments she owned had been purchased at the thrift store that hunkered uneasily on the north end of town. She doubted if Dan had ever even been in a thrift store.

Kelly stroked her hand over the full skirt of the dress he'd bought her, the first new dress she'd had in six years. Now he was talking about buying more clothes. The thought made the breath catch in her throat.

"What's wrong?" Dan came back to stand next to her. Her head was bent, the smooth length of her hair falling forward in a dark curtain that concealed her face.

"I don't really *need* clothes," she said, her fingers lingering over the soft cotton of her dress.

"If you don't like that dress, that's okay. You can choose your own wardrobe. I won't say a word."

"Oh, no, I love the dress." She lifted wide eyes to him, afraid that she'd hurt his feelings. "It's the most beautiful thing I've ever owned."

"Then what's the problem? I can afford this, Kelly. You don't have to worry about my bank balance."

She gave in because it was easier than arguing, easier than trying to explain feelings she wasn't quite sure she understood herself. Everything in her life had changed so quickly she felt as if she was running to catch up with it. He was right. She was going to need a few more things. Some inexpensive, practical garments that would wear well. Not too much, just enough to keep her decent.

Dan, however, had other ideas. His idea of "enough" was quite a bit different from Kelly's. Leading her into the most expensive department store in the mall, he found the women's department and waved a vague hand, telling her to get whatever she wanted. He handed her a credit card, the first she'd ever held in her life. When he turned to leave, Kelly had to clench her hands to keep from grabbing his sleeve.

"Are you leaving?" There was an edge of panic in the question. Dan turned to look at her, his face full of concern.

"I was going to get a pair of shoes. I figured you'd probably rather do this without me. You want me to stay?"

"No. No, of course not. I just..." She trailed off, drawing a deep breath before continuing. "How much should I spend?"

"Whatever you need to spend. I don't think you're likely to break me."

She watched him leave with the feeling that she was a shipwreck victim watching the last lifeboat sail away. The strength of the feeling bothered her. She was depending on him too much. If she was going to put her life in some kind of order, she had to remember to depend only on herself.

Drawing in a deep breath, she turned toward the racks of clothes. The array of colors and styles was dazzling, the prices shocking. She wandered through the aisles, her head spinning with the choices in front of her. It was almost ten minutes before she found the courage to touch anything. The royal-blue silk of a blouse spilled over her hand, almost too beautiful to be real. The price tag was very real, however.

With a sigh, she turned away from the blouse and went to find a less expensive selection of merchandise. She'd been clutching the credit card so tightly, it had left marks in her hand. Easing her grip, she slipped it carefully into her dress pocket.

When Dan found her half an hour later, Kelly was standing by the doors, one bag sitting on the floor next to her.

"Is that all you bought?"

"Yes. Did you find your shoes?"

"Shoes? Oh, I didn't need shoes. I just thought you might prefer to shop on your own." He frowned down at the bag. "Did you get enough?"

"Yes. Here's your receipt. I hope I didn't spend too much." She handed him the credit card and receipt as if handing over the royal treasury. She chewed at her lower lip as Dan read the receipt. Her heart sank when his frown deepened.

"Forty dollars? You spent forty dollars?"

"I'm sorry. Everything was so expensive." Her voice shook. How many times had she stood before her father while he castigated her for extravagance at the grocery store? For an instant, Dan's broad shoulders were replaced by her father's more wiry frame, his deep voice booming out at her, telling her she'd failed yet again.

"What did you buy?"

"I can return it. I knew it was too much." Her hands twisted together, her eyes reflected her distress.

"Kelly." Dan reached out to catch her hands, holding them despite her automatic withdrawal. "Kelly, I'm not upset with you for spending too much money. I'm not angry."

"You're not?" She stopped trying to pull back, her eyes lifting to his.

"No, I'm not. Just tell me what you bought."

"Two blouses and a pair of pants. They have elastic at the waist, so they'll stretch when I...I mean when my..." She broke off, feeling her cheeks warm as they always did at any reference to her pregnancy.

"Two blouses and a pair of pants. No dresses? Underwear? Shoes?" When she shook her head in answer to each of his questions, his hands tightened momentarily on hers, something close to anger flickering in his eyes before he released her. "Why didn't you buy any of those things?"

"Well, I don't really need them," she said uncertainly. This whole conversation was confusing. He wasn't angry that she'd spent what seemed to her to be an extraordinary sum of money. Instead, he seemed upset that she hadn't bought more.

"Kelly, you need a complete wardrobe," Dan said at last, his voice carefully level. He thrust his fingers through his hair. "You can't get by on only one pair of pants, two blouses and this dress." He waved his hand in the direction of the dress she was wearing. "And the shoes I bought you are too big."

Kelly curled her toes inside the flats he'd bought to go with the dress. There were blisters forming on the backs of her heels where the shoes had rubbed but she hadn't thought he could know that.

"I've got my old dress," she offered, not quite sure why he was upset.

"No, you don't. I threw it away." Kelly gasped. "And I threw away that hideous coat, too," he added with satisfaction.

"You threw away my clothes?"

"You said they didn't have any sentimental value."

"There was nothing wrong with them."

"Did you want to wear them?"

"I...there was nothing wrong with them," she repeated.

"They didn't fit and they were ugly," he said bluntly. "And you're going to need more clothes than what you've bought."

"No, I don't." She didn't move when he bent to pick up the bag and turned back into the store. "I can manage with what I've got."

"Kelly, I don't want you to 'manage.'" Dan set the bag down again. "I want you to be comfortable. I want you to be happy."

Kelly lowered her eyes, blinking back tears. It had been a long time since anyone had worried about whether or not she was happy. "I have enough."

"No, you don't. I told you I could afford this. I wouldn't tell you I could if I couldn't."

"It's not that." She was aware of the woman behind the makeup counter giving them curious looks. She felt awkward and self-conscious.

"Are we back to the problem of not taking charity?" Dan asked. "You can look on the clothes as part of a salary, if you like. You have to have something to wear while you're cooking and cleaning. And I might as well confess right up front that I'm going to give you money, too."

"It's too much," she protested in a strangled tone, blinking rapidly to hold back the tears.

"I haven't even said how much I'm going to give you. How can it be too much?"

"Not just that. The clothes, everything." She shook her head when she couldn't find the words. "It's not right."

"What isn't right?" He leaned closer, shielding her from prying eyes, his voice gentle.

"All this. I don't deserve all this. It's sinful," she burst out at last.

"Why is it sinful? You're not hurting anyone."

"What I did was wrong and now it's like I'm being rewarded for it."

"Stop it." Dan's voice held more force than seemed possible for such a quiet tone. He reached out to catch her chin, tilting her face up to his. "*We* did something foolish, but it *wasn't* a sin. God's not lurking on high to smack us for it.

"You didn't do anything that deserves punishment, and if you had then surely what your father did was punishment enough. We made a mistake and we're doing the best we can to make things right. We can't do anything more than that, right? Right?" he repeated when she didn't respond.

"I guess." Caught in the brilliant blue of his eyes, Kelly would have agreed with almost anything he said. She felt an odd tingling where his hand touched her chin, a tingle that seemed to spread throughout her body, making her almost dizzy. It must be because she was pregnant, she thought. Hormones or something.

"Now we're going to go buy you clothes. And you're not going to look at price tags. We're not going to buy anything remotely practical. And nothing in gray," he added firmly, thinking of the baggy gray dress that she'd come to him in.

"It just doesn't seem right," she said, not really protesting.

"Let me worry about it." Dan's hand shifted, cupping her cheek as he leaned down, so close that she could feel his breath against her mouth. "If there's a sin, it will be mine. Okay?"

"Okay," she said hesitantly, aware that it was an argument she didn't truly want to win. If she were honest, then she had to admit to a bubble of excitement at the thought of actually owning some of the wonderfully beautiful clothes she'd hardly dared to touch.

"Good." Dan's smile started in his eyes. Kelly felt an actual shiver run up her spine. His hand still lingered against her cheek. He'd held her face like that on New Year's Eve, his palm against her cheek as he'd kissed her. For an instant, the memory was so vivid she felt her mouth softening as if in anticipation of his.

Dan's smile faded, his eyes suddenly searching. She wondered if he remembered, too. The thought made her skin heat and she lowered her eyes, afraid of what he might see.

"Kelly." There was an intensity in his voice that hadn't been there a moment ago.

She wasn't destined to find out what he might have said.

"Dan?"

The voice was light and feminine. Kelly felt the sudden tension in Dan's fingers before they fell away from her cheeks. Her gaze swept up to his face, seeing the same tension there in the instant before he turned toward the voice.

## Chapter 8

"Dan. I thought it was you." The woman who spoke was quite simply the most beautiful woman Kelly had ever seen. Wide-set gray eyes dominated beautifully chiseled features topped by a thick chignon of glossy black hair. The man with her was dark haired also but his eyes were blue. Perched on his hip was a little girl of three or four, her eyes blue like her father's, her hair lighter than either of her parents'.

"Hello, Brittany," Dan said. His eyes flicked over to the man. "Michael." His face softened, something akin to pain in his eyes as he looked at the child. "Hi, Danielle."

She stared at him for a moment with eyes wide and then ducked her head, burying her face against her father's shoulder. There was a moment of silence that seemed fraught with more tension than was warranted by a child's shyness.

"She's just at that age where she's shy with strangers. Not that you're a stranger," Brittany added hastily. "She's just in a shy stage."

"It's okay, Brittany," Dan said, his mouth kicking up on one side.

The look she threw her husband seemed to hold a plea. For

what, Kelly couldn't guess. "How have you been?" Michael asked, the words flat.

"Not bad," Dan said. He seemed to suddenly remember Kelly and reached out to take her arm, drawing her forward. "Kelly, this is Michael and Brittany Sinclair and—their daughter, Danielle."

There was an odd hesitation in the way he added the little girl's name, a flash of something unreadable in Michael's eyes and visible distress in Brittany's.

"This is Kelly Russell," Dan continued. She could feel the tension that radiated from him in the too-tight grip on her arm.

"Hello," she said quietly. Tension surrounded the little group and she almost envied Danielle the ability to duck her head and hide her face.

"Kelly. It's nice to meet you." Kelly took the hand Brittany held out, feeling the tension revealed in the other woman's eyes. "Have you and Dan known each other long?"

"Not long," Kelly said, feeling as if she were swimming in dangerous waters without the least idea where the danger might come from.

"Actually, Kelly is staying with me," Dan said, his words bringing instant silence. Kelly flushed.

"Dan has been living like such a hermit these past few months. I'm surprised he managed to meet anyone," Brittany said brightly—too brightly.

"Nosiness does not become you," Michael told her dryly. He hitched the little girl farther up on his hip. "We ought to be going. We're expected at my parents' house."

The two men stared at each other for a long moment. Glancing at Brittany, Kelly saw the anxiety that was so evident in her eyes. Just when Kelly was sure that the tension was going to reach an unbearable level, Dan glanced away, smiling.

Brittany looked as if she might want to say something more but Michael set his hand against the small of her back, urging her toward the door.

"It was nice to meet you, Kelly. Maybe we'll get a chance to talk next time."

"That would be nice," Kelly replied, thinking that there wasn't likely to be a next time.

She turned to watch the little family as they walked toward the parking lot. Glancing at Dan, she saw that he was watching them, also, his expression hard with some emotion she could only guess at.

"Friends of yours?" she asked.

"More or less." Dan was still staring outside, though Michael and Brittany were no longer in sight.

"Brittany seemed nice," she ventured, watching his profile.

"Yes."

"And Michael."

"Hmm."

"And Danielle is very cute."

"Yes." He turned away from the door abruptly. "If we're going to buy you a wardrobe to rival Princess Di's, we should get started."

It was obvious that the subject was closed. Kelly filed the odd little meeting in the back of her mind. She knew so little about Dan. The incident only emphasized just how little. It was something she could think about later.

At the moment, there was no time to think about anything but shopping. Dan hadn't been kidding when he'd said they were going to buy a complete wardrobe. It might not quite match British royalty's, but it was enough to make Kelly feel like the princess in a fairy tale.

She had been determined to add only a few more things to her meager wardrobe; however, Dan was even more determined to outfit her with everything she could possibly need. In the end, Kelly couldn't stick to her resolve. Not only was Dan aligned against her, but the temptation he was presenting was simply too much for her beauty-starved soul to resist.

Dan watched her pick through the racks, saw the way she'd hesitate over a particular garment and then turn away as if shunning temptation. He followed along behind her, pulling each item off the rack and handing it to the saleswoman who had become their affectionate shadow as soon as she realized the kind of money Dan was planning on spending.

When Kelly reached the changing rooms, she had four or five items in her hand and the saleswoman had another fifteen. When she would have protested, Dan gave her a bland look that dared her to argue with him. He might have felt guilty about the way he was half bullying her into buying clothes, but his determination to see her outfitted won out over the mild twinge of conscience.

He roamed restlessly through the women's wear while Kelly tried on clothes. Seeing Brittany and Michael had been a shock, not so much for what he'd felt but for what he hadn't felt. Seeing them together no longer hurt. He hadn't been overwhelmed by a wave of regret. Even seeing Danielle hadn't caused the ache in his gut that it usually did.

It still hurt that he'd lost her. But he'd let go. It wasn't until now that it occurred to him that he hadn't been by her school since Kelly had burst into his life. He didn't feel the need to watch Danielle play in the school yard and wonder what might have been. He had a future now, something to look forward to, something to build dreams around. The past could recede to its proper place.

And a part of him felt he owed it all to Kelly. Not only did she hold the key to all his dreams in the child she carried, but she'd made him see how he'd been wallowing in his own misery. Seeing what she'd been through and the way she was trying to put it behind her had made him realize what a fool he'd been to waste so many months regretting things that couldn't be changed.

He turned as Kelly came out of the dressing room wearing a dress in an odd bluish green that the saleswoman called teal. The soft wool fabric—just right for spring—draped Kelly's body as if meant for her alone. The color made her skin seem translucent and made her eyes look even bigger and darker. Or maybe it was the price tag that had widened her eyes.

"I like it," Dan said, noticing the way the skirt swirled around her knees.

Kelly crossed the few feet that separated them, one of the only occasions he could recall when she'd approached him voluntarily.

"Do you know how much this costs?" she asked in a strangled whisper.

"No and I don't care. Do you like it?"

"Of course I like it. Who wouldn't like it?" She stroked her hand over the skirt as if it were made of something very delicate and precious. "But it costs much too much," she said firmly.

The saleswoman watched discreetly from a few feet away, wondering if she was about to lose what had promised to be a fat commission.

"I thought we agreed that you needed clothes," Dan said, taking an angled approach to the question.

"We did. But this dress costs too much." She fiddled with the tag that dangled from the end of one sleeve. "You can't spend this much on one dress."

"Yes, I can. It looks terrific on you and you like it."

"But..." She broke off when he raised a cautioning hand.

"If you argue about it, I'll buy seven of them, one for every day of the week."

"Where would I wear it?" she protested, knowing she was losing the battle and not entirely regretful about the defeat.

"Shopping or out to dinner or something." He waved a vague hand, unconcerned with the specifics.

"If I buy this dress, can we be more careful about the rest of the clothes?"

"No." Dan smiled at her, softening the flat refusal. "I don't like being careful."

He could see in her eyes that she knew she'd lost the battle. He also saw the way her hand trembled as she fingered the full sweep of a skirt.

"Kelly, do you like the dress?"

"It's beautiful," she said, her voice shaky. "I never thought I would have anything so beautiful."

He felt a surge of anger that something as simple as buying a dress should move her to tears. He forced the feeling down and smiled at her.

"You ain't seen nothin' yet. We're just getting started."

It was a promise he kept. Clothes piled up at a rate that

made Kelly's head spin. Skirts, slacks, blouses, dresses and lingerie. He wasn't buying anything more than the average woman might have in her closet, but to go from owning one dress and one pair of shoes to owning an entire closet full of garments was a little difficult for Kelly to absorb.

Dan had never shopped for a woman before and he found it surprisingly fun. At least, shopping for Kelly was fun. She was so cautious, so determined to be practical. It was fun to coax her into admitting that she really preferred the hot-pink top to the more practical ivory one she'd picked out.

After an hour, she had all but given up protesting his extravagance. The worried little frown that puckered her forehead had been replaced by pleasure, underlaid with a certain resignation.

It became Dan's mission to coax a smile out of her, and when he achieved that he wanted a laugh. He couldn't ever remember hearing her laugh out loud. Not even on New Year's Eve. He finally achieved his goal when he held a particularly frilly dress up to himself, raised his brows haughtily and suggested that the hem needed to come up just a trifle.

Kelly had been looking at something else and turned to see him with the pink-and-white confection draped around his rugged frame. The contrast was so ludicrous that she was momentarily struck dumb. When he reached out and removed a pillbox hat, complete with veil, from its stand and plunked it on his rumpled blond hair, the picture was complete. She pressed her hands to her mouth, laughter bubbling up inside.

"Dahling, don't you think this is just perfect for the governor's ball," he asked her in a very bad British accent.

Kelly's muffled giggle became full-blown laughter. Dan couldn't have felt more pleased with himself if he'd just won the lottery. With her eyes sparkling and her face flushed with laughter, Kelly looked young and happy.

And pretty. He'd been so focused on her health and on making sure that the baby was going to be all right, that he sometimes managed to forget how pretty she was, especially when she smiled. Her eyes weren't just brown. Up close, he could see little gold flecks in them. Her hair swung full and thick against her shoulders, the color of tobacco and looking like silk. Her mouth was soft, with a full lower lip that seemed just made for kissing.

He could remember the feel of that mouth beneath his, the way she'd responded, her body melting against him. It was odd how, the more time he spent with her, the more vivid those memories became.

What was he thinking? He dragged his gaze from her mouth. He had no business thinking like that, no business feeling that particular kind of awareness. She was under his protection, to use an old-fashioned phrase. He'd promised to take care of her, not lust after her. All he had to do was keep that in mind and he'd do just fine.

It got harder to remember his proper role as the afternoon wore on. The twinkle in Kelly's eyes was so inviting. The excitement she was trying so hard to contain was infectious. With her face flushed with color and her hair mussed from trying on clothes, she looked sweet and desirable.

Only he had no right to find her desirable. Through his carelessness she'd found herself carrying his child. Oh, it was true that he hadn't forced her and she could argue that the situation was as much her fault as his, but Dan didn't see it that way.

He was the one with the experience, the one who should have known better. And the fact that he'd consumed enough alcohol to knock an elephant to its knees was no excuse. If he couldn't hold his liquor, he'd had no business drinking it.

No, the responsibility was entirely his. Now he had to do his best to make sure that Kelly didn't have to suffer the consequences of his stupidity alone. And he'd make sure that the child they'd so carelessly conceived never wanted for anything.

In the meantime, he simply had to view Kelly as his responsibility—like a little sister. He frowned at a rack of dresses. No, not like a sister. There was nothing brotherly in the way he felt when he looked at her. Okay, so he just had to keep in mind that she was pregnant. No, that wasn't quite the right approach, either. Just the thought that she carried his child stirred feelings he shouldn't be having.

Did she have to be so damned pretty, so vulnerable? Those

soft brown eyes made him want to put his arms around her and keep her safe from the world. Unfortunately they also stirred thoughts that had nothing to do with keeping her safe and everything to do with desire.

He shoved his hands into the pockets of his jeans and tried to force his thoughts away from Kelly. Maybe this was part of his penance—to have her so close and so out of reach. Maybe this was his just deserts for having been so foolish. Maybe if he looked on having her underfoot but untouchable as a kind of medicine he had to take, it would be easier.

But medicine generally didn't come in such an attractive package.

By the time they'd bought all the clothes Dan felt she needed and far more than Kelly could ever imagine wearing, it was late afternoon. They'd eaten lunch early and Kelly's stomach was sending up a polite inquiry as to the condition of her throat. She was thankful when Dan suggested an early dinner.

They ate at the mall, coffee-shop food that was plain and filling. Kelly ate a hearty meal, trying not to think that her sudden appetite might have something to do with the baby, just as she generally tried to avoid any thought of the baby.

Today, more than ever, she didn't want to think about it. She felt almost pretty today, wearing one of the ridiculously expensive outfits Dan had insisted on buying. She'd changed in the store, putting on a pair of trim gray slacks and a soft sweater in a delicious shade of raspberry pink. She could pretend that she was an ordinary girl out for a date with a handsome man. It was almost possible to forget the real reason she was here, the reason she had the beautiful new wardrobe, the reason Dan was with her at all.

The meal was hardly finished when Kelly became aware of a sweeping tiredness. She stifled a yawn. Dr. Linden had told her that she was likely to find herself sleeping more.

"You look beat," Dan commented, pulling out a bill and slipping it under the check. "Maybe we tried to do too much today."

"I'm fine." She tried to look bright eyed and alert as she

slid out of the booth, but the truth was she was suddenly exhausted.

"I shouldn't have tried to get this all done in one day," Dan said, seeing the dark tint under her eyes.

"I'm not that tired," she said, spoiling the protest with another yawn.

"Sure you're not. Let's get you home." He reached out to take her arm in a gesture so natural Kelly hardly noticed it.

Outside, the air was chill with evening's approach. Kelly felt the cold, but she was snuggly wrapped in her new coat. She turned the collar up higher, enjoying the feel of the soft ivory wool against her face. She'd never owned anything so luxurious in her life. She pulled a pair of black leather gloves out of a deep pocket and slowly drew them on. The short walk to the car hardly warranted the gloves but she couldn't resist the supple feel of them.

When they had gone into the mall, they'd had to circle around a small construction crew making repairs to the roadway that ran between the mall and the parking lot. The crew was packing up for the day as Dan and Kelly left the mall.

"Dan! Dan Remington!" Dan turned, his face breaking into a smile when he saw the heavyset man who'd called his name.

"Larry Welch! You old dog."

The other man covered the distance between them with a speed that belied both his age and his weight. Dan thrust out his hand.

"I heard you hadn't been killed in that crash, after all, but by the time the rumors got around to me, you'd left town again. How the hell have you been, boy?"

Kelly watched as the two men shook hands fervently. *Killed in a crash? Dan?* What was he talking about?

"I've been okay. How about yourself?"

"Not bad, not bad." Larry shook his head, his broad face sobering. "Sorry about your dad. He was a good man. Musta been tough on you."

"Yeah, well, it was a long time ago," Dan said.

"Best damn boss I ever had," Larry said.

"He thought you were the best damn foreman he ever had."

*Dan's father was dead, apparently.* Kelly drew back a little, pushing her hands into her coat pockets. It had never occurred to her to ask about his family; she was realizing more and more that she knew so little about him.

"Your mom sold the business right after he died. Offered me first bid but you know I ain't got that kind of dough. Said she was real sorry but she just wasn't up to running a construction outfit."

"She told me," Dan said. "I don't think Mom is the construction type."

"Guess not. A mite too elegant for it, I'd say."

"What have you been up to, Larry? Who are you working for?"

"The county." Larry's tone expressed his disgust.

"Good pensions."

"Yeah, but it ain't the same. Too many bureaucrats. Say, you wouldn't be thinking about starting up your dad's old business, would you? You got the know-how. You have plenty of experience working on the crews."

Kelly was as curious about Dan's answer as Larry was. Dan had told her that his job at the mechanic's garage had been more a favor to a friend than real employment. He hadn't said anything about wanting to do something else. They'd talked so little.

"I don't know, Larry," he said slowly. "I've been giving it some thought, actually. I'll give you a call if I do."

"You'd better." Larry's eyes shifted past Dan's shoulder to where Kelly waited. "Friend of yours?"

"Sorry." Dan turned, giving Kelly an apologetic smile. "I didn't mean to be rude."

"That's okay." She let him draw her forward.

"Larry, this is Kelly, a friend of mine."

"I wish all of *my* friends were so pretty," Larry said. His hand engulfed Kelly's.

"It's nice to meet you," she said, giving him a shy smile. It was more than a little unnerving to meet Dan's friends. Though at least with Larry Welch there wasn't the disturbing undercurrents she'd felt with the Sinclairs.

"How about the old crews?" Dan asked Larry, his mind still on their earlier conversation.

Kelly tuned the conversation out, letting her mind and her eyes wander. Dan's hand rested lightly against the small of her back. She wondered if he felt the same awareness at the casual touch that she did. Probably not. It had to be the pregnancy that made her feel warm where he touched her. It was probably just her hormones acting up again.

Dan wondered if Kelly was even aware that he was touching her. She was usually so skittish about even the most casual of contacts. Keeping up the train of conversation with Larry, he was still aware of the feel of her under his hand. Even through the layers of coat and clothes, it seemed as if he could feel the warmth of her.

He didn't think he'd ever been quite so aware of anyone in his life. Was it the fact that she was carrying his child? Did that create some sort of primal link between them?

Whether it was that or something else, he didn't know, but he instantly felt the odd little shudder that went through her. He broke off in midsentence, turning to her, aware that something was wrong.

"Kelly?"

She was looking past Larry, her eyes wide and dark. Seeing her pallor, he felt his stomach clench.

"Is it the baby?" he asked urgently.

"I want to go home," she choked out.

She seemed to sway and Dan's arm came up, ready to catch her if she fainted.

"Something wrong? Something I can do?" Larry's rugged face creased with concern.

"I want to go home," Kelly repeated. It seemed as if she had to drag her eyes away from whatever she'd been looking at. She looked up at Dan, her eyes wide and terrified. Terrified?

Dan turned his head to follow the direction she'd been looking. There didn't seem to be much to see. Some of Larry's crew putting away the last of the equipment, the truck they were loading and the parking lot beyond that. He was about to turn his attention back to Kelly when his eyes were caught by a lanky old man who seemed to be staring in their direction.

Unkempt iron-gray hair straggled over his ears. The coveralls he was wearing looked nearly as old as he was, and even over the distance that separated them it was plain to see that he didn't have more than a nodding acquaintance with bath water.

But there was something about his steady gaze, something fierce and oddly compelling. Dan had to pull his eyes away. He seemed to be staring at Kelly, his eyes glittering with an emotion Dan couldn't read.

"Kelly?"

"I just want to go home," she whispered without lifting her head.

Through the arm that half encircled her, Dan could feel her trembling. He looked back at the old man, a sudden suspicion flaring.

"Who is that?"

Larry turned, following the direction of Dan's gaze. "The old man?" He shrugged. "That's Russell. Hardly worth a day's wages. Spends most of his time muttering about sin and saviors. Why?"

Dan hadn't heard anything beyond the name. There, not fifteen feet away, was the man responsible for hurting Kelly. Rage blossomed in his gut, rising in his throat to nearly choke him. His hands actually ached with the need to feel that filthy neck between them.

He took a quick step forward, the movement so deadly that Larry took a half step out of his way.

"No!" Kelly grabbed at his arm. "No, please."

Dan stopped, looking down at her, his eyes a cold, angry blue. "You can't let him get away with what he did."

"Please. Please, I just want to go home." Her eyes were wide, pleading with him not to do what every instinct was screaming at him to do.

"What's the problem?" Larry asked uneasily.

"No problem," Dan said at last. He slipped his arm more solidly about her, glancing to where her father had been. But the old man was gone and Dan wasn't sure whether to be glad or sorry.

He made quick farewells to Larry, knowing the other man must be puzzled, to say the least. His only concern right now was Kelly. Recently the shadows had receded from her eyes and she'd looked happy, at least for a little while. But now the shadows were back. One glimpse of her father and all the color was gone from her cheeks; her eyes were haunted. She almost seemed to shrink in size, as if pulling into herself physically as well as emotionally.

Dan said nothing as he settled her into his car, shutting the door with more force than was necessary. He strode around to the driver's door, his hand clenched so tight that the keys gouged into his palm. The engine roared to life, a deep growl that fitted his mood.

Kelly's huddled pose reminded him of the night he'd picked her up. The thought fed into the rage gnawing at his gut. *He should have beaten the bastard to a pulp while he had him within reach.* His hands tightened on the steering wheel. If he had been alone, he would have taken the Corvette out of town, found some lonely stretch of road and floored it, hurtling down the pavement until he'd left some of his fury behind.

But he wasn't alone. And it was time he learned to deal with his anger in some less childish fashion. He had responsibilities now. Kelly and the child she carried—they depended on him. *Which was exactly why he should have beaten her father to a pulp,* his more primitive side argued.

Neither of them spoke on the drive home, each wrestling with their private demons. Darkness had drifted over the town by the time Dan parked the car. Kelly walked up the pathway ahead of him, her movements mechanical.

Dan unlocked the front door, ushering Kelly in ahead of him. She still looked as if she'd seen a ghost. Or had a glimpse of hell.

Kelly hardly seemed aware of her surroundings. She stood in the hallway, still wearing the coat and gloves she had taken so much pleasure in. She might as well have been wearing sackcloth and ashes.

Just that one glimpse of her father had been enough to show her how fragile her security was. She'd almost managed to convince herself that she was safe—but she had only to look at him to know she'd never be safe. He was always going to be there. He would find her wherever she went, waiting to punish her for her sins.

She turned abruptly, her eyes blind. Dan stood just inside the doorway, taking off his coat, his face grim. She hardly saw him.

"I've got to go," she muttered as much to herself as to him.

"Wait a minute." Dan stepped in front of the door, blocking her way. "Where are you going?"

"I don't know. Out. Away. Somewhere he can't find me."

"Kelly, he's not going to find you here."

She looked at him as if in a trance. "I have to go," she repeated, wondering why he didn't see the obvious.

"No, you don't. I'm not going to let him hurt you ever again."

"You can't stop him," she whispered. "He thinks I have to be punished and he'll find me. Oh, God, maybe he's right." She turned away, wringing her hands. Fear had taken over, blotting out every other emotion. She didn't have to close her eyes to see her father standing over her, that terrible, terrible madness in his eyes, his fist lifted to strike her. The image was so vivid, so real, that she buried her face in her hands, her shoulders shaking with dry sobs.

"Stop it," Dan's voice made the command gentle but firm. He caught her shoulder, ignoring her attempt to pull away as he turned her to face him. "We've had this discussion before. You didn't do anything wrong. I want you to stop thinking that."

When she didn't respond, he put one hand under her chin, forcing her face up until he could look directly into her eyes.

"Kelly, listen to me. I'm not going to let him hurt you. I'll kill him before I let him near you again. No one's ever going to hurt you like that again. Do you hear me? I'd kill him before I would let him hurt you."

It may have been the force of the words that got through. It may have been her own desperate need for reassurance—for someone to believe in. Whatever it was, he saw the frozen mask of despair slowly dissolve. She pressed her fingers against her mouth as it began to shake.

"I couldn't stand it again."

Dan had to lean close to her the muffled words. His heart ached for her pain. Slipping his hand to the back of her neck, he drew her forward to rest her head against his chest. She remained stiff for only a moment before giving in to the very human need for comfort, for someone to share the burden.

"It's going to be okay, Kelly. I'll take care of you. I promise. You don't have to be afraid anymore." He stroked his hand over the back of her head, murmuring reassurance, hardly aware of what he was saying. What he said wasn't important. What was important was that Kelly felt safe, that she understood he would take care of her.

She didn't cry. She only leaned against him like a tired child, all her strength seemingly gone. She allowed him to slip the thick coat from her shoulders, tossing it over a hook in the open coat closet.

If she had been tired before, it was nothing compared to the exhaustion she felt now. The emotional turmoil of seeing her father had drained the last bit of energy from her. In the back of her mind was the thought that she should move, should do something to prove that she was strong and that she could handle this little scare. Except she didn't feel strong. And it felt so wonderful to have Dan holding her, protecting her.

Dan bent, sliding his hand beneath her knees and lifting her into his arms. He carried her into the living room, settling in the big overstuffed chair with her on his lap.

Grunge jumped up on the coffee table, his battered face alight with curiosity. The big tomcat had shown an immediate devotion to Kelly. From the moment she'd moved in, Dan might as well have ceased to exist. The fact that Kelly admitted she'd never had anything to do with animals didn't seem to bother Grunge at all. It simply made her easier to train in the proper way of doing things.

Now he watched Dan settle into the chair before making the

leap from the coffee table to the arm of the chair. When h
stepped down onto Kelly's knee, Dan moved to push him of
but Kelly grumbled a protest.

"It's okay. I like him."

"You spoil him," he told her without heat. Grunge picke
his way delicately onto Kelly's lap, pausing to knead his paw
against her thigh.

"Everybody ought to be spoiled," she said, her voice drag
ging with sleepiness.

Then why hadn't anyone spoiled her? he wondered, watch
ing the cat find a spot and settle in.

He leaned his head back, closing his eyes. How long was
going to take for her to heal, inside as well as out? How lon
before she could believe that she'd committed no wrong, unles
loneliness was considered a sin? And if loneliness *was* a sin
heaven knew he was guilty.

# Chapter 9

It was after ten o'clock when Kelly awoke. With only the hall light burning, the apartment was dim. And it was quiet. She didn't have any of that momentary disorientation that occasionally comes on waking. She knew exactly where she was, exactly why she felt so warm and safe.

Dan was sprawled in the big wing chair, his feet on the coffee table, his arms holding her even in sleep. Grunge lay stretched over her legs, his torn ear twitching in response to some feline dream.

She lifted her head slowly, careful not to disturb either of them. Dan's head had settled into the corner where the back of the chair met the arm. She studied him in the sparse light. He looked younger in sleep, almost vulnerable.

*Vulnerable.* It wasn't a word she would normally have applied to Dan Remington. Her acquaintance with him had been relatively brief in terms of time but it had been eventful. In that time, he'd shown her nothing but strength. And kindness.

She mustn't forget just *why* he'd been so kind. He wanted the child she carried. That was the only reason she was here, the only reason he was so determined to help her.

Dan stirred in his sleep, one hand shifting until it lay just beneath her breast. Kelly flushed at the feel of his long fingers. Even though she knew he was asleep, the touch seemed intimate, warming her skin. She was suddenly aware of the way his body cradled hers, the feel of his thighs beneath her, the muscled width of his chest against her shoulder.

The heaviness she felt in the pit of her stomach had nothing to do with the child she carried and everything to do with its father. Her flush deepened until her face burned.

Moving carefully, she tried to slide off Dan's lap without waking him. At her first move, Grunge meowed, digging his claws into her leg as a gentle suggestion that she might like to stay where she was. When Kelly persisted, he got up and jumped off her lap, turning to give her a reproving glance.

Kelly ignored him. Dan stirred as her feet found the floor. Seeing his lashes starting to lift, she abandoned her attempt at stealth, sliding off his lap with more speed than grace.

"Hello." His voice was just-awakened rough. His eyes held a sleepy awareness that made her flush anew. There was nothing offensive in the look, but there was something in it that made her suddenly aware of the lateness of the hour and the intimacies they'd shared.

"Hello." She ran a hand over her hair, smoothing the tangle out. "I guess we fell asleep."

"Guess so." Dan stood, arching his back in a deep stretch. Kelly backed up a step, wanting a little distance between herself and the maleness that she was so suddenly aware of. She glanced away, tugging the hem of her sweater down over her slacks.

"Well, it's late. I guess I ought to go to bed."

"How are you feeling?"

"Okay. I'm sorry I made such a fuss earlier. It's just that it was a bit of a shock to see him."

"You've got nothing to apologize for," Dan said easily.

"I overreacted."

"I think you're entitled to a little overreaction."

"Maybe." She hesitated, not sure why she was lingering. "Well, I should probably get to bed," she said again.

"You want a cup of cocoa?"

"Cocoa?"

"You know, the brown chocolatey stuff that you drink?"

"I know what it is. I haven't had cocoa since...in a long time."

Since her mother died? Dan wondered.

"Well, I'm a moderately skilled cocoa maker" was all he said.

"I...sure, it sounds nice."

It was, he thought, like having a half-wild kitten in the house. She wanted to be friends but she was wary of being hurt—with good cause, heaven knows. But he was going to do his damnedest to make sure she didn't get hurt.

"Can I help?" She'd trailed after him to the kitchen and leaned against the corner of the counter. Glancing at her, Dan could see that she was still too pale and there was a tired droop to her eyes. Obviously her lengthy nap hadn't been enough to recharge her energy. Weren't pregnant women supposed to get lots of sleep?

"I've got it," he told her as he got out the milk and found a pan. "Why don't you sit down. You look like a strong wind would blow you over."

"I feel fine." But she walked over to the table and pulled out a chair.

She watched Dan make the hot cocoa, his movements efficient. It occurred to her that he probably knew his way around a kitchen as well as she did, which meant that their deal that she would do the cooking and cleaning might not be as much to his advantage as she'd thought.

That didn't disturb her as much as it might have twenty-four hours before. Maybe it was having clothes like a real person. Or maybe it was that seeing her father had made her realize nothing was as important as the fact that she'd gotten away from him. Maybe it was just that she was too tired to care. She'd worry about pulling her own weight tomorrow. It would be soon enough.

"Here we go." Dan set a steaming mug in front of her.

"World-famous cocoa at a moment's notice. That's ou motto."

"World famous?" She drew the mug closer, inhaling th dark, earthy scent that drifted up from it.

"Okay, 'locally pretty well-known' might be a more accu rate description," he admitted as he sat down in the chai across from her. "It's my dad's recipe, and when the construc tion business got him down he used to threaten to chuck th whole thing and open a cocoa stand."

"It's very good," Kelly assured him after taking a sip.

"Thanks."

Silence drifted between them, a surprisingly companionabl silence. Somewhere during the course of the day, she'd lost he wariness of him, or at least her vague fear. Whether it was th way he'd clowned around while they were buying clothes, o the rage she'd felt boiling inside him when they saw her fathe or the way he'd held her while she slept, she couldn't hav said. Maybe it was nothing more than the way his hair insiste on falling onto his forehead in a dark blond wave.

"When did your father die?" she asked, thinking that sh knew too little about him.

"Almost four years ago."

"Were you close?"

"Yes. We had our ups and downs but we were close. H had a great sense of humor. We had just begun to get past lot of the father-son garbage. I think we were beginning to b real friends."

Kelly tried to imagine what it was like to be able to say tha about either parent and failed. She'd loved her mother but sh couldn't imagine that they would ever have managed to b friends. Sara Russell had always been too fragile, too turne into herself, to be friends with anyone, even her own daughte

"What about your mother?" she asked, following her ow train of thought.

"She lives in Europe. After Dad died, she didn't want t stay here with all the memories so she packed up and took tour of Europe."

"And she decided to stay?"

"More or less. She fell in love with someone. He's a count or a baron or something. Very old family. He even owns a molding castle. He apparently took one look at Mom and decided that the sun rose and set for her. Took him nearly a year to convince her but she finally married him. They live in France."

"Do you mind? Her remarrying like that, I mean?"

"No. Dad would have been the last person to want her to mope around after he died. And Henri treats her as if she were made of spun glass. I'm happy for her."

"It sounds nice," Kelly said, feeling a little wistful.

"It is." Dan lifted his mug, watching her over the rim. "What about your mother? What was she like?" He made the question so casual it didn't occur to Kelly not to answer.

"She was pretty. Long dark hair and the biggest brown eyes you've ever seen."

"Sounds a lot like you," he said.

She looked up, surprised. "Oh, no. She was really pretty," she repeated, as if he couldn't have heard her the first time.

"So are you."

"Thank you." The words were perfunctory. Clearly she thought he was only saying it to be polite. Dan was torn between amusement that she could dismiss his opinion so easily and irritation that she couldn't see herself as he did. He wanted to march her to a mirror and make her look at her reflection, make her see the sweet lines of her face, the way the dark sweep of her lashes created soft shadows on her cheeks, the perfect molding of her mouth. But now was not the time to pursue that particular issue.

"So what was she like besides being pretty?"

"She was nice." Kelly frowned down into her half-empty mug as if dissatisfied with that description. "Sweet, really."

"Did you spend a lot of time together?"

"Not really. Mama was...well, she was delicate, I guess. My father..." She stumbled over the word, her fingers tightening on the warm mug. "My father wasn't very easy to get along with, even when I was little. I think Mama sort of withdrew because she couldn't cope with his temper. She used to spend a lot of time in her room, reading or just staring out the window. I guess it was her way of dealing with him.''

And of leaving her children to cope with a lunatic, Dan thought sourly but he didn't say as much. It was obvious that Kelly's memories of her mother were pleasant. He wasn't going to spoil them by pointing out that retreating was hardly the best way to deal with a bully.

"What about Devlin? You said he left home when you were little. Were you close to him?"

"Oh, yes." Her smile was sweet, with none of the sadness that usually haunted her expression. "He's ten years older than I am, but we were always close. He never seemed to mind having me tag along. Mama wasn't well for a long time after I was born and Devlin watched over me quite a bit. I guess that's what made us so close."

*In other words, her mother had allowed a ten-year-old boy to take on the responsibility for his infant sister.* Dan concealed his sour expression by swallowing the last of his cocoa.

"When did Devlin leave home?" he asked, wanting to take advantage of her unusually talkative mood. He almost regretted asking when her soft expression faded, replaced by the familiar tightness around her eyes.

"He was eighteen."

"And you were eight," he calculated. "That must have been tough, losing your older brother."

"I cried for days. I couldn't understand why he left, not then, anyway. Later, when I got older, I realized that he'd probably stayed as long as he had because of me. I think if it hadn't been for me he might have left even sooner."

"Why?"

She shrugged without answering but Dan didn't really need an answer. He could guess the answer on his own.

"Did your father beat him, too?" he asked softly, watching her face. She winced and started to shake her head. Her eyes flickered over his face and the gesture changed to the merest hint of a nod.

"I think so," she whispered. "Sometimes Devlin would have bruises, and when I asked him about them he always said he'd fallen or run into something. But later I thought maybe he hadn't fallen at all.''

"'Later' being when your father began to beat you?" he questioned boldly. "When did that start, Kelly? After Devlin left?"

She didn't answer at first. The silence stretched until Dan could hear the faint hiss of a soft rain falling outside.

Kelly stared at the tabletop, quiet for so long that Dan thought maybe he'd tried to go too far too fast. Perhaps she wasn't ready for this. But he'd always believed that the best way to get rid of an infection was to lance the wound. What her father had done to her was festering inside her. Maybe talking about it, getting it all out in the clean air, would help start the healing process.

"He wasn't a bad father," she said, just when he'd begun to give up hope. Her voice was husky, the words a little fast as if she had to rush to get them out. "Not really bad, not when I was little. He wasn't an affectionate man but that was just his way. He was never the sort to hug and kiss or play silly games with you or anything.

"He was always very involved with the church. Mama never went and neither did Devlin and me. Most nights he went to church to pray and every Sunday he was gone. He didn't have much patience with children—some people don't, you know," she said as if he had suggested otherwise.

Dan said nothing, his expression neutral. Kelly waited for a moment before continuing.

"I didn't see all that much of him, really. He was usually gone early in the morning, then he'd come home for supper and go out again and he usually didn't get home before I'd gone to bed. I don't think I missed him all that much. I had Devlin. And Mama," she added.

Dan wondered if it was just his imagination that made the addition seem perfunctory, as if she included her mother more out of loyalty than conviction.

"Devlin sounds like a brother in a million," he said, the one sincere positive comment he could make.

"He was. I don't think it was easy for him. I never blamed

him for leaving, not once I got old enough to understand how
it must have been.''

"Was that when your father started beating you?" he aske
again, determined to get the subject around to her.

"No," she whispered. "That didn't start till after Mama wa
killed. He was so angry with her. I think maybe he took it ou
on me. He said that she was running away with a lover whe
she was killed." She pushed the empty mug away, lifting he
head to look at him, her eyes daring him to say anything. Da
wisely chose a noncommittal position.

"You don't believe that?"

"No. She wouldn't have left me there. If she *were* runnin
away she'd have taken me with her."

"Makes sense," he said, keeping his thoughts to himself. /
woman who'd lie in her bedroom staring out the window whil
her son took care of an infant, who had apparently let he
husband beat that same son, hardly struck him as the sort t
give much thought to her daughter if she decided to run awa
from what had undoubtedly been a less-than-pleasant life.

"What happened after she died?"

"He was very withdrawn for weeks," Kelly said, her eye
dropping back to the tabletop. She drew her finger through th
dark ring that marked the table where cocoa had sloshed ou
of the mug when Dan set it down. "I tried to talk to him.
was twelve and I was trying so hard to be an adult. He didn'
want to talk to me. He didn't even want to look at me. W
settled into a pattern, I guess. I took care of the house—w
had a house then, not a trailer. I thought we were doing okay

"And then, about six months after Mama died, I was clean
ing and I found her makeup case under the bed. I should hav
known better, really. I mean, it was so soon and I know h
must have missed her."

"What happened, Kelly? Was that the first time he hur
you?"

"Yes." She couldn't seem to get out any more than the on
syllable for a moment. "I was playing and he came home an
saw me with all the makeup on." She closed her eyes, twelv
again and seeing her father's face twist with rage.

"He was so angry," she whispered. "He said I looked like a painted hussy, a whore. He said one whore in the family was enough and he wasn't going to stand by while I became the second. He said that woman was born of sin and that the only means to prevent them from following the devil's ways was to beat the sin from them."

Dan became aware of pain in his hand. He had to force his fingers to relax their grip on the mug. Only the fact that it was made of thick, sturdy china prevented it from shattering beneath the pressure.

"Why didn't you tell someone? Why didn't you go to someone for help?"

"I don't know." She shook her head, looking older than her years in the light that slanted across the table. "He was all the family I had left. I was afraid to lose him, too. I was ashamed and I was scared. I ran away once, when I was almost sixteen."

"What happened?"

"He found me. I didn't dare try again." She didn't add anything to the simple statement. She didn't have to.

"Didn't anyone notice?" Dan asked, shoving away from the table to pace restlessly. "What about your teachers? Your friends?"

"I didn't have any friends. After he sold the house and bought the trailer, I was ashamed to bring them home, afraid they would find out we weren't a perfect family like I was sure they all had. I used to pretend we were a perfect family."

"What about Devlin? Didn't he ever come back, ever see what was happening?"

She shook her head. "He sent an address a few months after he left, a post-office box in South Carolina. I wrote there and he answered for the first few years. Then he stopped answering the letters. The only time I heard from him after that was when Mama died. He wrote and said he couldn't come to the funeral and that I shouldn't grieve too much."

"Did you ever tell him what was happening? What your life was like?"

"No. I didn't want him to worry. So I always let him believe everything was all right. I've written once a month."

"And you haven't had a response in—what—six years?"

"I know it seems foolish," she said, raising her chin. "But if he weren't getting the letters they'd be returned, wouldn't they? And I'm sure there's a good reason he hasn't written."

Dan sank back into his chair, staring at her. The story she'd just told him was the stuff of lurid headlines. She had lived a life that would have destroyed most people, left them embittered and scarred. A mother who'd abandoned her in mind if not in body, a father who'd ignored and then beaten her, even her beloved brother had left her. And yet she could still say that he must have had a good reason for not writing in six years.

Maybe she was only clinging to the last vestige of the family that had dissolved around her. Maybe she didn't dare believe that Devlin had left her just like her mother had.

And maybe she was strong in ways he was only just beginning to understand.

"I should never have let you go back there," he said as much to himself as to her, thinking that he could have saved her at least one beating.

Kelly reached across the table, her fingers touching his fleetingly, darting away almost as soon as they'd contacted his.

"It wasn't your fault."

Dan's mouth twisted. "Thanks. But it *was* my fault, almost as much as his. I shouldn't have brought you back here that night. Having done that, I shouldn't have let you go back to your father once you'd told me about the baby. I could see that you were scared. I should have tried to find out why."

"I wouldn't have told you then. I'm not sure why I've told you now," she said, half to herself. "I've never talked about it, not with anyone."

"Maybe it was time you got it out in the open," Dan suggested. "It's easier for things to heal in the fresh air."

"Maybe." She frowned and shook her head, getting back to the subject at hand. "You can't blame yourself for what happened."

"I don't see how you can be so forgiving about this." He stood again, emotions boiling inside him. He covered the distance to the kitchen counter in a few long strides, spinning on one heel to look at her.

"If it wasn't for me, none of this would have happened. The baby, your father." He gestured sharply with one hand, words failing him.

"That's true in a way," Kelly admitted slowly. "But that doesn't make it your fault." She stopped, her cheeks blushing brightly as her eyes dropped to the table. "No one forced me to come back here with you."

"I didn't force you but I should have known better. And even if I didn't know better, I could have at least used protection."

The color in her cheeks deepened, reminding Dan that this was undoubtedly the first time in her life that she had ever talked about contraception; reminding him that he was the one responsible for introducing her, rather dramatically, to the need for such things. Guilt, an all-too-frequent companion these days, washed over him in a new wave.

"If it wasn't for...what happened," Kelly said. "If it wasn't for the...baby." She stumbled over the word, getting it out with difficulty. "I might never have gotten the courage to leave. And it was my fault for going back to the trailer. I should have known better. I'd been sick in the mornings, I knew I couldn't keep it from him forever."

"Why *did* you go back?" Dan leaned back against the counter and stared at her intently.

"There were some things I wanted to get. Silly things." She shook her head, dismissing something that must have been important to her.

"Keepsakes?"

"Nothing really important. There was a loose panel in my closet and a place to hide things under it."

"If you want them, I'll get them for you."

His offer brought her head up, her eyes wide. "There's nothing of value."

"If you want your things, I'll get them for you," he repeated, his jaw set. There was something in his eyes that suggested he wasn't averse to the idea of a chance to confront her father.

"No." Kelly shook her head. "It's nice of you to ask but I'd rather you didn't. I don't want to stir up any trouble. I just want to put it behind me."

A sudden yawn caught her unawares. She pressed her hand over her mouth. "Excuse me."

Glancing at the clock, Dan saw that it was nearly midnight. He pushed away from the counter, moving to the table. "It's late. You ought to be in bed."

Kelly stood. "I am tired."

She reached for her empty mug, her hand colliding with his as he did the same. For a moment, their fingers were nearly entwined. There was an instant of silence, too tense for such a minor incident, and then Kelly pulled her hand back.

"Well, it's late," she said, as if it were news. "I guess I'll go to bed. Good night."

"Good night."

Dan watched her leave, his eyes skimming the slender line of her back, somehow emphasized by the bulky sweater she wore. He didn't move until he heard the bedroom door shut behind her. Absently he picked up the mugs and carried them to the sink.

He had the feeling that Kelly Russell was going to bring even more changes to his life than he'd originally expected.

# Chapter 10

"Your friend Brittany stopped by this afternoon." Kelly was reaching for a plate on the bottom rack of the dishwasher as she spoke, her back to Dan, so she missed his startled look.

"Brittany Sinclair?" The bank statement he'd been reading was forgotten. *What had Brittany been doing here?*

"Yes. She seems very nice." Kelly shut the empty dishwasher. Running a towel over the counters, she stepped back to make sure the kitchen was returned to its usual immaculate condition—a condition to which Dan still wasn't quite accustomed.

"What did Brittany want?"

"I guess she just wanted to get acquainted."

"Did she stay long?" Dan toyed with the edge of the bank statement, trying to sound only mildly interested.

"Almost an hour. I liked her."

"Oh, Brittany's great."

*Except when she's up to something.*

Kelly turned to leave the kitchen but she didn't go into the living room, as had become her habit. Though she didn't actively avoid him anymore, she rarely sought out his company.

Dan hadn't been able to decide whether that was because she didn't want to bother him or because being near him made her uncomfortable. The fact that she was lingering suggested that something was on her mind.

"She's pregnant. Did you know that? Her baby is due the beginning of September." Though her tone was casual, there was nothing casual in her eyes.

*Just a month before her own baby was due,* Dan filled in.

Though proximity had forced them to develop a certain intimacy over the past month, the one subject that was still taboo was, ironically, the reason Kelly was here. They didn't discuss her pregnancy; the baby was never mentioned. It couldn't go on forever, of course, but Dan tried to respect her privacy. So much had changed for her. She deserved a little time to try to come to terms with those changes.

"Yes, I knew Brittany was pregnant," he said casually, as if there had been no awkward pause in the conversation. The look Kelly threw him was unreadable, but he thought she might have mentioned Brittany's pregnancy on an impulse she immediately regretted. It was too strong a reminder of her own situation.

"She said you two had known each other a long time."

"Quite a while."

"She's very pretty."

"Yes, she is."

"Beautiful, really."

Dan leaned back in his chair, watching Kelly needlessly dust the corner of the table. Was she wondering about his relationship with Brittany? Unless Brittany had said something about their rather convoluted past, which didn't seem likely, there was no reason for Kelly to think there was anything to wonder about.

"Don't you think she's beautiful?"

"Yes, I suppose she is," he answered cautiously, wondering just where the conversation was leading. But having gotten his agreement, she changed the subject, seemingly satisfied with his answer.

"She said her husband is an architect."

"He works with his father, Donovan. Sinclair Associates is one of the best design firms in this part of the country. They've done work over a good part of the United States."

"Would you be working with them when you start up your father's business again?"

"Possible but not likely. The Sinclairs only work with the best. Remington Construction was the best once and we will be again, but it will take a while to get the reputation back."

*Not to mention that his past history with the family was likely to make things a little awkward.*

"'When' I get the company going again?" he questioned, registering her choice of words. "You don't seem to have much doubt about it."

She shrugged. "It's what you want to do, isn't it? And you strike me as someone who generally does what they truly want to do."

"You mean I'm pigheaded," he said, his mouth turning up in a half smile.

"Determined is a more polite word," she suggested, giving him that shy smile that never failed to stir something in his chest. "I suspect you can do just about anything you set your mind to."

"Thanks." Her simple faith in him felt good. Especially since, at the moment, he wasn't sure whether the idea of re-building Remington Construction was inspiration or insanity.

Their eyes met and, for a moment, something seemed to pass between them. Kelly looked away before Dan could quite get hold of what it might be.

"Well, I should let you get back to your paperwork," she said. She turned to pick up a stack of library books from the counter. Dan frowned at them.

"Did you walk to the library again? I told you I could drive you there."

"You weren't here. And it's not that far."

"It's almost two miles."

"I'm used to walking."

"Not when you're pregnant."

The word hung in the air between them, as if painted in neon letters. Kelly's cheeks reddened and then paled, her hands tightening around the books. He'd broken a cardinal rule by saying it out loud. Generally he abided by Kelly's obvious wish to pretend that the baby didn't exist. But they couldn't go on pretending forever.

"Dr. Linden says walking is good for me," she said in a strained voice.

"Fine. But only if it's what you want to do. You should have a car. But first you've got to get your driver's license. Maybe this weekend I could start teaching you."

"All right." But the animation was gone from her voice.

Dan watched her leave the room before turning back to the paperwork in front of him. He stared at the forms for a moment before muttering a curse. Tossing down his pen, he shoved his chair back from the table. Stalking to the window, he stared out at the park across the street. It was empty now, swathed in darkness. But it wouldn't be long before the lights on the soft ball field would be turned on at dusk, symbolic proof that spring had fully arrived and summer couldn't be far behind.

And not long after summer ended, he'd be a father.

Kelly's stubborn denial of that reality was frustrating. They couldn't keep ignoring the fact. Already he could see small changes in her body—a slight thickening of her waist, hardly visible if you weren't looking for it, an extra fullness in her breasts. Soon it was going to be obvious that she was carrying a child—his child.

The thought was shockingly erotic.

His frown became a scowl as he felt a familiar tightness in his body. He wanted her. Was that such a terrible thing? After all, if he hadn't found her attractive three months ago, he wouldn't have brought her back here and none of this would be happening now.

She was soft and feminine, all big brown eyes and milky white skin. He'd have to be half dead *not* to want her. And the fact that she was pregnant with his child only added to the attraction. This primitive reaction was one he hadn't bargained on when he'd suggested that she stay here with him.

It was a small apartment and a certain amount of intimacy

was unavoidable. There was no way to avoid seeing her just after a bath, her skin scrubbed fresh and damp, her hair curling around her face. His eyes couldn't help but trace the perfectly modest neckline of her robe. What would she do if he reached out and loosened the belt she'd snugged around her waist? Would she be frightened and angry or would she melt the way she'd melted on New Year's Eve?

Cursing himself, he spun away from the window. He had no business standing here letting his imagination run wild like a randy teenager. He'd promised to take care of her, not lust after her.

Had he been wrong to insist that she have the baby? Should he have given her the money she'd asked for and walked away? He stopped next to the table, neatening the stacks of paper with one hand, his expression moody. How could he have walked away once she'd told him she was pregnant? It was his child. She'd made him a part of the decision by coming to him— even if she'd only done it because she had nowhere else to go.

He wanted this baby. That much he'd known from the beginning. What he hadn't expected was to find himself wanting its mother quite as much as he did.

Kelly shut the bedroom door behind her and leaned back against it, the library books held to her chest. She was an idiot to get so upset just because Dan had mentioned that she was pregnant. It was a reality and no amount of pretending was going to change it.

Pretending was exactly what she'd been doing. She'd been pretending she was someone else, pretending she was here for another reason, pretending she wasn't carrying a child she'd promised to give away.

Angry at the tears that blurred her vision, she straightened away from the door. She tossed the books on the bed and reached for the buttons of her blouse. It was time she made herself look at things as they really were. This wasn't a fairy tale she was living in. This was real life, and she didn't dare forget the reason Dan was taking care of her—the only reason.

A few minutes later she stood in front of the full-length

mirror. She still wasn't accustomed to seeing so much of herself at one time. Her father had allowed only one small mirror in her tiny bedroom, saying that mirrors only encouraged vanity and vanity was sin. But it wasn't vanity that drove her now

She'd turned on all three lamps in the room and light spilled over her nude body, illuminating it so clearly that Kelly cringed. She'd never stood naked in front of a mirror before and it seemed shocking to do so. She stifled the urge to turn away, forcing herself to really look at her reflection.

The bruises her father had inflicted had faded, leaving only memories. Her skin was pale and smooth, unblemished. She touched her hand lightly to her waist. It was thicker than i used to be. She'd put on weight this past month. Some of i could be attributed to the fact that she was eating well for the first time in her life, but not all of it. Her breasts seemed heavier, more tender, and that had nothing to do with how well she was eating. The baby was making its presence known, no matter how much she tried to ignore it.

Kelly spun away from the mirror, grabbing the robe she'd draped over the foot of the bed and thrusting her arms into it not daring to look in the mirror again until she had it securely belted around her waist.

Crossing to the window, she stared out at the park across the street. When she'd first come here, frost had crisped the grass at night. But spring was elbowing winter out of the way and the grass didn't carry a carpet of white in the morning anymore.

Time was passing. Summer wasn't far off. Soon her pregnancy would be obvious. She leaned her forehead against the cold glass, closing her eyes against the tears that threatened She cried much more easily now—another sign of pregnancy she supposed.

She'd felt so odd today, listening to Brittany Sinclair say she was pregnant. For a moment, she'd felt an intense connection with the other woman. She'd wanted to tell Brittany about her own pregnancy, to strengthen the tentative bonds of friendship that had only just begun to grow. She'd felt excited, eager to share it with another woman, someone who could understand the changes she was going through.

She'd never really had a female friend, someone to share things with. The few friendships she'd had when she was a girl had ended so long ago. She hadn't quite realized how lonely she'd been until Brittany had shown up on the doorstep, apologizing for dropping in unannounced.

With someone else, there might have been awkward moments. Brittany didn't allow such things. She freely admitted that she was nosy. She'd said she'd known Dan forever and she wanted to get to know Kelly.

She'd invited herself to lunch, then helped prepare it. It was like being run over by a cheerful steamroller, Kelly thought now. Brittany might have admitted to nosiness but she hadn't asked a lot of questions; at least, not about Kelly's relationship with Dan. She'd seemed to have nothing more in mind than just what she'd said—she wanted to get to know Kelly.

Kelly hadn't realized how starved she'd been for feminine companionship until Brittany's visit. They barely knew each other and their conversation was not deeply personal, but it was pleasant to talk to another woman. It was pleasant to talk to someone with whom she did *not* share a tangled past.

She'd had the urge to tell Brittany about the baby, another link in the fledgling friendship. But then she'd remembered. She couldn't tell Brittany about the baby. How could she tell her about the baby when it wasn't even hers to keep? What would Brittany say to that? Would she understand something Kelly herself couldn't really understand?

She turned away from the window, glancing again at her reflection in the mirror. She had to keep some distance between herself and this child. For the sake of her own emotional health, she couldn't begin to think of this child as hers. Not in any real sense.

This was all a temporary arrangement. It was as if she was putting her life on hold, just long enough to have this baby. Once she'd had it, the child—and Dan—would be out of her life forever. She couldn't afford to lose sight of that. She couldn't become attached, not to the baby or to Dan. She had to keep a certain distance. Though whether or not that was possible...

Dan had been kind to her. He was giving her a chance at a new life. But he was only doing that because of the baby. It wasn't that he had any deep personal interest in her. The moments when it seemed as if there was a connection between them—something more than the child they'd so foolishly created—those moments were undoubtedly tricks of an overactive imagination.

Kelly sat on the edge of the bed, running her fingers over the nubby surface of the tan bedspread. She'd made the right choices—the best choices for her and this child she didn't dare love. It might not be easy to walk away from either Dan or the baby, but she'd have to find the strength to do it.

She realized that she'd set one hand over her stomach, cradling the life she carried. This time there was no stopping the tears that sprang to her eyes. Curling up on her side, she buried her face in the pillow, letting it absorb her tears.

Spring came on full of gentle promise. Winter-browned grass sprang to life. The trees leafed out seemingly overnight. The birds returned from their winter nesting places, making the air sing with their calls as they courted and built nests. The last traces of winter disappeared beneath a barrage of greenery.

To Kelly it seemed as if time was racing by. Her life had changed so quickly, she felt as if she was still trying to catch up with it. There had been no gradual period of change when she could adjust to a new life, new circumstances. In the space of a week, her old life had been left behind and a new life begun.

True to his promise, Dan provided her with her first driving lesson—and it was nearly her last. It would have been hard to say which made more noise—the grinding of gears or the grinding of Dan's teeth.

The Corvette lurched down the street like a drunken rabbit as Kelly struggled to keep in mind the proper sequence of clutch and gearshift. It wasn't easy when half her attention was on Dan's increasingly anguished expression.

"Clutch, then shift," he got out in a voice that was clearly trying for patience. Flustered, Kelly stepped on the brakes instead, nearly throwing them both through the narrow windshield.

"Clutch! Put the clutch in," Dan all but moaned.

The car mercifully stalled. Kelly dropped her hands from the wheel, letting them rest in her lap. Though the temperature had barely reached seventy, she felt beads of perspiration on her forehead. The short-sleeved sweater and slacks that had seemed so comfortable earlier suddenly felt as if they were made of heavy wool instead of soft cotton.

Neither of them spoke for a moment. Dan stared out the windshield, a vaguely shell-shocked look about his eyes. Kelly stole one glance at him and then stared at the steering wheel.

"Okay," Dan said finally, his voice weak. "Let's try it again."

"Maybe this isn't a good idea," Kelly suggested. "I don't have to have a driver's license."

"Yes, you do. This town isn't set up for someone who doesn't have a car and you can't keep walking everywhere. Besides, driving is really simple, and once you've learned to drive a standard, an automatic will be a breeze."

Kelly stifled the urge to suggest that she'd rather learn the easy version first.

Pushing the clutch in, she turned the key, aware that her hands were moist with nervousness. The engine started with a roar that never failed to startle her. She tried to tune out Dan's continuous stream of instructions, the way his hands clutched at the edges of his seat, and concentrate on the simple pattern— or what should have been a simple pattern.

The gears ground together with a pained shriek of metal on metal. Echoing it was Dan's moan of pain. Panicked, Kelly hit the brake, remembering too late to push the clutch in. The car lurched to a shuddering stop.

For several seconds, neither of them spoke. Kelly's stomach churned with a mixture of nerves and anger. If only he'd *shut up* for a few minutes, she might be able to figure it out.

"Look, it's really very simple," Dan said in a tone that was so reasonable it was an insult.

"I don't want to learn to drive," she said, aware that she sounded childish and beyond caring.

"It's not hard. I'll go over it one more time."

"I don't want to learn to drive." She fumbled with the latch on her seat belt.

"It's not hard," Dan repeated through gritted teeth. "Look at all the idiots on the road who have managed to get licenses. If they can do it, you certainly won't have a problem."

"I may not have a high-school diploma," she told him in a trembling voice, "and I may have done some pretty stupid things recently, but I do *not* like being called an idiot." Kelly got the seat belt loose and jerked the door open. She was halfway out of the car before Dan realized what she was talking about.

"Wait a minute!"

She didn't pause. Dan yanked open his own door, thrusting his long legs out and then muttering a curse when he realized he hadn't undone the seat belt. He stepped in front of her as she came around the hood.

"I didn't mean that *you* were an idiot," he protested.

She stopped in front of him since it was either that or make it a point to walk around him. In defiance, she didn't lift her eyes above the third button on his shirt.

"Kelly, I wasn't saying that I thought you were an idiot," he repeated. "I was trying to make you feel more confident."

"It's supposed to make me feel more confident to be compared to the other idiots on the road? If they can do it, heaven knows even *I* should be able to manage."

"That's not what I meant at all." Dan thrust his fingers through his hair, looking around as if hoping for an inspiration. They hadn't made it more than a few yards away from the apartment building, and he didn't have to look to know that nosy neighbor Mrs. Barnett was watching this whole operation from her window. Since Kelly had moved in with him, his every move was once again being carefully scrutinized.

"I was just trying to get you to relax by telling you how

simple driving is. Any fool can learn." He immediately regretted his choice of words but it was too late to take them back.

"Any fool but not me, right?" Kelly tried to step around him but he sidestepped, blocking her path.

"I didn't mean that. Oh, damn. Look, I don't think you're an idiot, okay? I didn't mean to hint, imply, suggest or say that you were. I just want you to see how simple it is. If you would just relax a little."

"If you'd stop bellowing instructions at me, it would be a lot easier," she flared, lifting her head to glare at him. Dan couldn't have been more startled if the car itself had risen up to chastise him.

"Bellowing?"

"You keep telling me what to do. You never give me a chance to think. How am I supposed to figure out when to step on the stupid clutch when you're always talking? And the clutch is too hard for me to push, anyway."

She looked harried and irritable. What she didn't look was frightened. Dan felt a smile tugging at the corners of his mouth. She wasn't afraid he would be angry that she had snapped at him. She was reacting like any normal person would.

"Why are you looking at me like that?" she snapped, her frown deepening as she caught the hint of a smile.

"You're absolutely right," he said, sidestepping her question. "I have been yammering on at you. It's a wonder you didn't scream at me."

"Well, you weren't really yammering," she said, softening now that he showed some understanding.

"Why didn't you tell me that the clutch was too hard?"

"It's not that hard."

"But it's difficult for you to push?"

"I think my legs are too short." Moments ago, she'd been ready to consign him and his car to the devil. But all it had taken was for him to show a little understanding and she could forget her annoyance.

"I could offer a solution." They both turned as a new voice

entered the conversation. Ben Masters leaned against the side of Dan's car.

"How long have you been here?" Dan asked, not entirely pleased to see his friend.

"Long enough to catch the tail end of what looked like a not-too-successful driving lesson. Hi, Kelly."

"Hello."

The smile she gave Ben held none of the wariness she so often showed toward him, Dan noted. From the beginning, Kelly had been comfortable with Ben in a way she'd never been with him.

"We were doing all right," Dan said.

"Oh, then you intended to teach Kelly how to strip the gears?"

"I'm not a very good student," Kelly said, coming to Dan's defense.

"I've heard it said that there are no bad students, only poor teachers," Ben said to no one in particular.

"Did you have a reason for coming over or did you just want to be obnoxious?" Dan asked sourly, catching the laughter in Ben's eyes. The problem with Ben was that he was almost impossible to insult.

"Well, actually, I was just dropping by for a visit. A beautiful Sunday afternoon and all." He swept out one hand in a gesture that encompassed the sunshine and sparkling blue skies. "But it occurs to me that I might be of some use."

"That would be nice for a change," Dan muttered.

The amusement in Ben's eyes only deepened. "I have some experience as a driving coach. I taught both my little sisters to drive and there was no blood shed during the process. My car is a bit less...finicky than yours. And I would be happy to take over the lessons."

"Your car is a heap of junk," Dan said bluntly, looking at the battered blue vehicle in question.

"True, but it runs." Ben was not in the least disturbed by Dan's assessment of his car. "Kelly won't have to worry about doing it any more damage."

Dan shoved his hands into his pockets. "It's up to Kelly," he said at last, aware that he probably sounded a bit sullen.

"Kelly?" Ben looked at her, his brows raised.

Kelly hesitated, glancing at Dan as if trying to gauge what he would prefer. But he wasn't looking at her and there was nothing to be read from the firm line of his jaw, which was about all she could see.

He would probably be glad to be out from under the commitment to teach her to drive—a commitment he'd insisted on. He hadn't expected it to be quite so difficult, she was sure. If he didn't have to worry about this, he'd have more time to devote to getting his business of the ground.

Besides, it wasn't good for her to get too dependent on him. The time was going to come when she was on her own and wouldn't have him to lean on. She should start getting used to it now.

"Are you sure you wouldn't mind?" she asked Ben.

"It would be a pleasure."

"Is it okay with you?" Dan shrugged in answer to her question.

"Sure. Whatever you'll be comfortable with."

If Kelly felt any disappointment at his answer, she refused to admit to it. This was really the best arrangement. And if she was going to miss the time spent with Dan, then that was just more proof that it was better this way.

# Chapter 11

So Ben took over the driving lessons. As it turned out, Dan was home more often than not when Ben came to pick her up. Ben was an old friend, a good friend. And it was really great that he was doing such a good job of teaching Kelly to drive. So why was it that he'd like nothing better than to land good friend Ben a punch on the nose everytime he saw Kelly going off with him?

Dan restrained the urge, showing nothing but enthusiasm over Kelly's progress. And when she passed her driver's test the first time through, no one could have been happier than Dan. Seeing the feeling of accomplishment that made her eyes glow, Dan promptly forgave Ben for interfering and invited him to the celebration dinner.

But there had been a specific method to Ben's madness in interfering as he had. If Dan didn't have the sense to recognize what was under his nose, a little nudge had seemed in order. From the green glow in Dan's eyes everytime Kelly returned from her lesson, Ben had reason to hope that maybe his friend wasn't as dense as he'd been acting lately.

So he bowed out of the celebration dinner, hoping that, given some time alone and a congenial atmosphere, maybe the two of them could see what was so obvious to him.

It was the first time in her life that Kelly had been to an elegant restaurant. As she walked in on Dan's arm, she half expected to see the other patrons giving her sidelong glances as if wondering what she was doing there. But the only looks she noticed were one or two admiring female glances directed toward Dan. Despite herself, she felt a small glow of possessive pride.

There were also several approving looks thrown Kelly's way. And if Kelly was oblivious to them, Dan was not. He'd never thought of himself as the possessive sort until now. But seeing the admiration in other men's eyes, he was torn between a definite pride and the urge to throw a blanket over Kelly's head to keep their eyes off her.

"You're drawing a bit of attention," he said, after they were seated.

"I am?" She looked uneasy, her small spurt of self-confidence ebbing. "What's wrong?"

"Nothing's wrong," Dan said, laughing.

"Then why am I drawing attention?"

"Because you look beautiful."

She couldn't have looked more surprised if a chimpanzee had leaped onto the table and started to sing.

"Don't be silly." Rather than reassure her, the compliment seemed to make her even more uneasy.

"I'm not," Dan protested. "You look beautiful tonight."

"It's just the dress," she said uncomfortably. "It's lovely."

"The dress is nice but that's not what all the men were looking at."

"Men were looking at me?" She was torn between disbelief and a surge of purely feminine pleasure.

"Well, I hope they weren't looking at me," Dan said dryly. "You looked in the mirror. Didn't you see how you looked?"

She lowered her eyes, her fingers shifting the silverware. "I look okay."

"You look beautiful. Don't argue," he said when she opened her mouth to do just that. "The only polite way to deal with a compliment is to accept it graciously. Say 'thank you,' Kelly.''

For a moment, he thought she was going to protest again. She must have decided it was a losing battle, though he didn't think she was any closer to believing she was beautiful.

"Thank you, Kelly," she parroted. Though her eyes were demurely lowered, there was a tuck in her cheek that was pure mischief. Dan wondered what she'd do if he were to lean across the table and kiss that hint of a smile from her mouth. He pushed the thought away, reminding himself that he shouldn't even be thinking such things.

Maybe it was just the lingering effects of having accomplished a major milestone in her life that made the evening seem almost blessed. Kelly certainly preferred to believe it was the new driver's license tucked snugly in her purse that gave everything a rosy glow, rather than to think that it was the company.

The evening couldn't have gone more perfectly if it had been part of a movie script. The service was wonderful, the food was better and the ambience was relaxed and intimate. Until now, the closest Kelly had been to ambience was a vase of plastic flowers set on a peeling table in a diner.

They talked mostly of unimportant things, avoiding anything too personal by mutual, unspoken consent. Dan told her some of his dreams for the newly revived Remington Construction. He wanted to build a reputation for quality as opposed to quantity. Not the largest number of houses or the fastest to go up, but the best houses and the ones that would still be standing in a hundred years.

They were lingering over dessert when Dan broke off in the middle of a sentence and laughed self-consciously.

"I've been rambling on for hours. You must be sick of hearing about this whole thing."

"I like hearing people talk about their dreams. You can learn a lot about someone by learning about their dreams." Kelly took a last bite of chocolate mousse pie and set down her fork, sure that she could never eat another bite.

"What about your dreams, Kelly? What do you dream of doing?"

*A real family. A home. Someone to love who loved her.*

Those weren't the kind of dreams he was talking about. She shrugged.

"I always thought that if I could have any job in the world, I'd want to be a librarian."

"A librarian? You mean stout shoes, ankle-length dresses and hair screwed in a knot?" Dan sat back in his chair, eyeing her as if trying to picture her as he'd described.

Kelly chuckled. "It must have been a while since you were in a library."

"Not since college," he agreed, nodding his thanks to the waiter as his coffee was refilled.

"Librarians aren't all maiden ladies anymore, if they ever were."

"I'm sure they're not. I just remember the stern looks I used to get. Why a librarian? I mean, as opposed to a rocket scientist?"

"For one thing, I don't have a technical turn of mind, which would make rocket science a poor choice." Her smile became more wistful. "Besides, I've always loved libraries. They're so peaceful. And some of my best friends have been books. Come to think of it, just about all my friends have been books." Her smile took any hint of self-pity from her words. "I always thought the best job in the world would be working with books all day."

"So why not do it?"

Kelly looked at Dan to see if he was making fun of her. There was nothing but honest inquiry in his eyes. Her laughter held an edge of self-deprecation.

"I don't think a pregnant high-school dropout is a good candidate for college." She stopped, aware that it was the first time she'd referred to her pregnancy so casually.

"I don't see why not," Dan said, apparently unaware that he'd said anything significant.

"Even if I had the money, I don't have a high-school diploma."

"You could take an equivalency exam," he suggested.

"I could, but I've probably forgotten everything I ever knew. Even if I did pass, colleges aren't all that easy to get into these days. Anyway, it was just one of those childish fantasies. Most girls dream of being cheerleaders or movie stars. I was just a little weird."

Dan let the subject drop, but he filed it away for future consideration.

Driving home, they spoke little, but it was a comfortable silence, without undercurrents. Kelly was pleasantly tired and more content than she'd ever been in her life.

It was after ten when they got back to the apartment. Kelly stifled a yawn as they climbed the stairs. The click of Dan's key in the lock sounded too loud in the quiet courtyard.

"Here, I'll hang up your coat."

"Thank you." Kelly loosened the oversize button that held the coat together, feeling the brush of Dan's hands as he lifted it from her shoulders. She turned toward him as he hung her coat on a hook in the hall closet before slipping off his own jacket.

"I had a wonderful time," she said, pitching her voice low in deference to the hour, though there was no one but the two of them to be disturbed.

"I did, too." Dan pushed the closet door shut and turned to smile at her.

He hadn't bothered to turn on the hall light, relying on the illumination provided by the lamp they'd left burning in the living room. The dim light seemed to play tricks with the imagination, turning the plain little hall into an intimate setting.

Kelly was suddenly vividly aware of Dan's size, the width of his shoulders, the way he towered over her. She hadn't realized how close they were when she'd turned. Only inches separated them and he was too close, too large, too male. She could smell his after-shave, something crisp and tantalizing.

She saw his hand lift, moving as if in slow motion toward her face. She wanted to move away but her feet didn't seem to be cooperating. His palm was pleasantly rough against her cheek and she felt her eyelids drooping as she leaned into the light touch.

Dan wondered how it was possible for someone's skin to feel so incredibly soft. He could feel the brush of her hair where it swung forward against her cheek and his hand slipped to the back of her neck, losing itself in the silk of her hair.

He lowered his head slowly, aware of the fragility of the moment, of how little it would take to frighten her. That was the last thing he wanted. He wanted her to lean into him; he wanted her to melt for him.

She trembled at the first touch of his mouth against hers but she didn't draw back. He deepened the kiss slowly, feeling her mouth quiver and then soften for him. She swayed as if her knees were unsteady and he slid his arm around her waist.

Her hands came up to rest against his chest. He could feel the tension in them and knew she was a breath away from pushing herself free. If she did, he was sure he'd crack into a thousand pieces. Communicating only by touch, he tried, with mouth and hands, to still her fears, to reassure her uncertainties.

For a trembling moment, he wasn't sure she'd understood and then her hands slowly slid up his chest to his shoulders. She took a tiny step forward and Dan's arm tightened around her, drawing her the rest of the way.

She felt right in his arms, right with her mouth all soft and shaking beneath his. His tongue traced her lower lip, half plea, half command, and her mouth opened for him. He slipped inside, taking possession, making her his. She made a tiny sound that was part moan, part plea, and melted into him, her hands slipping up to twine in the soft hair at the base of his neck.

This was the way it was meant to be. Dan could feel it deep in his soul. This was how it had been on New Year's Eve. She'd felt like this then, as if his arms had been waiting for her to fill them. His hands slid down her sides, pulling her still closer. Holding her like this, he could feel the slight thickening at her waist, visible proof that she carried his child.

The thought made him ache with a primitive need that started deep inside. He shifted his stance, bracing his feet apart, easing

Kelly forward, one hand sliding beneath her buttocks to lift her into the cradle of his thighs.

Kelly gasped at the feel of his arousal pressed against her femininity. The thin layers of clothing did little to conceal the hard ridges of him. Dan's mouth slid across her cheek, his teeth finding the sensitive lobe of her ear.

Her body felt warm all over. Her head was spinning and she could see colored lights dancing beneath her eyelids. There was a heavy ache in the pit of her stomach, a rhythmic pulsing that made her want to press herself closer, that made her resent the barriers presented by their clothing.

Dimly she was aware that she'd felt like this once before, that these same uncontrollable fires had burned in her. New Year's Eve. The night her child had been conceived.

With a gasp, she pushed herself away from Dan, the move so sudden that she tripped and would have fallen if he hadn't caught her by the arms, steadying her. Her eyes wide, she jerked away from even that touch.

Dan shook his head, struggling to adjust to the abrupt change in mood. His body still pulsed with awareness, a primitive demand that he pull her back into his arms and prove to her that this was meant to be.

Kelly watched him warily, one hand pressed to her swollen mouth, her eyes wide above it. It was the fear in those eyes that helped him control the need still pounding in his veins. It was like a dash of icy water on his overheated skin.

"Kelly." He took a step toward her, reaching out one hand. She backed away as if it were a cobra. A huge fist clamped itself around his chest, squeezing all the air out. Never in his life had he thought he'd see a woman look at him with such fear. He let his hand drop, careful not to move any closer.

"Kelly, I would never hurt you."

She seemed to relax slightly, though he had the feeling it was more the fact that he kept his distance than his words. Her hand dropped from her mouth as she eased a step backward.

"I don't want...that."

"Okay," he said, as if his body wasn't still screaming a need for "that." "I would never force you to do anything you didn't want."

"I'm not going to sleep with you."

"It's your choice." Looking at her, he had a sudden flash of memory—a gasp of pain, a body that trembled more with fear than passion.

"Kelly, what happened that night—it isn't always like that. I was drunk and I didn't know that it was your first time." A slow flush mantled his cheekbones, concealed by the dim light. No man likes admitting to having been something less than a terrific lover. But he didn't want her to think that it was always going to be painful.

"I know it hurt you. I should have taken more time. It wouldn't be like that again."

Kelly pressed one hand to her heated cheeks, her eyes skittering away from his. "I don't want to talk about it. It was a long time ago. I...it's late. I'm going to bed."

"Kelly."

But she was gone, shutting the bedroom door behind her. Dan stared at the blank panel for a long time, his fists clenched at his sides.

Over the next few days, Kelly tried to pretend that nothing had changed. After one attempt to talk about what had happened, Dan accepted her lead and didn't mention the kiss and its aftermath again.

It was really nothing more than a simple little kiss, Kelly told herself as she scrubbed vigorously at an already clean sink. Just like Krakatoa was a simple little firecracker. The truth was that one kiss had changed everything. She couldn't pretend that he and Dan were ever going to be friends when all he had to do was kiss her and her knees melted.

And what business did she have letting her knees melt? Hadn't she learned anything the first time? Casual sex was a dangerous game and she had no intention of toying with it again.

Not that there would be anything casual about sex with Dan. She felt her cheeks warm, remembering the feel of his mouth, the way his hands had molded her spine. No, it wouldn't be casual, at least not for her. But that wasn't to say that he'd feel the same.

Oh, he liked her well enough, she supposed. But that wasn't enough. Next time she got involved with someone—if there was a next time—it was going to be something rich and deep, something that offered a future. There was no future in getting involved with Dan Remington.

As if she wasn't already involved with him, she thought, her hand brushing fleetingly over her disappearing waistline.

She welcomed the sound of the doorbell, glad for a distraction. Even if it was a salesman, she'd rather listen to him pitch a vacuum than continue on the tangled path her thoughts insisted on taking.

But it wasn't a salesman. It was Brittany Sinclair, looking just as lovely as ever, her thick black hair drawn back from her face in a casual twist that didn't look anything like the haphazard knot Kelly had pulled her own hair into.

"Hi." Brittany smiled, her eyes questioning. "I suppose I should have called first but I was in the area and I thought you might not mind too much if I dropped by. I can go away if it's a bad time."

"It's not a bad time." Kelly stepped back, her smile warming as the other woman stepped inside. Really, it was nice to see someone, even if it was Brittany who just happened to be disgustingly beautiful.

It wasn't until they were settled in the living room with glasses of iced tea that Kelly noticed that the other woman's pregnancy was now obvious. And if the small bulge of Brittany's stomach hadn't given it away, the look of glowing contentment might have.

"It must be nice to be so happy about your baby," she said without thinking. There was a wistful note to the comment that sharpened Brittany's eyes.

"It is. My first pregnancy was a little more…complicated. was thrilled with Danielle, of course, but I didn't get a chance to really enjoy the pregnancy as much as I would have liked

This time, I'm enjoying it to the hilt.'' She smoothed her hand over her stomach, her smile soft.

For a moment, Kelly had the urge to confide that she was also expecting a child. It would be nice to have another woman to talk to, someone who understood what she was going through in a way no man ever could.

Nevertheless, if she told Brittany about the baby, it was going to open the door to questions she didn't feel like trying to answer. She'd told Brittany little more than that she and Dan had only known each other a few months, leaving the other woman to draw her own conclusions as to why she was living with him. If she announced her pregnancy, it was going to bring up a whole new set of problems.

The subject changed and the opportunity was gone. Brittany was, as Kelly had found on her last visit, easy to talk to. She was comfortable chatting about recipes for chicken, discussing a book she'd just read or commenting on the latest political follies.

Kelly had spent most of her life with no one to talk to, with little beyond an active imagination to fulfill the needs usually fulfilled by friendships. There were too many emotional entanglements lying between her and Dan for her to be able to relax completely with him. Though on the rare occasions she was able to forget all that had happened, she enjoyed talking to him.

There were no such entanglements with Brittany. She was able to relax and enjoy herself without seeking out hidden meanings or trying to avoid pitfalls. It had occurred to her once or twice to wonder why Brittany had made it a point to seek her out, but it was hardly the sort of question she could ask. She finally decided that there didn't have to be a particular reason, beyond the fact that Brittany was a friend of Dan's. It was natural that she'd be curious about the woman who was living with him.

"Has Dan talked to you very much about Michael and me?"

Kelly glanced up from the fresh iced tea she was pouring into Brittany's glass. The question seemed odd. What was there to tell?

"Not much. He said that you were friends of his."

"Well, I'm glad he still considers us that."

"Why wouldn't he?" Kelly asked, wondering at the sudden turn in the conversation.

"There were some problems a couple of years ago—nothing insurmountable," she added, hoping that was true. "When Dan came back from prison, he—"

"Prison!" Kelly set her glass down so hard it drew a protesting ping from the glass-topped table. "Dan was in prison?"

"Oh, dear." Brittany stared at her in dismay. It had never occurred to her that Kelly wouldn't know that much. After all, she was living with him. What had happened between the three of them might be too painful for him to share with anyone. But the odd turn of events that had led up to it was certainly nothing to hide.

"Maybe I shouldn't have brought this up," she said, wishing she had listened a little more carefully when Michael had told her to let the issue of him and Dan alone.

"Dan was in prison," Kelly repeated, dazed. "Why?"

"It was really a sort of misunderstanding," Brittany said weakly. There was no way she could back out of this now. She could hardly leave Kelly wondering if she was living with an ax murderer.

"A misunderstanding? What sort of a misunderstanding put a man in prison?"

"It's not as difficult as it might seem in other parts of the world." She sighed, cursing her own big mouth before continuing. She spoke rapidly. "Dan was going on an archaeological expedition with his father. This was about four years ago. It was all legal and aboveboard, arranged through a university in Los Angeles. They were going to spend the summer assisting professional archaeologists on a site in Central America.

"It had been a dream of Dan's father, and I think Dan went along more to keep him happy than because he was passionately interested. Unfortunately the plane crashed in a rather isolated area, killing everyone on board, or so everyone here thought."

"Dan's father was killed," Kelly said, half to herself, re

membering the conversation Dan had had with his father's old foreman.

"His father was killed," Brittany confirmed. "And everyone thought Dan had been killed, too. Only he'd been thrown clear of the plane. He was hurt and not thinking too clearly and he wandered away from the site. Some villagers took him in and tended his wounds. They turned out to be hostile to the local government, which just happened to mount a cleanup campaign. Dan was swept up in the middle of it and accused of being an American spy sent to assist the rebels."

"Didn't he tell them who he was?"

"Of course, but they knew all about the crash. An *American* rescue team had confirmed that there were no survivors. Obviously Dan was lying to conceal his real purpose. So they threw him in prison."

"That's horrible," Kelly said, trying to imagine the frustration he must have felt, the fear. "How long was he there?"

"Almost two years," Brittany said, her expression sober as she remembered the thin, hardened man who'd come home on a snowy Christmas Eve.

"Two years," Kelly whispered.

"He's never really talked to me about it—hasn't talked to anyone as far as I know. He was changed when he came back—older, a touch bitter."

She broke off when she saw that Kelly wasn't listening, her vision turned inward as if trying to imagine what Dan must have gone through.

"Look, I shouldn't have mentioned it. It certainly wasn't my place to be the one to tell you about this. I know Dan would rather have done it in his own way."

"That's all right," Kelly assured her, thinking that she was the last person Dan was likely to tell.

"Still, I didn't mean to poke my nose in where it didn't belong," Brittany said, guilt coloring her voice.

Kelly shook her head, filing away what she'd just learned to pull out later, when she was alone and could really think. She forced a wider smile.

"Don't worry about it. But you asked if he'd said anything about you and Michael. Why?"

"Oh, it's a long story. Maybe I shouldn't go into it," Brittany backtracked. If Dan found out what she'd done, he'd be justifiably furious. And Michael—it didn't bear thinking what Michael would say. That she deserved Dan's fury was about the kindest comment he was likely to make.

"What could be worse than what you've already told me?"

"Well." Brittany hesitated and then gave a mental shrug. In for a penny, in for a pound. Some good might as well come of her blundering. "Dan has sort of cut himself off from most of his friends since he came back. I just wondered if he'd said anything about it."

"Not to me. But then there are obviously a lot of things he doesn't tell me," Kelly said lightly.

"Men can be peculiar," Brittany offered. "I'm still finding out things I'd never known about Michael."

Kelly was willing to bet that she wasn't finding out things quite as startling as the fact that he'd spent time in a prison. But then Brittany's relationship with Michael was obviously based on love and trust. Her relationship with Dan was based on—what on earth was it based on?

Brittany rose to leave. "I was thinking that it might be nice if the four of us got together."

Kelly was touched. Perhaps Brittany really did want to be her friend. Or perhaps she wanted to try to ease the tension that surrounded them all when they'd bumped into one another in the mall.

"I don't know," Kelly said slowly. "I couldn't speak for Dan."

"Why don't you ask him? It would be nice to get together as couples, wouldn't it?"

"It would have to be up to Dan," Kelly said, thinking it unlikely that he'd have any interest in taking her out among his friends.

"Why don't you ask him? Maybe dinner at El Gato Gordo a week from Saturday?"

"Maybe. I'll ask him," Kelly promised, though she was sure she already knew what his answer would be.

Considering their strained relationship these past few days, it was difficult to imagine even approaching him on the subject.

# Chapter 12

Dan fingered the envelope in his pocket as he climbed the stairs. It had seemed like such a good idea when he first thought of it. Kelly wanted to get a degree so she could be a librarian. But she couldn't think about college until she had her high-school diploma. And to get that she had to take a high-school equivalency test.

When he'd picked up the application, it had seemed like a good way to break down the barrier that Kelly had forced between them. She would be excited by the idea of taking a step toward getting her degree, she'd think it was thoughtful of him to have gotten her started. They would be able to put this awkwardness behind them and get on with life. Now he wasn't quite so sure.

She might look on this as interference on his part. Lord knows, he'd interfered with her life in some pretty major ways already. Maybe he should just ditch the application and pretend he'd never had the idea in the first place.

But she had looked so wistful when she'd talked about becoming a librarian, as if she were talking about something she could only dream of doing. She'd had so little in her life. He didn't see any reason why she shouldn't have this.

Besides, he needed something to get her talking to him again. He missed her. He missed that shy smile; he missed talking to her about what he was doing, listening to her tell him how she'd spent her day. They might be still sharing the same place, but she'd pulled back so that there were times when he felt almost as if he lived alone.

They'd come close to…to what? He stopped halfway up the stairs, frowning into space. Just what had they been heading for? Not exactly friendship. A certain acceptance, maybe. Whatever it was, it had taken only that one little kiss to shatter it into a million pieces.

Of course, calling it "one little kiss" was rather like calling *War and Peace* an interesting little story. It didn't even begin to describe what had happened. The minute he'd touched her, he had forgotten everything but the need to have her in his arms, to feel her melt for him.

He'd forgotten everything that had gone between them, including her pregnancy. It wasn't the idea that she was carrying his child that had made his head swim with desire. It had been the scent of her, the taste of her, the feel of her against him.

If she hadn't pulled back, he didn't have any doubt that they would have ended up in bed. Which, of course, wasn't at all what their arrangement had been. He scowled at a potted geranium that sat in front of old Mr. Tancredi's door.

That arrangement was beginning to annoy him. It seemed that every time he and Kelly began to really develop an understanding, something happened to remind one or the other of them of that damned arrangement.

He had no intention of expecting Kelly to simply hand her child over to him and then walk out of their lives. It was important for a child to know both parents. They had created a child together. Why couldn't they just go from there and see what happened?

He drew the envelope out of his pocket, tapping it absently against his thigh. The application could either help melt the wall between them or it could build it even higher. He wanted

Kelly to have her dream. And to do that, she had to start somewhere.

When Kelly heard the front door open she looked up from the lettuce she'd been tearing up for a salad. She knew Dan had gone to Indianapolis for the day to talk to an old friend of his father's—another contractor. Nearly an hour ago, she'd heard a news report on the radio that said there'd been a major accident on the highway. Since then, her imagination had been filled with pictures of the sleek black Corvette crushed and broken.

She nearly sagged with relief when she saw him come in the door. He looked hot and tired but he was unhurt. Without a word, she took a pitcher of iced tea out of the refrigerator and poured him a tall glass. Dan muttered his thanks as he took it from her, tilting back his head to drink.

"You'd think it was summer already from the heat out there," he said, lowering the empty glass.

"I heard on the radio today that we're probably going to get an unusually hot summer."

It was the sort of conversation they'd been having this past week. Friendly but impersonal. No chance of touching on any awkward subjects.

Dan watched Kelly cutting a cucumber into neat slices, feeling a surge of impatience. He didn't want friendly, impersonal little chats with her. He wanted... Hell, he didn't know exactly what he wanted, but he wanted to break this odd little dead end they'd hit.

"I've got something for you," he said abruptly, his tone almost challenging.

Kelly glanced over her shoulder, setting down the knife when she saw the envelope he was holding out. There was something in his expression, something—was it defensive or hostile? Nervous now, she wiped her hand on a towel and reached for the envelope. What could it be that would make him look like that?

She slipped the papers out of the envelope, skimming over them before lifting her eyes to his, her confusion obvious.

"This is an application to take the high-school equivalency

test,'' she said, as if he might not have realized what he'd given her.

"If you're going to go to college, you've got to have your high-school diploma." He said it almost casually.

"I'm not going to college."

"Yes, you are. It's what you want, isn't it?"

"Well, yes. But it's not that simple."

"I don't see why not. Once the baby is born, there's no reason you couldn't go to school."

*Of course there wasn't.* Kelly's hand trembled as she slipped the application back into the envelope. *After all, she wouldn't have to worry about day care or any of the things most new mothers had to worry about. Because she wasn't going to be a new mother, not in the most important sense of the word.* She kept her head lowered, forcing back the tears that blurred her vision.

Dan, sensing her distress and misinterpreting it, tried to assure her. "Look, I'll pay for your tuition and things. All you'll have to worry about is getting your degree. This is your dream, Kelly. Isn't it?"

It had been, not that long ago. That was before her life had changed. Before she'd found herself pregnant. Before she'd gotten to know Dan in more ways than just the one that got them into their predicament. Before her dreams had begun to revolve around little houses and perfect little families.

"Yes, of course it is," she said slowly. He'd done this because he thought it was what she wanted, because he thought it would make her happy. It wasn't his fault that she'd set her sights so much higher.

The thought brought a new rush of tears to her eyes and she forced them back, cursing her unaccustomed weepiness.

Dan watched her downbent head, wishing he could see something of her face, get some idea of what she was thinking. Was she angry? Happy?

"And if you're nervous about taking the test, don't be," he said finally, when it seemed as if she was never going to speak. "You'll ace it. You've got plenty of time to study up on anything you're not sure of."

He believed in her. The thought eased its way into Kelly's muddled thinking, bringing with it a sweet pang that was both pleasure and pain. He believed she could do this. No questions. No doubts. His confidence made her at once proud and uneasy. What if he was wrong? What if she failed?

"Look, you don't have to take the test if you don't want to," Dan said uneasily. "Just say something. Or you can slug me if you want to."

Kelly shook her head, lifting her eyes to his at last. "I don't want to hit you. I'm just a little overwhelmed, I guess. I've never had anyone try to make one of my dreams come true."

"It was no big deal," Dan said modestly, but quite pleased with himself. "I just picked up the forms. You're the one who's going to have to do all the work."

"Thank you." Surprising herself as much as him, she rose on tiptoe and brushed a quick kiss over his cheek. She drew back hastily, her cheeks pink. Her lips tingled from the brief contact. She cleared her throat. "You've got time to clean up before dinner if you want."

"Sure. Thanks." Dan lingered as if to say something more. But apparently he changed his mind and turned away.

Kelly picked up the knife and began slicing the cucumber again, concentrating on the simple action as if her life depended on it. The envelope he'd given her lay on the counter, just visible out of the corner of her eye.

Her dream. Six months ago, nothing would have made her happier than a chance at going to college. Nothing had seemed farther out of reach. Now she just wanted to put her head down and howl.

Everything had changed since then. She wasn't the same person. Those dreams belonged to someone else, someone who hadn't known Dan Remington. Someone who wasn't carrying a child—a child she'd promised to give up.

It wasn't Dan's fault that the dream he was willing to help her achieve was no longer the one that held the key to her happiness. She brushed the back of her hand angrily across her cheek, wiping away the single tear that had escaped.

Well, it was the only dream she had much chance of achievng. She might as well get used to that. Wishing for the moon wasn't likely to get her anything but hurt.

While the application didn't have precisely the effect Dan had hoped, it did serve to break the tension between the two of them. Kelly's reaction, which seemed more resigned than excited, was confusing, but he decided not to push his luck by questioning it. For now, it was enough that they were able to talk again.

When Kelly told him about Brittany's suggestion that the two couples get together for dinner, his first urge was to do exactly what Kelly had expected—make some excuse not to go. But not for the reasons she'd thought.

It had nothing to do with a reluctance to introduce her to his friends. It had everything to do with knowing exactly what Brittany was up to. She'd had this bee in her bonnet about his relationship with her and Michael ever since he'd come back from Europe. She wanted them all to be friends.

She just couldn't seem to accept that things had changed. No matter how civilized they were all being about it, there was still a certain strain between the three of them.

There was the fact that he and Brittany had been lovers, that it was *his* child she'd been carrying when Michael fell in love with her. And there was the fact that it had been Michael who'd married her, become a real father to that same child. Michael who'd ended up with the home and family Dan had always thought would be his.

He didn't feel any anger or bitterness anymore, but he wasn't such a fool as to think that all that had happened could simply be written off and friendships resumed as if nothing had happened. And the last thing he wanted was a strained dinner with Michael, who was not likely to be any happier about this than he was.

Yet there was more to think about than simply what *he* wanted to do. There was Kelly to consider. No matter what Brittany's motives might have been when she suggested this dinner, she and Kelly were apparently on their way toward developing a real friendship, something Kelly hadn't had much of in her life. He didn't want to do anything to discourage that friendship.

If anyone could understand what Kelly had gone through, it might be Brittany. Though her parents had not been abusive, they'd failed her when she needed them most—more concerned with what people might think than with their daughter's well-being. And she had also been young and alone at the start of her pregnancy.

Besides, if he made an excuse not to go and didn't tell Kelly the real reason, she was likely to decide that it was because he didn't want to be seen with her or something equally foolish. It was going to be a long time before she regained the self-confidence that should have been hers.

So he smiled and told Kelly that dinner sounded wonderful. He did suggest adding Ben Masters to the mix. No one was better than Ben at keeping things from getting too sticky in a social situation.

On the other hand, not even Emily Post could have completely overcome the tensions that stretched over the small group that gathered at El Gato Gordo.

For Kelly, the evening started off on a sour note when she discovered that her stomach had grown—seemingly overnight—so that there was no longer any graceful way to conceal her condition. Nervous already, the last thing she wanted was to go public with her pregnancy.

She stood sideways to the mirror and experimented with trying to suck the small bulge in, but all it did was make her feel breathless. Her hand trembled as she stroked it over the rounded line of her stomach.

Nearly five months pregnant. Halfway there. Most women could consider this point halfway to fulfillment. For her, it was halfway to an ending, an ending she dreaded more with every passing day. No matter how hard she tried, she could no longer pretend that this baby wasn't real. She carried a life beneath her heart, a unique new person who was going to have all the strengths and weaknesses that went with being human.

Kelly shook her head, forcing her thoughts to the more immediate future. The dress she had planned to wear nipped in at the waist and the zipper had simply sneered at the suggestion that it might want to close. Going to the closet, she riffled through the garments there, sparing a thought—as always—to the wonderful luxury of having a choice. She finally settled on a dress of soft ivory jersey that draped softly from the neckline, skimming the body and hinting at curves—but not too strongly, she hoped.

Though he told her she looked nice, Dan had little to say on the way to the restaurant. Stealing glances at his face, Kelly was struck by the fact that his jaw seemed unusually tight, and there was a sternness about his eyes she couldn't remember seeing before.

They were the last of the group to arrive. Michael and Ben both rose with old-fashioned politeness as Dan and Kelly walked up to the table. Kelly sat next to Dan with Ben on her other side. Brittany was on Dan's other side with Michael next to her.

The round table allowed the conversation to flow easily among them. Or it would have if there had been enough conversation to flow. It was immediately apparent that Michael and Brittany were not completely on good terms with each other. Brittany was a little too flushed, her eyes a little too bright. And the little sidelong looks she stole toward her husband from time to time were nervous and just a touch angry.

This was only the second time Kelly had met Michael, but she had the feeling that he was not normally quite as taciturn as he was tonight. No one could have faulted his manners, but there was something about him that made it clear that he'd rather be elsewhere—perhaps shoveling coal in a mine.

There was actually little to choose between his attitude and Dan's. The tightness Kelly had noticed in Dan's jaw grew as the evening wore on until she could almost hear the sound of his teeth grinding.

Only Ben seemed comfortable, nudging the conversational ball when it showed signs of rolling to a halt, even managing to draw a laugh or two. But as the evening wore on, the ball got heavier and heavier until even Ben was having a hard time getting it to move.

Kelly felt as if she'd fallen into the middle of a movie for which everyone had a script but her. It was obvious that there was something more going on here than anyone had bothered to tell her. The atmosphere between Michael and Dan could have been cut with a knife.

Halfway through the meal, she came to the painful conclusion that Brittany had lied to her, by omission if nothing else. Whatever she'd had in mind when she'd suggested this dinner, it hadn't been anything as simple as strengthening a new friendship.

The realization hurt. She'd thought she and Brittany were becoming real friends. But you didn't use friends, and that was exactly what Brittany had done. Since it was obvious that Kelly was the only one at the table who didn't know what was going on, it was equally obvious that she was the only one who could have been conned into suggesting this dinner to Dan. Everyone here must know what a fool she had been.

Muttering an excuse, she pushed her chair back from the table and headed for the rest rooms. The ladies' room was bright with color but the soft light was soothing. There were low stools in front of a wide mirror and Kelly sank onto one of them, digging through her purse for a tissue. She kept her head bent when she heard the door open, in no mood for exchanging polite smiles with a stranger.

"Kelly?"

Kelly stiffened at the sound of Brittany's voice. Her fingers knotted over the soft leather of her purse. A surge of anger and embarrassment colored her cheeks, drying the tears that had been threatening.

"Yes?" She took a brush out of her purse and turned to the mirror, as if her only concern were to neaten her hair.

"Kelly, I'm sorry."

The simple apology was impossible to ignore, but it did little to cool Kelly's hurt.

"Sorry you played me for a fool or sorry that it doesn't seem to be working?'' she asked coolly. She put the brush away before turning to look at the other woman.

"Sorry that I didn't tell you up front what the situation was." Brittany's eyes were stormy gray with distress.

"Just what is the situation?"

"I can't tell you," Brittany said. "I've already interfered too much."

"That's great." Kelly's laughter held no humor. "You're sorry, but you won't tell me what's going on. Well, I'm sorry, too. I'm sorry I was such an idiot. I thought we were becoming friends."

"We were. We are. At least, I hope we will be again." Brittany stopped, her eyes pleading. "I was wrong to use you to help clear the air between Dan, Michael and myself. It's just that we were all such good friends and it hurts to see those two not speaking to each other. It hurts them, too," she added fiercely. "I know it does, even if they're too stubborn to admit it."

Despite herself, Kelly was impressed by her vehemence. "What happened between them?"

"I can't tell you. Wait." She caught Kelly's arm when she would have risen. "I've already interfered too much. Michael was furious with me about this and he was right. I was wrong to do it this way. I can't tell you anymore. That's got to be up to Dan."

"Fine." Kelly stood. "I hope you don't mind if I suggest to Dan that we leave. The evening isn't turning out to be what anyone had hoped."

Brittany rose also, her eyes searching Kelly's face. "I really am sorry, Kelly. I was wrong. I never meant to hurt you."

Looking at her, Kelly knew she was sincere. "Was this the only reason you wanted to get to know me? To get Dan and Michael to speak?"

"No!" Brittany reached out, touching her hand lightly. "When I first came over, I wanted to see what you were like. I've known Dan a long time. I wanted to know you, too. And I really liked you. You're fun and easy to talk to. This whole thing—" she waved one hand to encompass the evening

"—was an impulse. And a rotten one, at that. I never meant to hurt you. Can you forgive me?"

Kelly believed her, but that didn't make the hurt disappear. She shook her head. "I don't know," she said honestly. "I want to."

"Well, that's more than I deserve. I'll let you call me when you think you'd like to talk."

They didn't speak again as they walked back to the table. Dan looked up as they approached, his eyes concerned. The concern grated like sandpaper over her already stretched nerves, stemming as she knew it did solely from his interest in the baby.

"Are you all right?" He leaned close as she sat down, his breath brushing across her forehead.

"I'm a little tired, actually. Would you mind if we called it a night?" She was hardly surprised when he agreed instantly.

"No problem." He pushed his chair back and stood, reaching for the light jacket she'd draped over the back of her chair.

Kelly smiled at the table's other occupants. "I'm sorry to cut this short. It's been…very nice," she managed.

A brief silence fell over the table when they'd left. Ben toyed with his margarita glass. Michael stared at the flowers that occupied the center of the table. Brittany rearranged her silverware, waiting for someone to say something.

"So okay," she burst out at last. "It was a lousy idea and it was all mine."

"Your heart was in the right place," Ben told her soothingly.

"You meant well, honey." Michael reached out to catch her restless fingers. "But please don't do it again."

"I won't," she promised, her hand turning to clasp his.

## Chapter 13

Neither Kelly nor Dan had anything to say on the drive home. Dan asked her once if she was sure there was nothing wrong and she assured him that she was just tired, and that was the extent of their conversation.

Dan stared broodingly out the windshield while Kelly stared out the passenger window. She was getting more than a little bit tired of feeling like a pawn. Dan was using her to get the child he wanted. Brittany had used her to try and patch up her and Michael's relationship with Dan. Was she really so worthless that she didn't have any value in her own right?

By the time Dan shut the apartment door behind them, she was feeling annoyed, aggrieved and frustrated. Dan took her jacket, hanging it in the closet without a word. His expression was tight, unreadable.

"I'm sorry I suggested this evening," Kelly said, breaking the silence. "I had no idea there was any problem."

"It's not your fault." He moved past her into the dining room, pulling a bottle of bourbon out of the cupboard and splashing a small amount into a glass.

She followed him, stopping next to the table. "Brittany didn't tell me there were problems between the three of you."

"There aren't any problems," Dan said, his tone short. He took a sip of bourbon.

"Right. So the tension tonight was all my imagination."

"Look, it was all a long time ago." He finished the bourbon and poured himself another shot, a little larger this time. Putting the bottle back into the cupboard, he turned to give her a tight smile. "It's not important anymore."

"In other words, you're not going to tell me anything," she said.

"It doesn't have anything to do with you."

"It does when someone uses me to set up a disaster like tonight."

"Brittany can be a little impulsive," Dan said. "I doubt she meant to use you."

"That's what she said, but it doesn't make me feel any better. And I don't even know why."

"Look, I really don't want to talk about this."

"Fine." Kelly couldn't explain the anger welling up in her. Most of her life she'd let other people dictate where she was going, what she was going to do. Her father, and even Dan to a certain extent. That Brittany had manipulated her, too, seemed to have broken something loose inside, a long-suppressed resentment, an anger.

"Fine. Let's not talk about it." She turned away from him, wiping tears from her eyes. "I suppose there's no reason why you should tell me anything. I'm just the woman who happens to be carrying your child."

"Kelly." There was a weary kind of anger in Dan's voice, but Kelly was too mad herself to pay any attention to it.

"I'm nothing but a…brood mare to you."

"Stop it!" Dan set the glass down with a thump, splashing bourbon onto the table. "I've never thought of you like that."

"Well, that's how you treat me," she said with more emotion than justice.

"I do not! For God's sake, Kelly." Dan took a step toward

her, lifting his hand to push his fingers through his hair, feeling frustrated and tired.

Kelly saw the raised hand out of the corner of her eye and heard the anger in his voice. Her reaction was instinctive.

"No!" Throwing one hand up in a protective gesture, she ducked back, her shoulders hunched.

His hand in midair, Dan froze. The color slowly drained from his face, leaving him as pale as she was. He lowered his hand, aware that it was not quite steady. The room was as silent as a tomb.

When no blow fell, Kelly slowly straightened without looking at Dan. She clasped her shaking hands together in front of her, staring at them.

"You thought I was going to hit you," Dan said in a rasping whisper.

"No, of course not." But her voice shook.

"You thought I'd hit you," he repeated.

"I don't know," she whispered. She glanced at him, seeing the stunned shock in his eyes. "I'm sorry."

She lifted one hand to her face, pressing it to her trembling mouth.

"Kelly." He stopped, as if he wasn't sure where to go from there. "Kelly, I would never hurt you."

"I know." And she did know it. In her heart she knew he'd never raise a hand to her. "I'm sorry. It wasn't your fault."

"Are you afraid of me?" His eyes looked so hurt, a rare vulnerability darkening them to stormy blue.

"No. No, please. I just...I didn't mean to...I'm sorry," she repeated, not knowing what else to say.

"You couldn't ever make me angry enough to hit you. You've got to know that."

"I do. I do know that." She stepped toward him, her hand coming out to rest on his arm. "I know that. I don't know what happened. It was an upsetting evening. I didn't mean to overreact like that."

Dan's hand was still shaking as he lifted it to her face, his fingers brushing across the tears on her cheek. "I would never hurt you," he said again, as if repetition could make her believe it.

"I know. I'm sorry."

"You don't have to be sorry. Just don't ever look at me like that again. Please, don't ever look at me like that."

There was strength in the way he caught her to him but it was strangely reassuring. Tempered strength that would never hurt. Kelly held him, telling him without words that she knew he would never hurt her.

Dan buried his face in her hair, drawing in the clean, gentle scent of her. Nothing had ever hit him quite so hard as that one moment when she'd looked at him with absolute terror. That she could think, even for a moment, that he would strike her had rocked him to the bottom of his soul.

He drew back, reaching up to brush her hair back from her cheek, his eyes searching hers. "I'd never hit you, Kelly. You have to believe that."

"I do." His hand fell away from her face as she stepped back and, for a moment, she felt an almost painful sense of loss. "I didn't mean to be so snappish earlier. I mean, it's really none of my business," she said, hoping he couldn't see what the words cost her. "I guess I just felt like an idiot. Everyone but me knew what was going on."

"There's not much to know." Dan let his hand drop from her face.

"I'm not asking for any explanations. I don't have the right..."

"It's not about rights, Kelly," he interrupted her, his voice strained. "It's just something I don't like to talk about. But you deserve an explanation."

He leaned one hip against the table, his expression reflective.

"Michael and I practically grew up together," he said, his voice quick and clipped as if he wanted to get through the explanation as quickly as possible. "We were closer than most brothers ever get to be. About four years ago, I went to Central America."

"Brittany told me about the plane crash," Kelly said quietly. He slanted her a resigned look.

"Busy little bee, wasn't she," he said, more to himself than er. "Well, then she must have told you that I was presumed ead."

"Yes. And she told me about you spending time in prison. must have been terrible."

"It wasn't a whole lot of fun," he said, dismissing the hell-h months he'd spent in prison. "Did Brittany tell you that ie and I had been involved before I left?"

Kelly shook her head, feeling a twinge of something that she ought couldn't be jealousy.

"We were. In fact, she was pregnant with my child when I ft." He ignored her quick gasp. "She hadn't told me. After ie crash, she didn't have anyone to turn to. Her parents are a ouple of sanctimonious prigs and they all but threw her out hen they found out about the baby."

"What happened?" she asked in a whisper.

"Michael stepped in. I always said he had a noble streak iat was going to get him in trouble." Dan's mouth twisted ut there was no bitterness in the words. "He married her to elp her take care of the baby. Only they fell in love. By the me I got back, they had a good marriage and Danielle was alling Michael 'Daddy.'"

"The little girl that was with them when we first saw them? he's yours?"

"Technically." There were traces of pain in the casual con-rmation. "But by every important measure she's Michael's."

No wonder he wanted this child so desperately. Kelly's hand nconsciously sought the slight bulge of her stomach. No won-er he'd reacted so violently when she had asked him for ioney for an abortion. He'd already lost a child.

Later it might surprise her to realize that her first thought as for the pain he'd felt, the pain he still felt. Later she'd onder that her heart had seemed to crack a little over his hurt. ater she'd be able to see that this didn't really affect her own tuation.

But right now all she wanted was to ease the taut lines that racketed his mouth. She wanted to go back in time and change iings, make his hurt go away.

"That must have been terrible for you." She put her har up, touching the hard line of his cheek. The light touch mac him start. His eyes, which had been focused inward on thin only he could see, were suddenly seeing her.

Seeing the compassion in her eyes, he felt something brea loose inside him, some long-held wall he'd put up to block th pain. Putting his arms around her seemed the most natural thin in the world. He held her to him, her cheek pressed against th soft cotton of his shirt.

They stayed like that for a moment, saying nothing, holdir each other. It might have ended at that, a moment's comfo nothing more. But when Kelly started to draw back, she turne her head slightly and found her mouth a whisper away fro Dan's.

Her heart seemed to stop beating. He was so close. Tc close, her head whispered. Not close enough, her heart replie She had to move away. No, she wasn't close enough.

Their eyes met, so near his eyes seemed almost silver inste of blue. He seemed to be asking something, a question sl couldn't begin to answer. Her fingers flexed against his chest drawing him closer or pushing him away—she didn't know

But when he closed the tiny distance between them, h mouth was soft and ready for him. Her lashes drifted dow shutting out everything but the feel of Dan's lips on hers.

This was a kiss like no other they had shared. Emotio already stretched tight were suddenly all spinning into foc on this one kiss. There was no tentative exploration eith wanted or needed.

Kelly's mouth opened for his as a flower opening to the su He tasted of bourbon, a smoky taste that was strangely erot

Her scent filled his head until he could think of nothing b the need that had been burning in his gut for days. Weeks. fire that hadn't gone out since the first night he had touche her. His fingers found the zipper at the back of her dress, sli ing it downward with a soft rasp.

Kelly gasped at the first touch of his hands against her ba skin. She pulled her head back, her eyes meeting his. In h was passion and reassurance. If she chose, he'd stop. She cou only imagine what he read in her eyes. A confused tangle of emotion and thought.

His palm flattened against her spine, his fingers moving restlessly against her back. She could feel the need that hummed in him, making his body taut and hard against hers.

He wanted her. No one else had ever wanted her. No one in her life had ever needed her. No one but Dan. And she wanted and needed him. If that was a sin, then she'd answer for it later. For now, she didn't want to think of anything but how good it felt to be held in his arms.

He must have read her answer in her eyes. The look that flashed into his eyes made Kelly's bones melt. He bent to catch her behind the knees, scooping her up in his arms in a movement that stole what little breath she had left.

The bedroom was warm and dark. The curtains were open, letting moonlight spill into the room, creating silvery patterns of light and shadow. Dan set Kelly down next to the bed, cupping her face in his hands, holding her for the possession of his mouth.

Slowly his palms slid down to her shoulders, taking the dress with them as they stroked down her arms. It fell to lie around her feet in an ivory pool. Her bra straps lay across her upper arms but only for a moment. Dan found the back closing and slipped the hooks loose and the bra joined the dress on the floor.

Kelly shuddered as his hands came up to cup her breasts, his thumbs brushing across the sensitive peaks. He held her like that, his mouth exploring the delicate line of her throat, his hands teasing her nipples into hardness, until Kelly thought she would surely die of pleasure. And then his tongue swirled lazily across her breast to curl around one swollen nipple and she knew she was going to die.

Clothing seemed to melt away like wisps of fog, until nothing lay between them but the white-gold moonlight. Dan eased her back onto the bed but didn't immediately follow her down. He only looked at her as if wanting to imprint every inch of her on his memory.

Kelly's hands came up to cover the gentle swell of her belly, suddenly shy.

"No, don't." Dan's hands caught hers, drawing them away as he knelt next to the bed. His palms flattened over the swell that cradled his child. Still so slight that he could cover it with his two hands.

"I look fat," Kelly whispered.

"You look beautiful," he corrected. "So beautiful."

Kelly knew that it wasn't true, but he made her feel beautiful. The way he looked at her, the way he touched her—she could truly believe she was beautiful.

He made love to her as if they had all the time in the world, touching and teasing, coaxing a response she was helpless to prevent. Only when she was breathless with wanting, her nails digging into his arms in a plea she couldn't put into words, did he rise above her, his thighs slipping between hers.

Kelly felt the hard pressure of his desire against that most intimate part of her and she quivered with sudden uncertainty, remembering the last time, the pain, the confusion.

Dan felt her hesitation and he stopped. His body screamed with the need to join with hers but he didn't move, watching her in the moonlight, waiting for her decision.

Kelly was torn between the warm liquid weight that throbbed in the pit of her stomach—the part of her that knew this was right, that nothing could ever be so right again. And a deeply feminine fear.

But this was Dan, who had promised he'd never hurt her. And she believed him. With all her heart she believed him. Her hands relaxed on his shoulders, her body softening beneath him, giving him her trust without words.

Dan's head lowered, his mouth settling over hers as he flexed his hips, completing their union ever so slowly. He could taste Kelly's uncertainty changing to dawning pleasure as her body stretched to accommodate his. Beads of sweat marked his forehead when they were at last fully joined.

He waited, his muscles knotted with effort, giving Kelly time to adjust to this new sensation, determined that she would know the full potential of her woman's body. When her hips arched upward in an unconscious demand, he began to move, gently at first, letting her set the pace.

It wasn't long before she was trembling beneath him, her nails digging into his shoulders as the tension coiled tighter within her. His mouth caught hers, drinking in her sounds of wonder as the pleasure intensified.

Kelly could only cling to him, the only solid thing in the universe. With each movement, each thrust of his hips, she was drawn closer and closer to something she could only barely perceive.

And then suddenly it exploded inside her, pleasure so intense she nearly fainted. She held onto Dan as wave after wave of ecstasy shivered over her, each greater than the last, bringing her higher and higher until she was dizzy with the intensity of it.

Dan felt her body turn to liquid in his arms, felt the unmistakable tightening of her around him, caught the startled gasp that broke from her. With a groan, he released the iron control he'd been holding over his own needs.

Kelly felt him tremble above her and she was filled with a sense of purely feminine wonder and power that this man should tremble because of her.

It was a long time before Dan rolled to the side, drawing her close even as she murmured in protest at his leaving. She felt as if she had just battled a mighty storm and won. Now she lay exhausted on the battleground, wanting nothing more than sleep. She was sated and fulfilled in a way she'd never known before.

They fell asleep wrapped in each other's arms.

It was still early when Kelly woke. Sunshine spilled into the room, painting cheerful patterns across the floor before falling over the foot of the bed. She couldn't ever remember feeling quite so warm and cozy, she thought, blinking sleepily at the dust motes that danced in the stream of light.

She closed her eyes, not wanting to face the new day, wanting only to hold onto the vague but wonderful dreams that were fading from her mind. But the dreams wouldn't come back and the day wasn't going to go away. She couldn't pretend that she didn't know where she was or who was with her.

Dan was curled along her back, his chest pressed to her back, his legs drawn up beneath hers, wrapping her in his warmth. His arm lay over her side, one hand spread over the mound of her stomach, as if holding their child—his child, she corrected herself, feeling the last mists of sleep melting away.

He mumbled in his sleep as she eased out of the bed but he didn't wake. It struck her that she had snuck out of bed the last time they'd made love, too. There was a difference this time. This time she wasn't running away like a frightened little girl. There was nowhere to run even if she'd wanted to go.

She slipped on the robe that lay draped over the chair, belting it securely around her middle. Moving to the window, she looked out at the park. It was deserted this early on Sunday morning, but later in the day there would be plenty of people enjoying the sunshine and cool grass. Children, families, people who had commitments to one another.

She wrapped her arms around herself, feeling a chill that had nothing to do with the temperature. Behind her, Dan stirred, the sheets rustling as he turned over.

Last night had been a mistake.

Kelly had to force herself to think the words. The most incredible, wonderful experience of her life had been a mistake. For the first time in her life she'd felt beautiful, wanted, even loved, and it couldn't happen again.

She'd broken every promise she had made to herself to keep some distance between herself and Dan. She could no longer pretend to keep any emotional distance from the child she carried. Giving up this child was going to be like ripping away a piece of her soul. But she could do it because she knew it was the best thing for the baby.

She should have kept some distance from Dan. She could have saved a little piece of herself, kept just a little of the hurt away. Instead, she'd gone and made the biggest mistake of her life. Oh, not sleeping with him. That had only compounded an even bigger mistake.

She had fallen in love with him.

She closed her eyes against the sting of tears she refused to let fall. Okay, so she'd fallen in love with him. That didn't mean she had to walk headlong into more pain.

Opening her eyes, she blinked rapidly to dry her lashes. It wasn't too late to pull back, to protect herself, save some part of herself from hurt.

"Good morning." Dan's voice was husky with sleep, his arms still bed warmed as they stole around her, drawing her back against his hard body. He bent to kiss the side of her neck, sending shivers down her spine. "You're up early."

He turned her in his arms, his mouth closing over hers in a kiss that was both greeting and invitation. For a moment, Kelly allowed herself to melt against him, her mouth soft under his.

"Come back to bed," he whispered, his teeth nibbling at her lower lip.

"No." The word was weak at first but it was stronger when she repeated it. "No."

She pushed away, sidestepping around him, keeping her eyes turned from his magnificent naked body.

"No? Okay. I'm not going to push."

Kelly almost left it there, taking the easy way out. She could deal with it later. But it wasn't going to get any easier. She squared her shoulders, trying to look as if just the sight of him didn't turn her knees to jelly.

"I mean 'no' permanently." He had been reaching for the slacks he'd discarded the night before but her words made him turn, the slacks dangling from one hand, his brows arched.

"What do you mean?"

"I mean last night was a mistake," she said. Her voice held enough conviction to make him see that she was serious.

"A mistake? Why?"

"It's nothing you did," she said hastily, wishing he would put some clothes on. "I shouldn't have let it happen. It was a mistake."

"You keep saying that but you don't say why." To her relief, he stepped into the pants. It would be easier to talk with him at least partially dressed.

"It wasn't part of our deal."

"Damn the deal," Dan said, showing irritation for the first time. "We'll make a new deal."

"Not with sex as part of it," she said steadily. "I shouldn't have slept with you last night."

"Why not? It isn't like we don't know each other and like each other. At least, I thought we had developed a certain understanding between the two of us. Was I wrong?"

"It was a mistake," she repeated, hanging onto her control by the skin of her teeth.

"Would you stop saying that! Dammit, you didn't think it was a mistake last night when you were in my arms."

She turned her back to him, feeling her convictions wavering. She had to protect herself. And she couldn't do that if she remained his lover. She would begin to hope for too much, leave herself open for too much pain.

"It was a mistake. I won't do it again."

"Why the hell not!" He stared at her, exasperated. "It's not like it's the first time."

The words seemed to fall like stones into a quiet pool, their impact rippling endlessly outward. Kelly looked at him, her eyes showing the shock of their impact. That he could so callously refer to that first night, as though it had been a casual encounter. Which, of course, she supposed it had been, at least for him.

"Kelly…"

She turned as if he hadn't spoken, her back rigid as she walked away.

"Kelly, wait." When she didn't react, Dan stepped forward, catching her arm and drawing her to a stop.

"I'm sorry. I shouldn't have said that."

"Let go of me." Her voice was cool, completely expressionless.

"We need to talk."

"I don't feel like talking right now," she said politely, pulling her arm away. "If you'll excuse me."

He let her go, staying where he was until he heard the bathroom door close behind her and then the distinctly separate sound of the lock clicking into place.

"Idiot." He muttered to himself. "Open mouth—insert foot
l the way to the thigh." He stripped off last night's slacks,
rabbing jeans and a shirt and tugging them on with vicious
rce.

He had hurt her. The last thing on earth he'd wanted to do.
adn't he promised he would never hurt her? Of course, he'd
en specifically referring to physical hurts, but that didn't
ean he had the right to inflict emotional injuries.

After last night all he wanted to do was hold her in his arms.
ast night her response had been everything he'd ever dreamed
f, everything a man could possibly ask for. He had awakened
is morning, sure that they'd reached a new understanding.
hey could define just what that understanding was later. But
ere was no doubt that things had changed between them.

Obviously they had but not in the way he'd thought. He
ew last night had been as satisfying for her as it had been
r him. She didn't have the experience to know just how ex-
aordinary it had been, but he'd felt her shivering in his arms,
lt her reach a shuddering completion.

Dammit! She'd enjoyed their lovemaking and she'd fallen
leep in his arms as if she belonged there. There had been a
eling of rightness about it, a feeling that this was where they
ere meant to be.

Her attitude this morning had been completely unexpected.
had thrown him as off balance as if he'd walked off a step
at wasn't there. He hadn't been prepared to hear her say that
hat they'd shared had been a mistake. Even so, that was no
cuse for what he'd said.

Dressed, he hesitated, wondering if he should try to talk to
r. But she hadn't looked as if she was in any mood to talk,
least not to him. Maybe if he gave her a chance to forget
hat an idiot he'd been...

Angry with himself and the world in general, he stalked out
the apartment.

Kelly sagged against the bathroom door when she heard the
ont door shut behind him. She wasn't sure whether she was
lieved or sorry that he hadn't tried to talk to her again. Now
least she didn't have to worry about what to say to him.

Letting herself out of the bathroom, she walked back into the bedroom, feeling tears well up when she saw the tousled bed. She blinked them back furiously. Crying wasn't going to change anything.

Her first impulse was to pack a bag and leave. She didn't want to be here when Dan came home. She didn't want to have to see him again. She could just run away. She'd find some way to take care of herself.

And the baby?

Sinking down on the edge of the bed, Kelly set one hand on her stomach. A wave of despair washed over her. Things hadn't changed all that much, after all. She might have nicer clothes but she still didn't have anywhere to go. True, she had a driver's license and the little compact car Dan had bought from his friend Lee so that she'd have something to drive.

She could take the car and a few of the clothes. There was nearly a thousand dollars in the checking account Dan had opened for her. It sounded like a fortune. Surely it was enough to get her a start on a new life.

But a thousand dollars wasn't going to last very long. And then she'd be alone and without money, without a way to earn a decent living. Wasn't that why she'd come to Dan in the first place? Because she didn't want that for her baby?

Dan. He'd already lost a child. Could she take this one away from him? He hadn't meant to hurt her. Given time to think she knew that. It wasn't his fault she'd been foolish enough to fall in love with him. It wasn't his fault that the longer she carried this child, the more it was a part of her, the more impossible it began to seem that she could ever give it away, even to him.

She'd made a promise—a bargain. She'd agreed to what she truly believed to be best for her child. The only thing that had really changed was that she'd realized how hard it was going to be to go through with the bargain. But that didn't give her the right to break her promise.

Standing, she thrust her fingers through her hair, pushing back from her face. The gesture made her think of Dan brushing the hair back from her cheek, his hand gentle.

Kelly forced the memory away. Right now her emotions were a little too exposed for her to be trying to make rational decisions. She needed to get dressed, comb her hair, have a cup of tea. Maybe then she could think clearly again.

# Chapter 14

Time didn't change the situation. She was still in love with a man who didn't return her feelings and she had still made promises she was beginning to doubt her ability to keep.

Dan was gone until early evening, leaving Kelly plenty of time to decide how to react when he got home. She was going to be cool and calm, no emotional scenes. With luck, he wouldn't insist on discussing what had happened.

Luck was apparently not on her side at the moment.

When Dan came home, Kelly was at the table, a math textbook laid out in front of her. Ostensibly she was studying to take the high-school equivalency test in two weeks. In reality, at the moment, she couldn't have added two and two without considerable effort.

The sound of Dan's key in the lock caused her to jump, her pen skipping around the flower she'd been carefully doodling on a notepad. Her plans to remain calm and collected scattered like dry leaves before a breeze. Her heartbeat accelerated and she was suddenly breathless with nerves. Her fingers clenched around the pen as Dan stepped inside, shutting the door quietly behind him.

Kelly drew a deep breath. She couldn't just sit here staring at the table as if she didn't know he was there. That was hardly an adult way to handle things. And she couldn't stick her head under the table, which was what she really wanted to do.

Start as you mean to go on, she told herself. And she meant to go on in an intelligent fashion. Mature and controlled—those were her watchwords.

Kelly lifted her head, a polite smile ready to set distance between them. Her breath caught in surprise. She'd been so engrossed in her mental arguments that she hadn't realized how close Dan was. He stood right beside the table, not more than two feet away. But that wasn't what made her suddenly breathless. In his right hand, held out to her, was an enormous bouquet of spring flowers.

"Oh!" The small exclamation was startled from her.

She reached out, taking them from him hesitantly, her eyes lifting to his face. His mouth smiled but his eyes were searching and she looked away quickly, afraid of what he might see.

"Hi."

"Hi." She buried her nose in the bouquet, pretending total absorption with the flowers.

"I'm sorry for what I said this morning." There was no doubting the sincerity of his apology.

"That's okay," she said softly, keeping her gaze on the flowers.

"No, it's not okay. I hurt you and that's the last thing in the world I want to do."

"I know you didn't mean it. I should put these in water." She stood, still avoiding looking at him as she moved into the kitchen. She was aware of Dan's eyes following her. Since there were no vases, she got out a pitcher. She watched it fill with water as if the fate of the world depended on getting just the right amount of water in it. But once the flowers had been placed in the pitcher and a few unruly blossoms tweaked into order, she'd run out of excuses to avoid looking at Dan.

"Thank you for the flowers. They're beautiful," she said, still not turning around.

"I'm glad you like them." There was a brief silence. "Aren't you ever going to look at me again, Kelly?" There was a sort of gentle humor in the question that gave Kelly the courage to turn around.

"Of course I am." She was proud of the casual tone of voice she managed. "I was just thinking about what to make for dinner. Since it was so warm today how does a chef's salad sound?"

"Fine. But I'm not particularly interested in talking about food right now. We need to talk about last night."

Her eyes skittered away from his face. "I don't see why."

"Kelly, we can't just leave it like we did this morning."

"I think we said everything we needed to," she insisted. "I'm not sleeping with you."

"All right. Nobody said you had to." She would have relaxed at his calm agreement but she knew that wasn't the end of the discussion. "Do you mind telling me why not? And why you made the decision after we'd just spent a rather incredible night in bed? You enjoyed last night, Kelly. Don't try and tell me you didn't. I felt the way you trembled in my arms."

His words brought the color rushing into her cheeks. Memories she'd been trying to forget all day flooded in, making her knees suddenly weak. She reached back to grip the edge of the counter, holding it so tight that her fingers ached.

"This has nothing to do with whether or not I enjoyed last night," she got out, keeping her voice level with difficulty.

"Then what is it?"

"I don't want to get...involved with you." Dan's eyebrows rose, bringing a new wave of color to her face even before he spoke.

"Involved? I hate to point this out, but I think we're already pretty damned deeply involved."

"I don't want to get any more involved, then." She focused on the top button of his shirt, which was open at the throat. Just looking at him brought memories of how right it had felt to be in his arms—but it hadn't been right. Letting herself think that was setting the stage for disaster.

"I know we started off on the wrong foot," Dan said slowly. "But I really thought we'd gotten to know each other in the past few months. I thought we actually kind of liked each other." His crooked smile sought to lighten the conversation, to ease the tension.

But Kelly couldn't force an answering smile. *Like him?*

What was she supposed to say to that? *Like* didn't even begin to describe her feelings for him.

"It has nothing to do with whether or not I like you. We made a deal."

"To hell with the deal," Dan said, showing irritation for the first time. "Forget about the damned deal."

"I don't want to forget about it," she lied. "In a few months we're going to go our separate ways. I think it would be foolish to get our lives any more entangled than they already are. You're going to go on with your life, building your business, being...a father." She had to stop, forcing her voice under control before she continued. "And I'm going to be going to school, starting a new life."

"And that's what you want?"

"That's what I want." Kelly met his searching gaze calmly, hoping she looked as sure as she had sounded. If he could see the quivering wreck she was inside, he'd never believe she meant what she was saying.

"You want to just walk away when the baby's born, no strings attached?"

"That was the deal, wasn't it?"

"Yeah. That was the deal."

There was a long silence and then Dan seemed to shake himself. "Don't worry about fixing dinner for me. I told Ben I'd meet him at the gym."

"Fine." Kelly turned away, fiddling with the flowers as if they had to be arranged just so.

"Are you okay here?" Dan asked after a moment. "Do you need me to bring anything home?"

*A new heart would be nice.*

"No. I've got a lot of studying to do. I'll probably turn in early tonight."

"Well, then I'll see you later."

"Say hi to Ben for me," she said brightly.

"I'll do that."

Kelly didn't move until she heard the door shut behind him. Then her shoulders sagged. She stuffed a slightly mangled daffodil back into the bouquet at random. Tears blurred her vision, turning the flowers into an impressionistic painting.

She'd done exactly the right thing, she told herself. She really couldn't have done anything else. Which didn't seem to make it hurt any less.

On the surface, nothing changed. They continued to live in the apartment together. Kelly took care of the cooking and cleaning, which didn't amount to much. The rest of the time she studied for her exams, immersing herself in the subjects she was weakest in, retreating into books, just as she'd done most of her life.

Dan had applied for the necessary licenses and permits to resurrect Remington Construction and was slowly putting together a crew and exploring the market for the kind of construction he wanted to do.

Nothing had changed and yet everything was different. There was a tension between them that hadn't been there before, an awareness that made Kelly's skin tingle whenever Dan was in the room. She'd always felt a certain sexual awareness toward him. An awareness that had been easier to ignore when her only acquaintance with sex had been the confused and slightly painful experience the night the baby had been conceived.

Now she knew exactly what it felt like to make long, slow love with him. She didn't have to close her eyes to remember the feel of his hands on her skin, the way his mouth had felt at her breast. Even though her mind was telling her that to repeat the experience would be courting disaster, her body wasn't listening. And neither were her emotions. She wanted to experience that closeness with him again, even if she knew it didn't mean the same things to him that it did to her.

If it was difficult for Kelly to ignore the attraction between them, it was near torture for Dan. He knew, far more than she possibly could, about just how extraordinary their coming together had been. Never had a woman fit so perfectly in his arms. Never had he felt not only physically satisfied but completed in some deep way.

To experience that for the first time in his life and then to have her turn around and throw their "deal" in his face had hurt more than he liked to admit.

It didn't take him long to decide that there was something

more to Kelly's denial than what was on the surface. She was using their bargain as an excuse, but that wasn't the real reason she'd pushed him away. He hadn't quite figured out what the real reason was, but he knew he would. If two years in prison had taught him nothing else, they'd taught him the value of patience.

Kelly wasn't going anywhere for the next few months. He had time to work on the problem.

The compact slid neatly into the parking slot and Kelly turned off the engine, pulling the keys out and dropping them into her purse. She'd had her license for almost two months now but the experience was still new enough for her to enjoy it.

Dan had bought the compact two weeks after she passed her test, ignoring her protests that it was too much. A license wasn't going to do her any good if she didn't have something to drive, he'd pointed out. And the bright-blue compact was economical and easy to drive. He'd laughed at the way she'd carefully brushed dust off the fender before getting in it for the first time.

Kelly's smile faded. She hadn't heard Dan laugh in weeks. Not since—she broke the thought off and then forced herself to complete it. Not since the night they'd made love. There was no sense in pretending she didn't know what had caused the tension that stretched between them whenever they were together.

Dan was spending more time away from the apartment these days. True, he was about ready to launch his business and there were a lot of things to be arranged, but Kelly knew that wasn't the reason he ate out most nights, often not coming home until after she'd gone to bed. She would lie awake, unable to sleep until she heard the sound of his key in the lock.

She sighed as she opened her car door. Sometimes she wondered if she was nuts not to take advantage of the time she had with him. What if it was possible that Dan could come to care for her? She had come to know him well enough to know that he wouldn't try to shut her out of the baby's life.

Was it best for any of them for her to live on the fringes of their lives? Certainly it would all but destroy her. And it couldn't possibly be what Dan wanted. He'd signed on to take care of her until the baby was born and then make sure she was established in a new life. Would it be best for her child to have his or her mother lurking in the background, never quite a part of their life, never completely out of it?

Just thinking about it was enough to give her a headache. Sometimes she'd have given anything to have someone to talk to, another woman who could understand what she was feeling. Several times she'd picked up the phone to call Brittany but she always put it down with the number undialed.

She'd forgiven the other woman for her part in that disastrous dinner. The road to hell might be paved with good intentions but that didn't make them any less well intended. And Brittany's intentions had been good. That wasn't the reason Kelly couldn't bring herself to complete the connection.

Every time she thought of calling Brittany, she could hear Dan saying that they'd been *involved,* and she'd picture the beautiful blond-haired little girl who'd clung to Michael's neck the first time they'd met. Dan's little girl. She was ashamed to admit that she was jealous. Dan had probably loved Brittany very much, maybe secretly still did love her. And she'd had his child.

Shaking her head, Kelly slid out of the car, slamming the door behind her. Sitting in the parking lot of a grocery store was hardly the place to try and solve all the problems in her life.

She tugged the hem of her loose smock over the bulge of her stomach. At nearly six months into her pregnancy, it was no longer possible to hide her condition and she had given up trying.

Kelly couldn't have said what it was that made her suddenly look up. She had been searching through her purse for the list she knew she'd put in there when some sixth sense told her that someone was watching her.

She felt her heart bump when she saw who it was. Her father glared at her from the corner of the building. His hair was a filthy tangle of gray, his coveralls were torn at the knees and stained with weeks of living. She stopped so abruptly that the woman behind her nearly ran into her. She swerved past, giving

Kelly an annoyed glance as she dragged two whining children toward the doors.

Kelly stared at the grubby old man. It was as if seeing someone from another lifetime. Her steps slow, she walked forward, unsurprised when he moved to intercept her. She stopped a few feet away, letting him approach her.

Hadn't he been taller? More imposing? Surely he hadn't always been so thin and ragged—pathetic, really. He was just a scrawny old man, in need of a bath and a haircut. He'd loomed larger than life in her nightmares. Dominating everything around him, nearly invincible. He wasn't anything like the enormous giant of a man he'd become in her imagination.

"Hello." She felt almost light-headed with the realization that she didn't fear him anymore. She didn't have to cower in terror just because he was near.

"Your shame is plain for all to see," he said by way of greeting. Even his voice didn't seem quite as imposing as she remembered. It seemed lighter, less threatening. Not the voice of authority anymore, merely the voice of a sick old man.

"I don't happen to consider it a shame," Kelly said calmly, one hand touching her stomach.

"You're far gone in sin. I saw you with him, bold as day."

"I don't believe I wish to speak to you," she said.

"You'll listen or your soul will be doomed to eternal damnation," he boomed, causing a couple leaving the store to turn and look at him.

"No," Kelly said, her tone so confident that he seemed startled. "You're not God's mouthpiece. You're nothing but a lonely old man. You've destroyed your family and now you're left with nothing." She paused, feeling as if she were shedding a burden she'd carried all her life.

"You are nothing."

The flat statement had the impact of a blow. Her father actually backed a step, his face paling beneath the ragged growth of his beard. Then his skin reddened alarmingly and he took a step toward her, one hand raised.

"You're a whore, displaying your shame for all to see, feeling no shame for what you've done. You'll pay for your sins. You and the bastard you carry."

Kelly was peripherally aware that her father's booming accusations had drawn attention to their confrontation, but she didn't turn away from him. Meeting his eyes head on, she refused to quail in the face of his rage. If she backed away from him now, she'd spend the rest of her life regretting it.

Her silent defiance seemed to drive his rage to new heights. He was actually trembling from his anger. For a moment, Kelly thought he was going to strike her, despite the onlookers. A part of her shook with terror, but she refused to let him see her fear.

What he might have done she would never know. The manager of the store, called perhaps by a nervous customer, pushed his way through the doors. A short but burly man in his sixties, he'd spent time in Korea and still walked with a military bearing. He took in the confrontation between the young pregnant woman and the filthy old man in a glance. His chin thrust out.

"Here, now. What seems to be the problem, ma'am?"

Kelly waited a beat before turning to answer him, making it clear that she wasn't looking away out of fear.

"There's no problem, Mr. Johnson."

"Do you know this man?"

She glanced back at the man who'd spent so many years trying to destroy her spirit and shook her head.

"No," she said clearly. "He's no one."

She walked away without another glance, entering the cool store with her spine straight. She did her shopping in a daze, hardly aware of what she was buying. By the time she'd paid for her purchases and gotten them to the car, reaction was beginning to set in. She drove home automatically and carried the two sacks of groceries up to the apartment.

She'd confronted her father. Kelly collapsed onto one of the dining room chairs as the thought hit her. She'd looked him right in the eye and she hadn't backed down. Her heart was still beating a little too quickly. Her skin felt warm. Now that it was over she felt dizzy and slightly sick. Putting her head down on the table, she took deep, slow breaths, willing her pulse to steady.

And that was how Dan saw her when he opened the door.

"Kelly!" He reached her in two strides, his heart pounding. "What's wrong?"

She lifted her head to look at him.

"I saw my father," she told him, her eyes still dazed with the realization that she'd faced a nightmare and come off unscathed.

"Where? What happened? Are you all right?" Dan ran his hands over her arms, his eyes sharp as he sought some sign of injury. "Did he touch you? I'll kill him if he hurt you."

"I'm all right." Her smile was shaky around the edges but she could feel the shock fading. "I'm all right."

"Are you sure?" Dan sat back on his heels, his look still searching. "What happened?"

"I faced him. I looked him right in the eye and I didn't cringe in fear." The wonder of it was in her voice.

Hearing it, Dan let some of the tension ease out of his shoulders. His heart was still beating too fast. When he'd seen her with her head lying on the table, he'd thought for one terrifying moment that something was wrong.

"What happened?" he asked again, more calmly this time.

"I went to get groceries." She gestured vaguely to where the two bags still sat on the counter. "He was at the store. And I wasn't afraid of him. Not really. He's not nearly as big as I'd thought. In my mind he was huge. But he's really just average size. Nothing but a filthy, ragged old man. And that's what I told him."

"You *told* him that?" Despite the fact that his heart was still beating too fast, Dan's mouth twitched. "How did he react?"

"I think he was shocked that I hadn't collapsed at his feet. And then he was angry. For a minute, I thought he might hit me."

Dan's hands were loosely clasped around hers as he knelt in front of her. His fingers tightened. "He didn't, did he?"

"No. Mr. Johnson, the store manager, came out. He asked if I knew him. And I said he was no one."

"My God, you do like to live dangerously, don't you?"

Kelly's laughter was tremulous. "I guess I do. I wasn't afraid of him anymore. He can't hurt me again, can he?"

"No."

"I can't believe I said he was no one." Her giggle was more nerves than amusement.

"You're a lot tougher than you look," Dan said, smiling at her.

"I guess I am."

"You're sure you're okay?"

"I'm fine. In fact, I think I feel better than I have in weeks. Oh, Dan, I'm finally free of him." Without thinking she leaned forward, throwing her arms around his neck.

Dan caught her with one arm, balancing himself against the table with his free hand when her exuberance threatened to tumble them both to the floor. Laughing, he stood, lifting her off her feet with an arm about her waist.

Kelly's head fell back, her eyes smiling into his. It seemed the most natural thing in the world to bend his head and kiss her, tasting her smile with his mouth. For a moment, her lips relaxed under his, her body soft against him.

Only a moment and then she stiffened, turning her head to the side at the same time that her arms pushed away from him. Dan released her instantly, startled by her nearly violent rejection. She stared at him wide-eyed, something that could have been fear in her eyes. But, no, it couldn't be fear because the next instant it was gone. And so was the sparkle of pleasure.

Dan opened his mouth to apologize and then closed it with a snap. He was damned if he was going to apologize for a perfectly innocent kiss. She was the one who had thrown herself into his arms and there'd been nothing in that kiss to warrant her reaction.

"I wasn't going to ravish you on the table," he said irritably.

"I know. I…are you going to be home for dinner tonight?"

And so ends another deeply insightful discussion, Dan thought, surprised at the depth of his frustration. He'd told himself he could be patient, but his patience was wearing a bit thin around the edges.

"No, I'm not." The truth was he didn't have anywhere else to go. But he wasn't in the mood to spend the evening in this apartment, which seemed to be growing smaller every day. He didn't want to pretend to do paperwork or watch TV, while Kelly pretended to study.

He didn't want to watch her close the bathroom door behind her and hear the water come on in the shower and then sit there with his imagination running wild, picturing her all wet and inviting.

"I just came home to pick up a change of clothes and then

I was going to the gym. Unless you'd like me to stay," he offered, not sure whether or not he wanted her to take him up on it.

"No. I'm going to study."

"Are you sure? You're not feeling a little nervous after seeing your father?"

"No. I feel fine. I think it was really good for me. You go ahead and go to the gym."

There was no reading anything beneath the careful smile she wore. Dan swallowed the urge to curse roundly. Why was she so bloody determined to keep him at a distance?

He was no closer to an answer an hour later when Ben collapsed against the bleachers in the gym, holding up a weak hand for mercy.

"You're getting soft in your old age," Dan told him heartlessly. He sat down a few feet away, spinning the basketball between his hands. Patches of sweat darkened the back of his T-shirt and drew circles under his arms.

"I thought this was supposed to be a friendly game of one-on-one," Ben protested, dragging himself upright so that he could lean against the bleachers. "You were playing for blood."

"Was I?" Dan tossed the ball up in the air and caught it. Despite thirty minutes of brutal play, there was still a coiled restlessness about him. The physical exertion hadn't exorcised the demons riding him.

"You want to tell me what's going on with you and Kelly?"

"No."

"Well, that's honest enough," Ben said, nodding. "I could accept that and change the subject, but I don't think you're going to be safe to turn loose on a basketball court until you get it off your chest. What's going on?"

"Nothing's going on except that she's driving me crazy," Dan said moodily.

"I'm glad it's nothing serious."

"I don't know what she wants," Dan said, ignoring Ben's flippant remark. "I'm taking care of her. I've given her a home, have said I'll get her into college. We're going to have a kid together. And she still acts like she expects me to grow fangs and turn into Dracula one night. What does she want from me?"

"You really want my opinion?"

"No."

"Good." Ben settled himself more comfortably, eyeing his friend with a mixture of sympathy and amusement. "Have you told her you love her?"

The basketball shot into the air, landing in the bleachers with a thump. Dan paid it no attention, fixing Ben with a surprised look.

"No."

"Why not?"

"Why not? Well, because I don't. I like her. I admire her guts. She faced down her father today, did I tell you?"

"Twice." The dry interruption was ignored.

"She's got more courage than she realizes. And she's a fighter—but I'm not in love with her."

"Uh-huh."

"She's got a good sense of humor and sometimes, when she laughs, her nose wrinkles. It's kind of cute, really. And she's a hard worker. She's really worked on the stuff for the exam. She'll probably ace it. But she's too young."

"Some people are born old," Ben said to no one in particular.

"Sometimes she does seem almost older than I am. If I were planning on falling in love again..." He shook his head. "But I'm not."

"I wasn't aware that falling in love was something one put on an agenda."

"She's got her whole life ahead of her. School and a career and...stuff."

"You know, you're right." Ben seemed struck by this. "She's much too young. I bet, in a year or two, she'll meet some handsome guy—in college, perhaps—and they'll fall madly in love. They'll get married. She'll have other kids."

Out of the corner of his eye, he watched the flush slowly rise in Dan's face as he contemplated the future that had just been outlined.

"Maybe she'll even ask you to the wedding."

"Like hell!"

Ben looked at him, his eyes wide with surprise. "You know, if I didn't know better I might think that sounded like jealousy."

Dan stared at him, the flush slowly fading as he realized how neatly he'd been trapped. "You lousy son of a bitch!"

"I'm glad we're friends, too." Ben stood and stretched. Dan climbed to his feet more slowly, his eyes glazed. At another time, Ben might have felt sorry for him. As it was, he clapped him on the back with heartless good cheer. "Don't look so shocked. It happens to the best of us."

Dan watched him leave the gym, whistling softly under his breath. He felt as if he'd been struck in the solar plexus, driving all the air from his lungs.

He was in love with Kelly. Why hadn't he realized it before? Of course he was in love with her. He felt a foolish grin stretch his mouth. How could he not be in love with her?

But did she feel the same? The grin faded. She had to love him. She simply had to. And if she didn't, well, then he'd just do his damnedest to make her fall in love with him.

He wanted to rush home and tell her immediately. He wanted to know if she felt the same. But he reined in the urge. He wanted everything to be perfect when he told her. He wanted to be able to make her see how much she meant to him, to show her how much they belonged together.

## Chapter 15

Kelly knew she'd overreacted to the kiss. She'd known it as soon as it happened, but it had been too late to change things then. There had been something in Dan's eyes—something like hurt. And if he was hurt, it was her fault. She'd reacted like an hysterical little fool. No wonder he'd gone out again. He probably didn't want to look at her. She had made it a point to be in bed before he got home, taking a book with her and not reading a word of it.

She didn't sleep well and woke later than usual, feeling groggy and out of sorts. Slipping into the bathroom, she caught a whiff of coffee, which meant Dan must already be up and about. Hopefully he'd be gone by the time she got out of the shower. He probably didn't want to see her any more than she wanted to see him.

Not even a shower could wash away the rumpled state of her mind. And it didn't improve her mood to hear Dan whistling in the kitchen. She debated ducking back into the bedroom and hiding there until he was gone, but that was hardly an adult way to behave. Smoothing one hand over the thick fall of her hair, she made her way toward the kitchen.

The scent of coffee had been joined by that of bacon and

eggs. As Kelly came around the breakfast bar, Dan was just slipping slices of bread into the toaster. He turned, his face creasing in a disgustingly cheerful smile when he saw her.

"Good morning. My timing is impeccable as usual. Pull up a chair. Breakfast will be on the table in a minute."

Kelly sat down at the table, watching him warily. Why was he suddenly so happy? Where was the tension that had been a constant companion these past weeks? He hadn't been in this kind of a mood last night. In fact, she'd never seen him like this.

The toast popped up and he lifted it onto a plate, buttering it with what could only be described as a flourish. A moment later, he set a plate of crisp bacon, fluffy scrambled eggs and golden-brown toast in front of her. It wasn't until then that Kelly noticed that the table was neatly set for two, including glasses of chilled orange juice and the omnipresent milk.

"Looks great, doesn't it?" Dan sat down across the table from her. "Hope you're hungry."

"It looks wonderful." On the contrary, what little appetite she might have had disappeared in the face of his unexplained good cheer. She picked up her fork and poked it into the eggs, sliding a glance at him from under her lashes.

What had happened between last night and this morning to change his mood? Whatever it was, he didn't seem to be interested in offering any explanations, leaving her imagination free reign.

Unfortunately the only thing her imagination came up with was that he must have met another woman and fallen madly in love. Probably some athletic blonde at the gym. Someone who didn't look as if she'd swallowed a basketball. Someone who didn't act like an idiot over a little kiss.

"Do you have any plans for this afternoon?" Dan's question dragged Kelly away from her evermore gloomy thoughts.

"No."

"Good. I have something I want to show you."

"What?"

"It's a surprise. Wear comfortable walking shoes and you'd better bring a jacket. They're threatening us with showers."

He glanced at his watch. "I've got to run. I'll pick you up about four. Is that okay?"

"Fine." Kelly watched him pick up his empty plate and carry it into the kitchen. Her own food was barely touched.

"Eat up. You need to keep up your strength," Dan told her on his way back through. "I'll see you this afternoon."

He was whistling under his breath as he lifted a stack of folders from the breakfast bar. Turning, he gave her a wide smile that somehow managed to hold secrets. Kelly couldn't manage more than a weak grimace in return but it didn't seem to bother him. With a lift of his hand, he disappeared into the entryway and a moment later she heard the door shut behind him.

It was only in the silence he left behind that she realized what he'd been whistling. "Some Enchanted Evening." The blond bimbo theory seemed to have some supporting evidence.

The hours between the time Dan left and four o'clock seemed to move by in slow motion. If Kelly glanced at the clock once, she glanced at it a hundred times. The textbook she was supposed to be studying remained open to the same page, her notebook filled with nothing more informative than lots of doodled lines.

He had something he wanted to show her. She tapped her pencil on the table, her eyes focused on nothing in particular. A surprise. What could he want to show her that was a surprise and that required comfortable shoes?

Did the surprise have something to do with him getting the business off the ground? After the tension that had been between them these past few weeks, why would he want to share that with her?

She changed clothes three times, trying to decide just what comfortable shoes implied. Did it mean sneakers or low pumps? Slacks or a soft skirt? She finally settled on a pale gray trousers and a pair of flat skimmers.

Despite her indecision, she was dressed and waiting at three-thirty, with nothing to do but stare at the clock and will the hands to move faster.

When there was a brisk knock on the door a few minutes before the appointed hour, Kelly jumped as if stung. She hurried to the door. Dan must have forgotten his keys.

But it wasn't Dan who stood on the other side of the door. Her father's lean frame was such a shock that it took her a moment to believe he was actually there. Stunned, she hesitated for one disastrous instant before moving to slam the door. He thrust a battered work boot into the door, blocking it open.

"I've come to talk to you," he said, pushing the door open despite her efforts to close it.

Breathless, she fell back. He stepped into the hallway, bringing a miasma of dirt and sweat with him. He pushed the door shut behind him, and Kelly felt her heart bump with something she didn't want to admit was fear. It was one thing to face him in the open, with people all around. It was something else completely to be alone with him, closed off from the rest of the world, closed off from help.

"What do you want?" She was proud of the steadiness of her voice, determined that he would never know that her heart was beating double-time.

"It's my duty to try and turn you from the path of sin you've chosen to walk," he said, his voice booming out over her.

"I have nothing to say to you. I want you to go."

"You're my flesh," he said as if she hadn't spoken. "And I'd be failing the Lord if I didn't try to save you."

"The Lord has nothing to do with what you're doing," she told him.

"That child is born of sin," he said in a menacing voice, pointing one grimy finger at her stomach. "You must repent, lest you both burn in hell."

"Get out," Kelly spat, one hand pressed over her stomach as if to shield her unborn child from the venom her father was spewing.

"You've turned your back on the Lord and chosen to walk Satan's path. You must get down on your knees and beg His forgiveness."

"You're mad," she breathed, seeing that it was no more than the truth. The fierce light that burned in his eyes held little sanity. "You're completely insane. Get out. Get out before I call the police."

Madness burned in his eyes and she backed away, a coppery taste of fear in her mouth. Brought up short by the breakfast bar, she was afraid to turn away from him, as if the only thing holding him in check was the fact that she faced him.

"Repent. Repent and you may yet be saved."

"Get out." She groped behind her, trying to find the phone.

"The Lord has shown me the true path," he intoned, advancing toward her. Kelly choked back a sob of sheer terror. She knew that look, knew what followed it. Abandoning her search for the phone, she slid sideways, thinking perhaps she could dart around him and reach the door.

"I am the Lord's instrument," he told her, his eyes seeming to glow with a terrifying inner light.

Kelly didn't bother to answer, edging closer to the door, hoping he'd shift just a little bit farther. But she'd run out of time. She saw him reaching for her. With a terrified sob, she tried to dart past him. But pregnancy had slowed her and he was too close. His fingers closed over her upper arm, jerking her to a halt and spinning her around.

"Your sins must be punished," he thundered. Kelly saw the blow start to descend and she closed her eyes, both hands covering the swell of stomach.

The openhanded slap caught her across the cheek, jerking her head to one side. She felt her lip split and her mouth fill with the taste of blood. The force of the blow sent her stumbling backward. Only a wall stopped her from falling. Her breath coming in ragged sobs, she crouched down, making herself as small as possible, wrapping her arms around her swollen stomach, her only thought to protect the baby.

She heard him take a step toward her and whimpered, trying to brace herself for the next blow, knowing there was nothing she could do but endure.

She'd forgotten that Dan was due home, forgotten everything but the need to protect herself as best she could, the need to survive. At the sound of the door opening, she lifted her head, sensing more by instinct than by conscious thought that help had arrived.

The moment was forever frozen in Dan's mind. For one split second he stood poised in the doorway, while the camera in his mind registered the scene. Kelly was crouched against the base of the wall, curled into herself. A filthy old man with a shock of ragged gray hair stood over her, one hand drawn back as if to deliver a blow.

Kelly lifted her head, looking at him with eyes blinded by

fear. One cheek was livid and a thin trickle of blood marked where her lip had been torn.

Dan's vision was suddenly overcast with a thin, red haze. Somewhere in his subconscious he recognized that this was Kelly's father, but his only conscious thought was to kill the man who'd dared to lay a hand on his woman.

With a growl that was more animal than human, he launched himself forward. It was an unequal struggle. Dan was younger, larger and the fury that filled him magnified his strength. In a matter of seconds, he had the other man pinned to the floor, his neck caught in Dan's fingers. He proceeded to slowly choke the life out of him, feeling not a second's hesitation.

It took Kelly several seconds to realize that Dan wasn't merely choking her father into submission. He had every intention of choking him into oblivion. She scrambled toward them on her hands and knees, grabbing at Dan's wrists.

"Let go! You're killing him! For God's sake, let him go!"

She might as well have been trying to move an iron bar. He didn't seem to hear her and his hold didn't slacken. The old man's face was slowly turning purple. The blows he'd been directing at Dan's shoulders grew weaker. Dan's lips were drawn back from his teeth in a terrifying facsimile of a smile.

Frantic, Kelly tried to pull Dan away from him, her breath coming in deep sobs. "Stop it! Oh, please, you've got to stop."

Her father's hands began to claw weakly at Dan's.

"Dan. Listen to me. He's not worth it. Please, he's not worth it." Desperate, she caught his face in her hands, forcing him toward her. "Please don't do this. I beg you. He's not worth it."

Whether it was her words or the sight of the tears streaming down her face, she didn't know. But she saw the change in his eyes, saw awareness break through the primitive rage. His hands loosened, allowing his victim to draw a gasping breath.

"Are you all right?" he asked, his voice hoarse.

"I'm okay."

"You're sure?" He caught her shoulders, drawing her to her feet. He stepped away from the old man still gasping and choking on the floor. "You're not hurt?"

She nodded, her throat too full of tears for her to get words out.

"The baby? The baby's all right?"

"We're fine. We're both fine."

"Oh, God." He caught her to him, holding her so close it was hard to breathe. They stood like that, saying nothing, drawing comfort from the physical contact. Neither of them paid any attention as her father finally scrambled to his feet, one hand at his throat. He cast one terrified look in Dan's direction and scuttled out the door.

It was a long time before any coherent conversation was attempted. Dan insisted on putting an ice pack to Kelly's face, though she assured him that it didn't hurt. He hovered over her like a mother hen with only one chick. She allowed herself to revel in the attention, though a small voice in the back of her mind insisted on pointing out that of course he was concerned—he was worried about the baby. That didn't seem important at the moment. She'd been scared for the baby herself.

"I shouldn't have let him in," she said, her speech muffled by the presence of the ice pack she was holding to her cheek.

"You didn't know it was him when you opened the door. I shouldn't have let him go like that," he muttered. "I should have finished the job. I could *still* finish it."

"No." Kelly reached out to catch his hand, drawing him to a halt as he paced restlessly in front of her. "No. He's not worth it. He won't dare come back now. I think you gave him a closer look at the afterlife than he really wanted."

"How can you joke about it?" he asked. He bent over her, his hand gentle as he drew the ice pack away to look at her face. "Are you sure you're all right? We could call Ben."

"I don't need Ben. And if I'm joking about it, I guess it's just because I feel a little light-headed."

He didn't return her smile. "It's my fault. I should have known something like this could happen. I should have taken steps to prevent it." He spun away from her, pacing over to the window to stare out, his shoulders rigid.

"What could you have done?" she asked patiently.

"I don't know. I should have done something. I promised you I'd never let anyone hurt you again."

"This wasn't your fault. If anything it was mine. I was so proud of myself for standing up to him yesterday, but it was a stupid thing to do. I would have been better off ignoring him.

As long as he thought I was terrified of him, he wouldn't have felt the need to come looking for me.''

"You didn't do anything wrong." Dan turned away from the window, frowning at her. "You're sure you're all right? And the baby?"

"We're both fine." Her smile held a bittersweet edge. "Dr. Linden tells me babies are a lot tougher than most people think. Your son or daughter is just fine."

"Good." He said it absently as if his mind was on other things.

"You were going to show me something," she said, hoping to distract him.

"I can show it to you tomorrow," he said, still in that absent tone of voice. She waited but he didn't add anything more. Shrugging, she stood, rubbing one hand against the small ache in her lower back.

"I think I'm going to take a shower."

"Are you up to it?" Dan turned, his gaze sharp with concern.

"I'm okay. Stop worrying."

Dan watched her leave the room, thinking how impossible it was to follow that advice. He couldn't stop worrying. He'd only just realized how much she meant to him. When he'd walked in the door and seen her father standing over her, the blood on her mouth, the terror in her eyes...

He closed his eyes, feeling his body tighten with remembered rage. He should have killed the bastard. He should have choked the life from him, made sure he could never come near Kelly again. He could have done it without regret in that moment.

Looking out the window again, his thoughts wandered. He'd planned to tell her how he felt today. He'd had it all arranged. A picnic lunch on the site of what he hoped would be their new home. A proposal. He even had the ring in his pocket.

He could tell her, anyway, but he didn't want it to be like this. He wanted everything to be perfect, something they'd remember the rest of their lives. That was if she accepted him. Did she love him? She had to.

He noted vaguely that the shower had been turned off. Kelly was probably going to want to skip dinner and go to bed, though it was still early. She was bound to be worn out. This wasn't how he'd hoped to be spending this evening. But another day wasn't going to matter. Now that he thought about it, there was something he could do in the morning. Then he could get Kelly and take her out to the site.

He glanced up as the bathroom door opened. Shock swept across his face. Kelly stood in the bathroom doorway, her hair piled on top of her head, leaving a few ends free to trail against her neck. She was flushed from the shower, her skin moist as if she hadn't taken time to dry off thoroughly. And there was plenty of skin to see because all she wore was a bath towel that exposed a dangerous amount of leg.

Dan swallowed hard. He moved forward, telling himself that he was imagining the look in her eyes, that the invitation that seemed so clear wasn't really there. He stopped within inches of her, close enough to smell the fresh-washed scent of her skin.

"How was your shower?" he asked, his voice husky, his eyes questioning.

"Very nice." She blushed but met his gaze openly. When she reached up to loosen the knot that held the towel over her breasts, Dan thought his heart might stop. She hesitated, the knot undone but the towel still closed.

"I want you to make love to me."

Dan swallowed, wondering if he could possibly be dreaming. His hands were shaking as he reached out to take the ends of the towel from her. His eyes never left hers as he opened it, letting it fall to the floor.

"Are you sure?"

"Yes." She closed her eyes, a delicate shiver running over her as his hands came up to cup the full weight of her breasts.

"Yes." He echoed her agreement, his head spinning with the scent of her, the feel of her.

At another time, he might have wondered at her sudden decision. But not tonight. It fit so well with what he'd dreamed, what he'd hoped for, that he didn't think to question it, didn't think of anything beyond the warmth of her.

Carrying her into the bedroom, he made love to her with slow passion, telling her with his body what he hadn't yet said in words. If Kelly had had more experience, she might have recognized the message he was giving her, might have felt the love in his touch. But she didn't have the experience to know the difference between sex and making love, real love.

When she woke the next morning, Dan was gone, leaving a note on the pillow that said he'd be back before noon. He had signed it *Love, Dan.* She tried to convince herself that those words were significant but she knew it didn't mean anything. Kelly touched the note to her lips, blinking back the tears she refused to let fall. She didn't have time for tears. She had things to do.

She searched the closet until she found a duffle bag, probably a remnant of Dan's college days. Stuffing a few garments into it, she made what plans she could. She hadn't thought things out clearly, but she had realized last night that she couldn't stay here.

She'd made a promise she couldn't keep. She couldn't give up her child—not even for Dan. When her father had come at her, her only thought had been that she had to protect the baby. She'd tried to deny her feelings, tried to pretend that she could walk away from her child, but she couldn't do it.

Kelly sniffed back tears as she zipped up the duffle bag. She wouldn't keep the child from Dan. She couldn't do that to him. But neither could she just hand her baby over to him. She needed to get away, maybe try to establish herself a bit. She'd take the money Dan had given her. In a couple of weeks she would take the exam and get her high-school diploma. After that, she'd see about finding a job. First she had to find a place to stay.

The first problem came when she looked out the window and realized that Dan had taken her car, leaving the Corvette sitting at the curb. He sometimes took the compact if he was going to a site where the low-slung sports car wouldn't travel.

Kelly wasted only a moment cursing the fact that he'd taken it today of all days. She hesitated, frowning at the phone before picking it up. Brittany had said she wanted to patch up their friendship. Well, she could start by coming to her rescue.

"Hello?" It was Michael's voice on the other end of the line.

"This is Kelly Russell. Is Brittany there?"

"Hi, Kelly. Brittany isn't home. Can I give her a message?"

"I...no...no, I don't think so. Thanks, anyway."

Perhaps something in her voice sounded odd. "Kelly? Can I do anything?"

Kelly's fingers tightened over the receiver. It was eleven o'clock. Dan had said he'd be home by noon. She could call a cab but the taxi service was notoriously erratic. And Michael had kind eyes.

"I...could you come pick me up?" she asked in a rush. "I'm at Dan's."

There was a momentary pause while she waited for him to question why she needed someone to pick her up.

"I'll be right over."

True to his word, Michael was there in less than ten minutes. Kelly was waiting on the curb. Michael got out of the car, one dark brow arching when he saw the duffle bag at her feet. His eyes skimmed to her, widening in shock when he saw the bulge of her stomach. Kelly waited for him to say something but he only bent to pick up the duffle, tossing it in the back of his car without comment, shutting Kelly's door once she was settled.

She didn't dare to relax until they'd turned the corner and were out of sight of the apartment building. She stole a glance at Michael.

"I suppose this seems pretty odd."

"A bit."

"I suppose you'd like an explanation."

He slanted her an unreadable look out of dark blue eyes. "Only if you feel like giving me one. Do you have a destination in mind?"

"No."

"Then I guess you'd better come home with me. Brittany is out of town with my mother and Danielle until tomorrow. But you're welcome to stay at our place."

"Thank you."

"You're welcome."

Neither of them said anything for the space of several blocks.

"I promised Dan I'd give him this baby," Kelly said, as if he'd been questioning her.

"Did you? Why?"

"It seemed like the only thing to do at the time. But I can't do it. No matter what, I can't do it."

"I'm sure Dan isn't going to force you to do anything you don't want to do."

"I know, but I feel so terrible. I mean, he's already given up one child."

Michael's hands tightened on the steering wheel. "I know. It wasn't easy for him."

Somehow the whole story seemed to come tumbling out. She would never in a million years have imagined herself confiding in Michael Sinclair. But there was something so solid about him, something that said he could be depended on.

"Kelly?" Dan pushed the door open with his hip, maneuvering the dusty box through the opening. "Kelly?"

There was no answer. He set the box on the table, feeling a twinge of unease. Since he'd had her car, she couldn't have gone anywhere. He'd told her that he'd be home by noon. He was a little later than that but she'd forgive him when he showed her what he'd brought home.

The apartment was empty. It took him several minutes to convince himself of that fact. It wasn't until he was making his second circuit of the rooms that he noticed the note propped against the saltshaker. The box had all but obscured it.

He was aware that his hand was not quite steady as he reached out to pick up the note. It was short and simple. She couldn't give up her baby, after all, and she'd gone away for a little while. He wasn't to worry. She wouldn't try and keep him from his child. She'd be in touch.

Setting the note down, he stared around blankly. She couldn't go. Not now. Not when he'd gotten it all worked out. He'd been going to tell her how he felt today. The way she'd made such sweet love with him the night before had given him hope that she loved him, at least a little bit. And if she didn't love him as much as he loved her, he was willing to wait for that.

Thrusting his fingers through his hair, he forced himself to think clearly. He'd had her car, which meant she'd either called a cab or she'd walked. Or someone had picked her up. Only she didn't know anyone. Ben was out of town. He'd been leaving for some sort of convention this morning. Besides, Ben knew how he felt. Ben wouldn't help Kelly leave before he got a chance to talk to her.

Brittany. As far as he knew, she hadn't talked to Brittany since that disastrous dinner. Still, it was worth a try. He punched the buttons on the phone and then waited impatiently while the phone rang.

"Hello?" Michael's voice was unexpected but Dan didn't hesitate.

"Michael. It's Dan. Is Brittany there?"

"No. But Kelly is."

"Thank God. I'll be right over."

"Wait a minute," Michael protested. But Dan had already hung up the phone.

Dan pulled the Corvette up in front of the Sinclair house, paying no mind to the fact that he'd parked crookedly. Long strides carried him up the walkway and he took the three steps up to the porch as one. Michael opened the door before he had a chance to knock.

"Where is she?"

"She's upstairs, lying down. Wait a minute." Michael put his hand on Dan's chest, stopping him. "Before you go up there, I think we should talk."

"Later, Michael." Dan glanced impatiently up the stairs. He wasn't in the mood to talk to anyone but Kelly.

"Now," Michael said, the flat tone getting Dan's attention at last.

"What is it?" he asked impatiently.

"I think you should give some thought to what you're going to say to her."

"I think you should mind your own business."

"When Kelly called my home for help that made it my business. I don't know what the hell you were thinking of in the first place."

"What are you talking about?"

"Taking her home from that bar."

"She told you that, did she?" Dan felt color mantle his cheeks. It wasn't something he was proud of.

"She told me quite a bit. About this 'deal' the two of you struck. She seems very concerned that you not get hurt. I personally would like nothing better than to knock your teeth down your throat."

"I wouldn't advise trying."

They glared at each other for a moment. Michael was the first to soften, his eyes lighting with a trace of something approaching humor. "You always were the most pigheaded, stubborn s.o.b."

"And you always were poking your nose in where it didn't belong." There was no anger in Dan's tone.

"You're in love with her, aren't you?" It was only half a question but Dan answered it, anyway.

"More than I'd ever thought possible."

"Then why the hell haven't you told her so?"

"I was going to. Today. I had it all set up." Dan thrust his fingers through his hair, his smile rueful. "I guess I should have figured it out sooner."

"Yeah. You were always slow-witted, too." There was remembered affection in the insult.

"I can't argue this time around. Is she all right?"

"She's fine. But I think she'll be a lot better once you tell her you love her."

Dan started up the stairs and then stopped, turning back to look at Michael. "You know, you and Brittany are a lot happier than she and I ever would have been."

The words were a letting go—of old hurts, old losses, old bitterness. Michael's expression made it clear that he recognized them as such.

"Thanks."

Dan turned, taking the stairs two at a time. He stopped outside the door Michael had indicated, feeling suddenly uncertain. What if she didn't want to come back under any circumstances? What if she felt she could never love him?

He knocked quietly and then pushed open the door. Kelly had been looking out the window. She turned, color flooding her face when she saw him.

"Dan!"

"Hi."

"How did you find me so quickly? I wasn't running away," she added hastily. "I know how much this baby means to you."

"It doesn't mean half as much as you do."

"I'm sure we can work something out," she continued, oblivious to what he'd said. "Joint custody or something. I know it won't be easy but I can't give him up. I just can't."

Dan crossed the short distance between them, catching her hands in his. "Kelly, listen to me. I don't want you to give this baby up."

"You don't?" She stared at him, her eyes wide.

"I want you to marry me and we'll raise *our* child together."

"No." Her chin set and she shook her head. "I won't marry you for the sake of the baby."

He refused to let her pull away, drawing her closer, instead.

"I want you to marry me because I can't live without you, because my life was empty until you came into it."

She stared at him, feeling her heart start to pound a slow, hard rhythm.

"What?"

"I'm trying to tell you that I love you, Kelly. I'm trying to ask you to marry me and make a life with me for the two of us and our baby."

"You love me?"

"I love you," he repeated, with such conviction there could be no doubting that he meant it. She stared at him wide-eyed and silent. "You might say something about how you feel about me," he prompted when it seemed she might never speak again.

"I love you," she said, as if he had to have known it all along.

"And you'll marry me?"

"If it's what you want—but you don't have to."

"I want to. I want my ring on your finger so that everyone knows precisely who you belong to."

He slipped his arms around her, drawing her close. Kelly leaned her head on his chest, happier than she ever dreamed it possible to be.

"When I woke up this morning and you were gone, I was glad. Because I didn't know if I could look you in the eye and tell you I was leaving."

"I shouldn't have gone." His hand stroked her hair. "I went to see your father."

"No!" Kelly's head jerked up, her eyes showing a trace of ear. "I told you to just let it go."

"I didn't feel like letting it go. Don't worry, I didn't murder im, though that would have been no more than he deserved. merely suggested that he might find another part of the coun-y more comfortable."

"What did he say?"

"Well, a great deal about the wages of sin," Dan said dryly. But I think he's seen the wisdom of a fresh climate. And I lso got your box of keepsakes for you."

"You did?" Tears stung her eyes.

"I did. I was going to surprise you with them and then I vas going to take you out to a site I'd picked out. Remington construction's first project is going to be a house for the two f us. The three of us," he corrected, setting his hand against e swell of her stomach.

Kelly leaned against him, her heart swelling with happiness. had all happened so quickly. From despair to joy in a matter f minutes.

"We're going to be together always, Kelly." Dan put his and under her chin, tilting her head back until her eyes met is. "That's a promise you can believe."

And she did believe it. With all her heart, she believed.

# Epilogue

"Here's your veil." Kelly watched in the mirror as Brittany set the veil carefully in place. The delicate circlet of ivory silk roses was draped with a short fall of tulle.

"You look beautiful." Brittany blinked back sentimental tears.

"I look six and a half months pregnant," Kelly said. She stood, smoothing her hand over the fall of watered silk that failed to hide the bulge of her stomach.

"Well, you could look nearly eight months pregnant," Brittany pointed out, gesturing to her own bulging tummy.

"True. Do I really look all right?"

"You look gorgeous. Dan is going to be stunned. I wonder if that's the limo already." Brittany glanced at the clock as the doorbell rang. "They're early. You find your shoes and I'll tell them to wait."

She hurried from the room, leaving Kelly alone with her reflection. She was getting married today. Marrying the man she loved more than she'd ever dreamed she could, marrying the father of her child. And, miracle of miracles, he loved her. It hadn't been easy to convince herself of that, but she was finally beginning to believe it completely.

The wedding party was small. Brittany and Michael and Michael's parents, who had turned out to be just as wonderful as Dan had said they were. Ben, of course, who was acting as Dan's best man. Kelly knew that Brittany had hoped to see Michael in that role but it was too soon. He and Dan were working toward a friendship, but it was still in the early stages.

Brittany was her only attendant. If Kelly had one regret, it was that she had no one of her own to be at the wedding. She'd written Devlin when she first moved, though she'd hadn't told him the circumstances. There had been no reply, just as there hadn't been for nearly eight years. Maybe Dan was right. Maybe it was foolish to keep writing. For all she knew, Devlin wasn't even receiving her letters.

That was something to think about another time. Today she wanted to concentrate on her wedding, on a new beginning for her life.

"Kelly?" Brittany's tone was odd, almost strained. Kelly turned.

"What's wrong?"

"There's a man here who says that he's…well, actually, he says he's your brother."

"Devlin?" Kelly pressed one hand against her throat. Had thinking about him conjured up a hallucination? "Devlin is here?"

"That's what he says." Brittany glanced over her shoulder, stepping aside.

Kelly stared at the man who stepped into the doorway. He was older, taller, harder. There was nothing of the lanky boy who had left home so long ago in the rugged man before her.

"Kelly?"

Even the voice had changed, gotten rougher, deeper. But his eyes—the eyes were the same steely color that somehow managed to be both blue and gray.

"Dev?" she whispered, her voice trembling on the word.

"Hello, midget." The smile that softened his mouth seemed rusty, as if he didn't smile very much.

"Dev?" She took one step forward. "Dev."

He covered the remaining distance, catching her in his arms. Neither of them was aware of Brittany leaving them alone. They didn't speak for several minutes, just holding each other, absorbing the reality of being together again. It was Kelly who drew back first, brushing at the tears that dampened her cheeks.

"Where have you been? I missed you so much. Did you get my letters?"

"I got them," he said, ignoring the first part of the question. "But you didn't tell me everything that was going on." He gave her stomach a pointed glance.

Kelly flushed, smoothing her dress. "Yes, well, there didn't seem to be any need to tell you everything."

"You're getting married."

"Yes. In about fifteen minutes." She caught his hand. "There's so much I want to know, so much to tell you."

"Are you happy?"

"More than I ever dreamed of being," she told him with absolute sincerity.

"Good. I don't want to make you late for your wedding," he said. "We can talk afterward."

"Come to the wedding." Her fingers tightened over his. "You could give me away."

"I'm not really dressed for a wedding, Kelly." He glanced down at his jeans and short-sleeved shirt.

"I don't care. You can borrow one of Dan's jackets. Please, Dev. Please. It would mean so much to me to have you there. Someone of my very own. Please say you will."

The little church was a riot of flowers, courtesy of Beth and Donovan Sinclair. Dan hardly noticed them. Glancing at his watch for the tenth time in five minutes, he wondered uneasily what was taking Kelly so long. She was nearly ten minutes late.

Maybe the limo broke down. *Maybe she changed her mind.* She probably had a run in her stocking. *What if she'd gone into labor two and a half months early?*

Before he could work himself into a frenzy, the door at the back of the church opened and Brittany stepped in. The organist immediately began to play as she moved up the aisle at a slow pace. Her eyes sparkled with excitement, more than he'd expected to see. But he didn't have time to speculate. The familiar strains of the wedding march swelled and the doors opened again as the guests rose.

Dan's heart bumped. It was really happening. He and Kelly were really getting married. Kelly stepped into the church but she wasn't alone. Her hand rested on the arm of a tall man, wearing jeans, tennis shoes and—if he wasn't mistaken—one of his own jackets.

There was only one person it could be, though it was impossible to see any resemblance between the hard-jawed man and the delicate woman beside him. This had to be the elusive Devlin. Incredible as it seemed, Kelly's brother had made an appearance.

There would be time later to ask questions and exclaim over his arrival. Dan took Kelly's hand from Devlin's with a murmured thanks, his look only for her. Her smile shook around the edges and her eyes were bright with tears. But they were happy tears. And if he had anything to say about it, that would be the only kind of tears she'd ever shed again.

Breaking with tradition, he bent to kiss her gently before they both turned toward the minister who would bless their union. But it was really a formality. As far as Dan was concerned, he was already blessed. In having found Kelly, his life had been more blessed than he'd ever imagined it could be.

\* \* \* \* \*

Silhouette

SPECIAL EDITION™

*SPECIAL EDITION*

Stories of love and life, these powerful
novels are tales that you can identify with—
romances with "something special" added
in!

Fall in love with the stories of authors such
as **Nora Roberts, Diana Palmer, Ginna Gray**
and many more of your special favorites—as
well as wonderful new voices!

Special Edition brings you
entertainment for the heart!

SSE-GEN

# SILHOUETTE® Desire®

Do you want...

Dangerously handsome heroes

Evocative, everlasting love stories

Sizzling and tantalizing sensuality

Incredibly sexy miniseries like **MAN OF THE MONTH**

Red-hot romance

Enticing entertainment that can't be beat!

You'll find all of this, and much *more* each and every month in **SILHOUETTE DESIRE**. Don't miss these unforgettable love stories by some of romance's hottest authors. Silhouette Desire—where your fantasies will always come true....

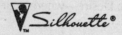